THE
MAN
YOUR
MOTHER
WARNED
YOU
ABOUT

LADIES MAN

KATY EVANS

NEW YORK TIMES & USA TODAY
BESTSELLING AUTHOR

First paperback edition April 2016

Cover design by James T. Egan, www.bookflydesign.com
Interior formatting by JT Formatting

10 9 8 7 6 5 4 2 1

Library of Congress Cataloguing-in-Publication Data is available

ISBN-13: 978-1530111640
ISBN-13: 978-0997263602 (ebook):

To that feeling you can't express,
but can't suppress.

TABLE OF CONTENTS

PLAYLIST

PRAYER IN C by Robin Schulz
DON'T GET ME WRONG by The Pretenders
WALK by Kwabs
SAME OLD LOVE by Selena Gomez
PHOTOGRAPH by Ed Sheeran
REALIZE by Colbie Caillat
BURNING LOVE by Elvis Presley
WAITING by Dash Berlin, featuring Emma Hewitt
RESOLUTION by Matt Corby

TONIGHT'S THE NIGHT

obin Schulz's "Prayer in C" reverberates through the club. It's an upscale place—to the point of being obnoxious. The walls are covered by frosted glass and sleek waterfalls. Long, cascading, modern crystal chandeliers hang from a domed, diamond-dusted ceiling. Everything is a different shade of blue—light blue drinks in crystal flutes, blue flashing lights, blue-hued water fountains.

Hundreds of guests yell and bounce on the dance floor. Artfully presented drinks are passed around on expensive trays.

Everyone is celebrating their host's twenty-sixth birthday. Guys have driven thousands of miles and flown in from around the world to be here. Girls have maxed out their credit cards to dress for this event.

My bestie Wynn and I push our way to the back rooms, where the pool and wet bar are.

We're probably the only ones who didn't have to sell our future firstborns for an invitation. We're also probably the only ones overdressed in dresses that are two sizes too small. But since the club is called Waves, and its main attractions are dozens of swimming pools in the back rooms, anything more than a skimpy swimsuit or cover-up is "overdressed."

I thought being this covered up in a room full of scantily clad girls would keep the wackos away.

Not so.

I've already had to fend off three butt-grabs and one blatant boob-cup.

Wynn squeaks every time someone touches her. I suspect she feels secretly flattered by the attention, but I'm starting to get tired of slapping away all the hands.

Seriously, this is not how I usually spend my Saturday nights. Me with a tub of salty light popcorn and my favorite TV show is more like it. Casual jeans and smaller, more intimate gatherings are my thing.

Wynn has been on some sort of crusade to entertain me almost daily since our other bestie (and my former roommate), Rachel, got married last weekend.

Why I let Wynn convince me to come here tonight, I don't know, but my heart has been pounding since we left.

God, what am I doing here?

"*Ginaaaaa!*" Wynn sounds frustrated as she squeezes my hand and tugs me forward.

She's trying to create a path for us. Trying to help me find…*him*. I have an urge to snatch my hand away and head straight back out the front door because…what am I doing here?

My attention is drawn to the naked women with blue-glitter moons on their nipples, hanging from the crystal chandeliers. They're basically humping the crystals, all shimmering bodies and exposed skin, squirming around like lizards, wiggling their perfect asses.

My outfit and makeup are the tamest things here. Why did I spend hours getting ready?

My heart is beating fast. Because HE is here. I saw his car parked in the lot—a white Rolls-Royce Ghost that screams money, and the off-road dirt clinging to the wheels that screams "I don't give a shit."

It's been a long time since I've been in such a packed club, but then, I should've *known* that a master partier would celebrate his 26th birthday in style.

His name is Tahoe Roth. And he's just a friend. That's the only reason I'm here. Because friends celebrate their friends' birthdays. Don't they?

"Look, we'll just walk up to him, say 'happy birthday,' and then be on our way," I say firmly in Wynn's ear.

She turns around, eyes flaring wide.

"So soon? Before Emmett gets here? No way!" Wynn shoots me a chiding frown and pulls me forward more firmly. "You're going to strut your stuff, say 'happy birthday,' and tell him that you have a present for his eyes only. Then you'll take him home for the night and get him out of your system once and for all."

"Um…that would be a hard no."

"Gina! That was the plan—to get him out of your system."

I bristle. "That *so* wasn't the plan. You can't work something out of your system that you don't have *in* your system!"

Wynn and I squeeze together as people bump past us and toward one of the pool rooms. For the twelfth time today, I regret telling Wynn that I don't know if I want to punch Tahoe or *do* him all night long. She's been on my case ever since.

I'm wearing the sexy underwear that I bought today, thinking of his blue eyes.

My stomach knots as I imagine his dimple.

And now I'm having an anxiety attack, wondering how many tequilas I need to get drunk enough to do what I've been fantasizing about all day.

"Let's get Tahoe in the pool—we need to get those clothes off!"

The whisper comes from my right as a girl and her friend push past us and head to the same pool room we're walking toward.

"Oooh! *Look!* There he is!" Wynn says.

I inhale sharply and feel that frustration I always experience when I look at him. He's infuriating. He's annoying. He's cocky. Selfish. Self-centered. Really, I don't even know why we're friends.

I stop a passing waiter and steal a tequila shot from his tray, toss it back in one gulp, then turn to where Tahoe is standing. And the tequila does nothing to soothe his effect on me.

He stands with a group of men. But Tahoe Roth is the only one I see.

Beneath the lights his blond hair gleams. His eyes are so blue they look electric. He's rugged, imperfectly raw. He has a day's growth of facial hair, and a primal, beastly look about him. *Vikings* is one of my favorite shows and I can't help but notice that he bears a striking resemblance to Ragnar. I'm breathless.

And then…his smile, his smile is so contagious and comes so easily. I've never seen a guy smile as much as he does. It's an irreverent smile, a mocking smile, because really, Tahoe never seems to respect anything.

My stomach twists up around my windpipe at the sight of him and that gorgeous, sometimes filthy mouth of his.

The two stalkers who wanted to undress him approach, and he curls his arms around each of them. Just like that, he's standing with a woman in each arm, and I feel a pang in my chest. An awful pang of fear, the kind that strikes when you're surrounded by hundreds of strangers, and they all keep dancing, and talking, and drinking...and you're staring at the guy who's been haunting your dreams, and you don't know what to do about it.

What to do about *him.*

"Gina!" Wynn nudges me. "Get on with the plan. Dude, you know he's a horny beast. He has a late-October birthday, which means he's Scorpio, and Scorpio is the sign of *sex.* And you're this sultry dark-haired Marilyn Monroe, screaming sex with that little dress and those crimson lips."

I inhale, trying to summon courage but failing, half turning back the way we came—but unable to leave because Wynn stops me.

"I can't, Wynn, I really don't want him, I don't even *like* him," I protest.

Scowling and mad at myself, I avoid looking at HIM when I spot a guy staring at me. He's short and looks harmless, so I flash him a small smile, praying that he's not a close friend of Tahoe's.

The guy grins back and starts walking toward me. I break our eye contact when I hear yells at the end of the room.

"Roth!"

I turn as a girl calls from under the waterfall, and I can't help but look at him again. Why can't I just ignore him?

He's standing with Callan Carmichael and two older men, and the two girls with him are stripping down to their bikinis. Carmichael and Tahoe are both just scorching hot. Callan is a copper-haired, tall athletic type, and then…Tahoe.

Tahoe, the beast.

He's dressed in black from head to toe, his tan accentuated by the flashing lights; his hair appears blonder, his scruff seems darker. My nipples pucker, my thighs clench.

Tahoe Roth is…

Hot to the extreme. Six feet four, at least two hundred pounds of man. At Rachel and Saint's wedding, even in a tux he looked raw. A power box of testosterone. The area around his eyes is a little crinkled from smiling too much, and maybe partying too hard, and not giving a shit about more than having a good time. His black jeans hang low on his narrow hips and give new meaning to sex-on-a-stick.

The two girls who are after Tahoe and the one who was just beneath the waterfall are tugging and whining and trying to cajole him into the pool.

"Hey."

Startled, I glance into the stranger's kind brown eyes and absently say, "Hey," as I hear a splash and squeals from the girls. I try to glance at the pool but a group that's come over to cheer blocks me.

A guy in front of me shifts slightly, and I get a glimpse of the pool. And inside…Tahoe, slicking his hair back, his wet shirt plastered to his muscled chest. Then he makes a grab for the ankles of the girls who are standing at the edge of the pool, and they squeal and leap away.

"You three are going to get it," Tahoe playfully teases them. His irreverent smile displays his dimple. As they giggle flirtatiously, he leaps out, scoops them up and tosses them in, one by one, and they fall into the pool with yelps of delight.

He dives in after them. One of the girls comes up to splash water in his face, but he's able to splash back more with his big hands. The girls start splashing each other when he stops playing along. He signals for a pool waiter to bring him a drink as he peels off his shirt and tosses it aside. He stretches his arms out on the pool ledge like Roman royalty and then he skims his gaze across the pool as if deciding whether to get out or not.

He pulls himself up, wraps a towel around his waist, and drops his jeans. He steps out of them, and—our eyes meet. Beads of water drip down his torso. He's cut and golden—cut and golden everywhere; his six-pack, his flat pecs, his muscular arms, even the sides of his calves peeking from under the towel.

He looks at me, his eyes sparkling with recognition, then he looks to the guy standing next to me. He stares at him, then at me, and one of his brows rises in question.

I stand here, amped up and nervous. He steps away from the pool in my direction, radiating heat. His smile quirks, and I see amusement in his eyes at my speechlessness.

I struggle with what to do next. Hug him? Oh god.

Just say happy birthday, Gina!

"Get over here," he growls under his breath.

"Excuse me?"

"I said come here."

"No," I say, scowling.

He smiles and cocks his head back, tilting it to the side just a little. "They're coming for you."

"What?" I ask. My nerves are making me shiver.

He signals at two men in swimsuits coming over with mischief in their eyes.

He steps over, grabs me by the waist, and says, "I got her." He lifts me up over his shoulder like a sack of rice, carries me to the edge of the pool, and then looks past his shoulder and shoots me a grin.

No. He is not going to do what I think he's going to do.

"Don't. You. Dare," I warn, clinging to his wet torso.

Before I know it, he throws me in. I don't have time to hold my breath. One moment I'm dry, the next I'm falling in an ungraceful splash, sinking.

Sputtering, I surface, and he just stands there, smirking at me.

He then drops his towel and dives in, a perfect dive. His head pops up out of the water and I splash him. I'm so mad I can't see straight.

"This was my favorite dress, you—"

He dips half of his face under the water as he floats in front of me, only his eyes and nose above the surface. His eyes reflect the water, luminescent.

Frustration is eating at me.

I want to grab his wet hair and kiss him.

I want to pull him underwater and kiss him.

I want to take him home and kiss him.

I want him to take me home and kiss me.

And then I want to forget I ever kissed him, and ever wanted to.

"Roth!" one of the girls calls from the pool steps. The moment Tahoe glances in her direction, she ceremoniously takes off her top.

"Very nice, baby," he says, smirking, getting a long look at her boobs.

Disgusted, I start to swim to the edge of the pool.

With one powerful stroke, he reaches it first.

He lifts his brows as both our hands curl on the ledge and again, our eyes meet.

His expression is unreadable.

"Fine, so you got me wet," I finally say, releasing my anger. "I know how you can make it up to me."

He lunges out of the pool. I pull myself up and he hands me a towel.

"I'm not a one-night-stand kind of girl, which is why I'm giving you the chance only a few others have ever had. One night with me. Happy birthday."

He scowls as he towels off his chest. "Is this some sort of joke?"

"Excuse me?"

He straightens as he wraps the towel around his hips, his lips quirking sardonically. "How many?"

"What? How many guys?"

"That's right."

"I...well, two, and my ex, Paul. But that wasn't a one-night stand; we were together for two years."

"In either case, that's nowhere near enough for you to recover after a night with me."

I blink in disbelief. "Oh wow, you're so full of yourself."

"Hey." He takes my chin and forces me to stare deeply—painfully—into those blue eyes. "You were vulnerable at

Saint's wedding, and I held you in my arms, and I liked it, but you were right to deny me. You were right and I was wrong."

I scowl and follow him. "You think I can't handle you?"

He stops and stands over me. I exhale.

His eyes darken a little.

I'm nervous and vulnerable, wondering if I completely misread him before.

But as we stand there, everything falls away until all I see are those blue eyes. Amusement is gone; something dark and watchful lurks in his gaze.

"Thanks for coming, Regina," he says.

His words pierce like an arrow through my chest.

"You're declining my birthday present...?"

He looks away, his jaw tight as he exhales. He draws me away from the crowd, and I see a flash of raw regret in his gaze. "I've got nothing good to offer you, Regina." His gaze holds mine, and he leans forward. He smiles against my ear, my knees turn to rubber. "Seeing you wet was gift enough for me."

He eases back then crooks a finger and signals for the floozies and the two stalker girls to follow him up a spiral staircase.

I grit my teeth and stare after him with an aching knot in my stomach, hating myself for putting myself in such a vulnerable position, hating that I didn't work him out of my system when I had the chance. Hating that I'm wet, that he ruined my dress and my evening.

Wynn is waving, standing with Emmett, her eyes filled with concern.

I smile a fake smile at her.

Tahoe is right, it's better that I rejected him, better to stay away from him. I've been hurt before, and knowing I'd have to see Tahoe again because of Saint and Rachel would make having sex an awkward mistake we would have to endure forever.

I just want to drink and forget him—how hard his chiseled muscles felt, forget the way he smelled, all wet and warm.

I'm ready to go home, but Wynn and Emmett are snuggled close together in a booth and I realize I still need sex, a one-night stand, a reminder that I'm human and alive and female.

As I turn to leave the pool room, I bump into the guy who'd been staring at me earlier in the night.

"Hey, you okay?" he asks, concerned.

"Oh, I'm perfect. Do you want to get a drink?"

"Hell yeah," he says.

I ask the guy for his name, and after a few drinks, I take him—Trent—back home.

We're in my bed. Hot lips on my neck, hands over my bare flesh. I removed my top but I'm still wearing my damp underwear. I tilt my neck to the side, and I'm transported to Rachel and Saint's wedding...

After the church ceremony, after a couple of drinks, I steal away from the party and walk for a few minutes toward the beach. I sit and stare at the waves, trying not to think about how much I'm going to miss living with Rachel.

Suddenly, I sense something on the back of my neck, and I know I'm not alone. I know who's sharing this moment with me.

Him.

Of all the people in the world I wouldn't like to see me weak, he is at the top of that list.

We're friends. I guess.

Otherwise I can't account for why he sits quietly beside me and puts his jacket over my shoulders.

"Thanks," I say, tugging at it. I feel like he's hugging me. It smells like him and I realize I've never touched something that he's touched. My skin tingles and my heart aches.

"Why are you crying?" he asks, staring ahead. We both do, as if eye contact would be too intimate.

He leans closer, puts his arm around me, and I feel guard-ed.

"What are you up to, Tahoe?"

"I'm up to many things."

I rest my head tentatively on his chest. It feels so nice. Nicer than you'd expect a wall of muscle to feel. "Then go…do them or something," I grumble.

His voice tickles the hair at my temple. "Do them? In the order I want them?"

My toes curl when he grins.

"I don't…" I shake my head.

I'm not sure if I'm shaking my head at him, or at the dull throb he's causing between my legs. He smells of expensive cologne.

I glance up at him as he watches me patiently. "Saint wants me to stay away from you."

All my hesitations flee when he gives me his wickedly devious smirk, and says, "I don't think I will."

His embrace tightens a little too noticeably around me, and he lifts my face. "My first priority is to look at you. Then I'm going to touch, and then I'm going to taste."

His eyes darken. He studies me for a reaction, and his smile fades as if he's seen something that he doesn't want to see. He wipes the tear from my cheek and then edges back. His nostrils flare, and he's frowning, deep in thought.

I groan in frustration. "Let's do something other than watch me cry. Any ideas?"

"Plenty."

He smirks as he pops open the top button of his shirt. My heart stops as he continues down the line, one by one.

"I was joking."

"I'm not. Come on, you'll look gorgeous naked."

"Close your eyes or it's not happening."

I ease off my dress. He pretended to turn away but I can feel him looking at me. I avoid his gaze. Oh god. *Please, moonlight, be nice to me!*

Why do I care what he thinks?

I walk to the water as fast as I can and notice his head tilt—he *is* looking at me fully. Completely. I feel his stare.

I dive in, and I gasp at the freezing water.

I rise to the surface to see him wading in, his eyes glimmering in the moonlight. I can feel his hunger calling out to me. I expect him to reach out and do something wicked. I'm prepared to stop him but I still want him to try.

"Why?" I blurt out.

"Why what?" His voice is thick against the crashing waves.

"Why haven't you made a pass at me?"

He sinks into the water and swims close to me. "You've been hurt before. I'm not a guy who can make a woman like you happy." He clenches his jaw and glances back at the party. "I don't get it. Being faithful to a woman your whole life like that."

"And here I thought you wanted me," I scoff.

His eyes darken. He cups my face. "Too much to fuck you up." He strokes my lips with one thumb.

I scowl. "The guy sitting at the table behind me was making eyes at me all night. I could go find him."

"Yeah, you could. And I could go after the girls who were looking at me and get more action than I'll get with you."

Neither of us moves though. We stay in the water for an hour, and when I crawl out onto the sand, he sighs and drops beside me.

We talk a little, but mostly we just stare at the sky. The bright stars shine above us but I barely notice them. I'm too aware of his hot wet body lying barely an inch away from mine. And his breaths, slow and even, both comforting and seductive.

We end up in his room, which is closer than mine. I slip into a plush resort bathrobe and he eases into his slacks, then joins me in bed. I can smell the vodka on his breath as I lift my head to look at him in the dark. He's so gorgeous and feels so predatory now that we're alone in his room. I can't stop staring at his rugged features. And he's staring right back.

He said he'd *look* and *touch* and *taste*…

"Do you want me?" His voice sounds brusque, and a little low, uneven. He looks at me with an intense gaze. "Do you?" His hand curls possessively over my hip.

In his eyes, there's a war. He's debating whether to make a pass at me. Whether to fuck me.

Do you want me? his eyes ask.

"No," I lie.

His eyes are dark and disbelieving for a moment. He nods and clenches his jaw. He pries himself away, rises, and puts on a shirt.

"Rest, call me if you need anything."

He sets the cordless phone on the bed, within my reach, and walks to the door.

He's going to see one of the other girls. I know it. And I stay in his bed, wondering if it's the vodka's fault that I care.

Hands on my breasts.

Wet lips on my neck.

Fingers try to tug my panties down my legs.

"Wait."

I stop his hand, bringing our make-out session to an abrupt halt. I'm pretty sure I'm ready to kick Trent out of my bed. It feels so wrong. Why does it feel so wrong?

"What the hell is wrong with you? I thought you were into it?"

"I wasn't…" Oh god, *why* wasn't I? "Look, you're a really nice guy but I'm not into one night stands, not really."

When he looks at me incredulously, I groan and rub my temples. Shit. He seems…a little too drunk to make sense of it.

"You're drunk, aren't you?" I ask him, and when he only stares at me, I sigh. "You can spend the night but...no spooning or cuddling or even breathing my air, okay?"

He's asleep within minutes, but I can't close my eyes. I'm afraid I'll see the blue eyes that I can't get out of my mind—the ones that have been popping into my dreams.

Why did I bring him to my apartment? No guy has ever been here. This used to be Rachel's and my sacred space, only Malcolm Saint dared venture here—and I hadn't been too happy about it.

At 5 a.m. I find myself wandering the apartment in my pajamas.

I hate the silence.

Rachel and I shared this apartment since the end of college. It's an industrial penthouse loft. Painted wood bookcases separate the living area from the kitchen. It's dark now but as soon as the sun comes up, it will be bright and sunny.

I stare at the ceiling then glance at the calendar. Next month, an *X* marks the day that Wynn is moving in with me. I'm glad she is; I can't afford to pay the rent on my own, and I don't want to leave this place. I also don't like being alone.

I've had three homes in twenty-three years, and I've always been the one left behind.

The first time, my parents told me they'd sold the house I'd grown up in, explaining, "We want to reconnect and get the spark back in our lives now that you're leaving for college." They left for Spain just after the sale closed. I finished packing and handed over the keys when I was done.

My next home was one I shared with my college boyfriend, Paul. He was definitely the first to leave.

I didn't used to be so anti-men, until Paul betrayed me. The worst part about being betrayed was that I hadn't seen it coming. I'd been blind, deaf, and stupid for such a long time.

Paul Addison Moore was good to me, but he was also *good* to two other girls at the same time. They both knew of me, and were content to be in the background. I didn't know about *them* for two years. Twenty-four months and nine days, to be exact.

One day, I received a call from an angry girl telling me she was his girlfriend and she'd been waiting for months for him to leave me, because he promised he would.

I hung up on her and told him some crazy girl had called to tell me this.

He grew very agitated—and suddenly began packing.

"Paul?" I asked. "It was a joke. Right?"

He just shook his head.

We were going to be late to class, so I went into the bathroom to brush my teeth and I heard drawers slamming.

"She's not the only one, there's someone else too," he suddenly yelled from the bedroom.

"Excuse me?" I walked to the doorway as I spoke through the toothpaste in my mouth.

The bedroom was empty.

I walked down the hall, my steps growing more hurried by the second, and I found him in the living room with his backpack and suitcase.

I froze.

"I don't love you, Regina."

That was the hundredth time he said the *L* word to me. He had said it while he lived with me, slept with me, called me just to tell me he was thinking of me.

He stood in the doorway as the toothbrush hung from my mouth. I must have looked awful. It felt like he'd shoved the toothbrush down my throat and stabbed my heart with it.

Finally, I took it from my mouth and sent it flying across the room at him.

"You!" I cried.

He picked it up and swiped the toothpaste from his shirt. "Very mature, Gina."

I couldn't talk to him, I couldn't breathe.

I'd prepared meals based on this guy's vegetarian tastes; I stopped eating *meat* for him. I had a map of my future and his name was splattered across every country. But on Paul's map, Gina was a wasteland, the thing you left behind.

I burst out crying and put my head in my hands.

He didn't say more. He left and closed the door. I heard the wheels of his luggage fade into the distance. And after two years together, after a hundred I love yous, after falling in love for the first time, I never heard from that cheating, lying asshole again.

I'm loyal to a fault. Even now, in an odd sense, I've been loyal to him. I've never been able to love again. He took my heart, the warm T-shirts that I used to sleep in, my trust, my hopes. He left me too scarred to ever feel that kind of happiness again. He walked out the door, leaving me to wonder if I was simply that foolish, or simply not enough.

MORNING AFTER

In the morning, I wake up after an hour of sleep, thinking about the night before. I really can't believe how wild and luxurious the club was and I'm obviously one of the few who wasn't completely wasted by the time I got home. I think about the drunk guy sleeping in my bed, and how, if I'd have gone through with it, the last man I'd slept with would no longer be Paul.

And then I think of Tahoe. God. Sexy, beastly Tahoe. I really hope I don't have to see him again, at least not until Rachel and Saint return from their honeymoon, which Rachel said in a short text they were extending for two weeks.

I climb off the sofa and make my way to the kitchen, turning on my cell phone. I see I have a message from Wynn and I click Play.

"So, the guy you brought home? Emmett knows him. How did that go? Tell me! Also, I have to talk to you. Call me, okay?"

I open the fridge to pull out my fresh coffee beans, grind them, and dial Wynn's number while I wait for my coffee to brew. "Hey, what's up?"

"Gina. Emmett asked me to move in."

I freeze while pulling out my artist mug. I set it down on the counter, softly. "What do you mean?"

"Well, you know I had that pregnancy scare at Rachel and Saint's wedding. And it got me thinking about, well, how serious this is. Emmett has been doing some thinking too because…ah! He wants me to move in!" she squeals.

What about me? I want to ask. But I cannot be that selfish. I mean, yes I can, but Wynn is my friend. Wynn has been wanting to find The One her entire life. I think she always imagined she'd be the first of us three to get married, and instead it was Rachel, who'd wanted nothing but a solid career. Why should Wynn be stuck with the young version of Old Maid who will forever be single? Why would she say no to her chef boyfriend because of me? No way.

But I say, suddenly afraid of Emmett hurting Wynn the way Paul hurt me, "Are you sure it's the right step, Wynn? You've been dating for…what?"

"A year! But Gina, I feel awful about not coming through for you after I told you I'd absolutely move in. I mean…what if you let me help with rent? Now that I'll be with Emmett, I won't be paying my own rent anymore…"

"Rotund no, Wynn."

"Rachel made me promise I'd move in with you. She won't be happy when she finds out. She'll want to pay your rent too."

"Nobody is paying my rent, okay? Except the person living here, which is me, alright!" I say.

But I stand there with my cell phone against my ear and stare at my lovely apartment, which I won't be able to afford anymore. "It'll be alright," I tell her, and because I'm too exhausted to deal with the worry of probably having to find a new place, I tell her I'll see her during the week and hang up.

I hear the sound of a door cracking open, and I turn to see the guy I brought home—Trent—standing fully dressed and ready to go. I smile at him, one of my regretful smiles, then pull out another coffee cup and a bottle of Advil. I bring it all to the table and push the Advil and the extra cup of coffee to the empty seat across from mine.

"God, thanks," he says, relieved. He pops open the Advil. "How bad was I?"

"You were that drunk?" I laugh. "Don't worry. Nothing happened."

"Well fuck, *that* bad, huh?"

"It was completely my fault. Cold feet after a long bout of…abstinence."

"Ahh." He sips his coffee. "I stole the invite to last night's party. I'd never be invited to those places."

"You did?" I laugh.

"How were you invited? Wait, I know. You're incredibly hot."

"Hahaha. Um, nope. Not half as hot as the other girls there. I just know the guy. Our best friends just married, so…"

"Wow, you've got friends in high places."

I end up chatting amicably with Trent. I find out that he does business with Emmett—he supplies some of the restaurant's produce—and I decide with a bit of regret that he's sweet and honest, and it's a shame that last night hadn't gone very far. Why can't you get your feelings where you want them? Why do I sit here and talk to Trent, all the while feeling the ache in my chest after Tahoe denied me?

I have to work at the department store that afternoon. Sundays aren't my rest days, usually Mondays or Tuesdays are, when sales are slower. It still boggles my mind how expensive everything we sell is. We cater to the rich of Chicago. The store is pristine and never really packed unless we have our yearly sale, which draws everyone in, if only to peek at our perfect holiday window displays and array of fashionable items. Black Friday and Christmas sales are still a month or two away and there are only so many people I can sell cosmetics to. I'm worrying about my living situation and wonder if I should a) put an ad on Craigslist for a roommate, or b) move.

The thought of moving doesn't thrill me, but the thought of having a strange roommate thrills me even less. I'm twenty-three, going on twenty-four, and I'm too old to live with a roommate.

My boss, Martha, calls me over. "Gina, let's organize this, I don't like seeing Pink Ecstasy on the Orange Flame holder."

Martha always makes sure the store is impeccable. I like working here because being with beautiful people, dressed well, makes me happy. Nobody is crying inside this store. Nobody is struggling inside this store. Everyone is blessed and leaves with huge smiles on their faces, and leaves us with one too. Everyone says thank you and that's that. I even have some regulars. So when I get a visit from Mrs. Darynda Kessler, telling me she has no time for me to do her makeup but she wishes I were available later, just before her big event, I seize the opportunity to expand my services.

"I would be happy to go to your place and do your face."

"That would be a dream! Nobody knows my face better than you. How's tonight at seven?"

"I get out at six, so seven works."

I'm relieved to have extra work. It'll keep my mind off...last night. And it'll help me pay my rent until my lease is up and I have to move. I write down her address and tell her I'll be there when my shift is over.

It isn't until I'm on my way to Darynda's place that I recognize the address. She lives in the exact same building Tahoe does. I can't help but feel a little bit nervous as I walk into the lobby. I've been here before, with Rachel and Wynn. Never alone. All I remember of his apartment is that it was too big for just one person. And somehow when I think of him, I always imagine him on the living room couch where I last saw him, watching a White Sox game with a White Sox cap and a White Sox shirt.

I board the elevator and press Mrs. Kessler's floor when I'm joined by two girls, both of them young and beautiful, who tell the elevator man who stands discreetly by the corner that they are going to HIS floor. He nods and slips in an access card.

"I could just die," one tells the other as the doors shut.

"God, I know. Is my hair okay?"

"Your hair is great. How about my makeup?"

I try not to judge her by her makeup, but it's hard not to when she's overdone her eyes so much. I *shouldn't* judge her. Our makeup is our mask. Good makeup can hide tired eyes, even sad eyes; nobody will ever know. Still, she looks beautiful, and I have to fight to keep myself from thinking *this is why he turned down your birthday present.*

My floor comes first, and they're still fixing their hair with the excitement of women who know they're seeing a very hot man whom they clearly want to see again and again.

I remember the last time I was in his apartment.

We were watching the White Sox game.

He's one of the most devoted fans I've ever seen. He was rubbing his sweaty palms on his jeans as he watched the game, yelling at the top of his lungs when they won. I laughed because it was funny, and then he looked at me and smirked. And then…he started to look at me the way he'd been looking at the TV, intensely.

Saint and Rachel left, Wynn gave me the eye signal that we should leave too. Tahoe made some signal to Callan, and soon Callan was striking up a conversation with Wynn, and Tahoe asked if he could show me something.

He led me to a massive room with all kinds of sports memorabilia.

"Wow."

Signed balls from the White Sox filled one shelf, while lacrosse gear spanned the opposite wall.

"You're a lacrosse fan?"

"I played in high school, college. I still play twice a month."

The blond beast was entirely too focused on me. He was killing me with that damn dimple.

"I've never watched lacrosse, not really."

"You should come to a game."

God, that dimple.

I started to hate that tiny hole in his cheek, though it felt so nice to have it trained on me that my toes were tingling.

"Sure," I said, with a shrug. "I'll go."

He's texted me twice a month every time there's a game: **Game tonight. Come see me.**

Or

Lax game tonight. I need some luck lady.

Or

Lax game. Kicking ass tonight, you'll enjoy it.

And I always make up some lame excuse.

I got home ready for bed, but didn't rest one bit. A night of no sleep really helps with the soul searching. By the time I wake up, I'm determined to call Wynn and ask her for Trent's number.

When Paul broke up with me, I never thought it possible to miss another human being like I missed him. I don't ever want to feel like that again. But I'm ready to move on. I want to give myself another chance.

Rachel and I, we always said we were the smart girls, the girls who know what guys really want from you. It's hard to stick to this belief when both of my friends have found true love. It's hard not to consider that maybeeee…just maybe…I can find it too.

I leave Wynn a message and head to work. I've felt…discontent ever since I came back from Rachel's wedding. *Restless.*

I'm questioning everything, what needs to stay and what I want to change in my life. And the more I question, the more I realize that what I want to change is—me.

So I try to soften; softer eyes, softer blush. I work on my face for the first half hour of my shift, since usually store hours are slower in the morning.

I brush a shimmery light pink Bobbi Brown shadow on my lids, a pale blush across my cheeks and a soft gloss on my lips. I finish, happy and curious to see my new look, but the girl who stares back at me has too big brown eyes, too soft pale skin, and looks too vulnerable, too young, and too innocent, like a girl fresh out of college. Which I guess I am….

Why did I end up at a cosmetics counter?

Because of Paul.

Because I couldn't get over being broken up with while at my worst, with a toothbrush in my mouth. It's the reason I never leave home without makeup. It comes on the second after I brush my teeth.

My makeup is definitely my mask, the mask that makes me strong, pretty, whatever I want to be. I like helping other women put on masks too.

I never want any woman in this world to be half-dressed and wearing no makeup, with a toothbrush in her mouth, when she's broken up with.

Because you never let him see you at your worst. Especially when he's discarding you like something old and worn.

Feeling vulnerable with my new look, I spend another half hour changing my face back to my heavy smoky eyes and red lips. And by the time Wynn calls back to give me Trent's number, I feel strong. I feel capable. I feel ready to see where it goes.

DATE NIGHT

Emmett said Trent wanted my number, but I called him instead. I'm giving myself a chance after encouragements from Wynn to "just see."

So I sit at a nice little round table at a well-known little restaurant, but I don't see Trent.

He's late.

I rub my palms over my black jeans. I'm nervous. You'd think I've never gone on a date before. And really I haven't. I've had one boyfriend and yeah, *that* went well.

"Anything to drink while you wait?"

I look up. Even the waitress is looking at me with pity. I'm having one of those crazy klutzy hair days, where my curly hair is reacting to the rain outside. I tried my best to flat-iron it into submission but I can feel the edges starting to curl already. *Please, Universe. Let me have a decent first date since Paul.*

"Do you have cabernet by the glass?"

"We absolutely do."

"Great. I'll have one. And if he's not here in five minutes, bring me the tab."

I try to distract myself. Across the table from mine, a man is twiddling his feet. Someone is eating a cinnamon-laced dessert and the scent teases my nostrils.

"See, you don't listen to me anymore. But if a man talks, you listen," a woman is complaining, three tables away to her partner. Behind me, another woman is saying she had to buy her shirts extra big so she didn't pop a button. The man she's with is assuring her she doesn't need to diet.

I feel a pang for her. Isn't that the way it always is? Spending our lives trying to improve, never quite happy with who we are?

"Sorry I'm late," Trent, in tan slacks and a pastel yellow shirt, says as he plops down. He waves a waiter over. "Bring us the house specialty, make them doubles, and keep those drinks coming." He looks around the restaurant then, narrowing his eyes. "Who's here, anyway? A couple girls were looking through the window."

That's when I see Tahoe.

I *see* him.

As if neon lights were flashing around him, as if every light in the restaurant were aimed at him.

My Tyrannosaurus rex, in the flesh, *in* the restaurant, heading toward a booth at the end with a candle, a candle reflecting very attractive shadows on his chiseled face.

His hair is in a state of subdued bed-head sexy. But it's the cocksure fucking smile that suddenly curls his lovely lips as he answers the waitress that gives me a little uncomfortable pinch between my legs.

He's with a group of guys. They're all wearing jeans and comfortable shirts, Tahoe in a white polo.

His lacrosse team?

"…well they all seem to be looking in that direction…" I hear Trent say, shifting to take a look. "Ah, thank you!" He's distracted by the incoming alcohol and delightedly watches the server pour.

Tahoe keeps flashing his beautiful smile, and when our eyes meet, his smile changes to a smirk as he glances meaningfully at Trent, then at me with a raised eyebrow.

He lifts his wine glass in a toast.

I can't help but feel my body respond, as if something or someone flipped the on switch.

"Alright, so…" Trent says. "Tell me about you. Gina."

I was going to ask him the same question. But with Tahoe in the restaurant, watching me with my awkward hair on an awkward first date, it's like I can't get my brain cells to cooperate.

I realize our eyes lock every time I glance in his direction. It's like he knows when I'm looking and catches me. He frowns every time he glances at Trent.

I toss back my cabernet and then smile at Trent. He sits there, with his red hair and kind face, and this time, at least, he's sober. He's still the nice guy I met at Tahoe's party, one of the only guys who wasn't totally wasted—at least he could still walk without stumbling. He's the kind of guy you could have a home and a dog with, not a threesome…like with *Tahoe Roth.*

"Excuse me, I'll be right back," I tell Trent, all the while staring at Tahoe.

I have to pass Tahoe's table as I head to the restroom at the end of a long hall, and I try to keep my eyes off him as I do.

I exhale when I finally turn around the corner, three steps away from the ladies' room, when I'm grabbed from behind.

"Where are you going?" a low voice whispers near my ear.

I freeze and squeeze my eyes shut in dread. My wrist feels tiny in his grip.

Please let it not be true. I'm not standing in a liquefying state with Tahoe Roth's body an inch from touching mine. I crack my eyes open and twist my body a little bit toward his. And it *is* Tahoe.

"Meet me outside," he says, looking at me with a smirky smile, then a puzzled frown. He walks away—and I stare at his back.

I follow my curiosity and head after him.

Parked seven feet away from the restaurant entrance is a vintage yellow Hummer. I can't see past the tinted windows but the passenger door flings open and T-Rex waits for me inside, behind the wheel.

I climb in, and then I slam the door shut and glare. "What are you doing here? Are you following me?" I narrow my eyes.

He narrows his eyes mockingly back at me. "Why? Do you need following?"

He looks boyish in those clothes, with a day's scruff on his jaw, a light smile.

But the smile doesn't last long.

Pretty soon he's frowning at me again. I swear this man smiles at everyone *but* me.

"Is he one of the club?" His voice sounds full of annoyance.

"My one-night stand club is very exclusive, so no, not yet. But he's hard for it; that counts for something."

"Does it?" He still sounds annoyed.

"It's a requisite for being in the club."

His eyebrows rise. "Don't be silly, Gina, he couldn't get it up with a tow truck pulling it."

"Don't be jealous, T-Rex, you had your chance, and you declined. Which is good though. I'd drunk too much Benadryl, allergies and stuff. And it makes me woozy," I lie. "But we don't really want to fool around—we'd have to look at each other when we're done, at all of Saint and Rachel's events. I've got enough awkward with my hair."

He looks at my hair, and I instantly drop my hand from the top of my head and become so self-aware and nervous. I'm not the type of girl to get nervous. But then he's not the type of guy I'm used to. He's like *nothing* I'm used to.

I end up studying him while he studies me.

"What's with the scruff?" I point at the dark blond shadow on his tan jaw.

"Letting it grow until we win." He sighs drearily and scrapes a hand over his stubbled jaw.

"Then I'm glad I haven't gone there just to see you lose."

"Gina Gina Gina." He releases a cocky laugh that almost shakes the car. "If you came, we wouldn't lose."

"Your pride would save your losing team?"

"No, you would."

I'm briefly taken aback by the comment then I make a brisk effort to dismiss it.

"So is lacrosse like your hobby?" I ask.

The frown is back again, his blue eyes laughingly incredulous. "Hobby? Lacrosse is my art. The fastest-growing sport in America. You'll understand when you go."

"Whatever." I kick his heel, and he kicks me back.

"So what, are you taking him home tonight?" he asks.

"I don't know, maybe." I shrug and glance out the window. "But if you keep me here, he won't even want to come."

"You're the one he won't know how to make come."

"Huh?"

"He'll leave you all strung up and wanting it," he says laughingly.

"Excuse me?!"

I kick him again, twice, and the third time he frowns and says, "Ouch," rubbing his heel. "Play nice, Regina," he chides.

"Well, this *has* been nice, but my prince charming awaits." I almost laugh at my own exaggeration. His voice stops me.

"You taking him home or not?"

I turn and stare at him.

I don't want to lie and say a definitive no, but I also find the idea of him thinking that other men find me attractive very appealing. "I don't know," I hedge again.

He reaches out and curls his hand around my upper arm. "Then I don't know how I'll manage to unwrap my hand from your—"

"Probably yes," I cry. "Yes! Go bother your fuck-friends. Go show them your lacrosse stick."

"The long one or the short one?"

I shove him, and he reaches over me, opens the door and rumples my hair. "You're too gorgeous for him, Regina."

"And you're full of it."

"I can tell he's a loser."

"I met him at *your* party, so…" I leave it at that.

He stops me again. "Hey. We're friends. Right?"

I force myself to meet his intense blue gaze. "Yes."

"We're good?" A muscle flexes along his jaw as he waits for my reply.

"We're good."

He grins, a devastating grin. "Good. Cause I don't want to hurt you. Alright?" His eyes are raw, clawing into me with some fierce emotion. "You need a guy who will always be there for you. One who will never let you down."

"I know." But where is he? I wonder. "And you need a thousand women to make you feel good, and I'm only one."

He laughs. "Friends then." He kisses my cheek. "You better come to my next game."

He pats the back of my head as I turn to go back inside. My heart hurting. Then I watch him head to his table. *Please don't appear in my stupid dreams tonight*, I think as I take my seat.

I think of having no one to talk to about this tonight when I go to my apartment. No one will be there. Rachel and I used to pass the Kleenex to each other whenever life threw us a curveball, when life threw me Paul and when Rachel nearly lost Saint.

There's no one to pass the Kleenex anymore.

And even though my best friend's reason for moving out was a happy one—she got married!—the feeling of loneliness is still strong. More than ever.

Paul helped me get over my parents' abandonment. Rachel helped me get over Paul's. But this time, I'm all I can count on.

I need to throw the Kleenex box in the trash, because I'm determined to be as happy as I can be.

So I drink another glass of wine and force myself to look at my date—Trent—as if nothing else in the world exists, and as if Tahoe Roth isn't only a few tables away, looking at me through the lowered, fierce lines of his eyebrows.

We are heading home from the restaurant.

"I can't believe he picked up the tab," Trent keeps saying as we ride in the back of a cab. We're supposed to drop me off first.

"He's loaded, trust me, he feels relieved."

Although to be honest, a part of me wonders if he did it merely to remind me that he was there, at the restaurant, watching me. I was good about not looking at him after I returned, except through the corner of my eye. Tahoe paying the bill almost felt like him staking some sort of claim over me. He doesn't want to hurt me but it almost feels as if he's determined to keep anyone else from hurting me as well.

"Huh." Trent scratches the back of his ear thoughtfully, still looking perplexed. "Something going on between the two of you?"

"Nope. We're friends."

Friends who annoy each other.

And sometimes want to have sex with one another.

But never do.

I laugh inwardly at that, surprised by the sudden relief I feel.

Whatever we almost had, it's all in the past. We're friends.

And I don't know why it matters this much.

In the back of the cab, I remind myself I have a guy next to me. He's not big, not overpowering, but it's comforting that he's not built that way, the opposite of Tahoe. So when he opens his mouth to ask me more about Tahoe—obviously still impressed—I press my lips to his.

Then break away.

"What was that for?" Trent is stunned and obviously thrilled.

The cab stops in front of my building, and I swing open the door, shrugging with a smile.

"Whoa, aren't you forgetting something? Don't you want to invite me up?" He sounds desperate.

A guy desperate to go to bed with me is *good.*

A refreshing change compared to Tahoe's rejection.

I look at him—good guy, genuinely interested, he doesn't even feel intimidated by my sometimes brusque ways. Wynn is with Emmett, Rachel's with Saint, and I really wanted to try to give myself another chance—even if I never again want to feel like I felt when Paul betrayed me.

But not yet. So I say, "Some other time."

I turn to walk away, and he calls me back, "Gina?"

He fishes in his pocket for money, then shoots me a look. "I don't have much cash. For when he…drops me off at my place."

I stare, then hear myself admit, "I'm not sure that I…have enough…"

I pull out money. Wads of bills, pennies, quarters, and he helps me count. "I think...yeah, I think I'll need the nickels too. Thanks."

"Okay," I say, then I start walking to the entrance to my building. "You know what?" I turn and look at him. "Yeah. Come in for coffee or something."

"Wow, thanks!" he says, jogging up to me.

The ride up to my floor is uneventful. I'm silent, wondering if I know what the hell I'm doing, and Trent is...well, he's fishing in his pockets as if he doesn't remember whether he has a condom or not. "I need to take this slow," I say.

"How slow?" He pulls out a crinkled condom packet and exhales in excitement.

"I haven't had the best time on the dating ride."

"Yeah," he scratches his chin, "I understand."

"So let's just try this and see how it goes."

It doesn't go well.

SOS!

Why is it that when something goes wrong, the differences we'd been having with others become trivial to the point of completely vanishing?

All I know right now is that, whatever my issues with Tahoe are, he's been the only thing on my mind for the past hour, the only thing helping me keep my sanity together.

I'm at the hospital. I've already been discharged, but I remain sitting alone on a bench outside. I'm torn between calling him or simply calling a cab. I decide not to call his cell phone, and I tell myself I'll simply call him at his place. If he's there, well...

Gathering what's left of my courage after the ordeal I just went through, I absently watch a man get wheeled into the emergency room and I dial his home number.

A female voice answers on the third ring, laughing as she picks up.

"Umm. Is Tahoe available?" Nervously, I change my cell phone from one ear to the other.

"He's busy, tying someone to his bed. Who's calling?"

Giggles, and a husky male laugh in the background. My stomach roils.

"No one important."

I hang up and exhale.

My phone rings less than five seconds later. I see *Tahoe Roth* flash on the screen and freeze.

One ring, two rings, three, and I still can't make up my mind whether to answer or let him go to voicemail.

Do I answer or not? Do I freaking answer or not? Do I want him to know or do I want the Earth to swallow me whole?

I decide to answer as naturally as possible. "I dialed by mistake, no need to call back."

There are giggles in the background and the sound of a closing door. "What's up, Regina?" He sounds amused.

"I just had sex with Trent and the condom broke."

Silence.

"It broke and I couldn't find it," I blurt out, my voice breaking unexpectedly. I scowl and stare into the glass doors of the hospital, my stupid voice still wavering. "I just had the most humiliating moment of my life at the hospital while some guy…" I shudder. "Anyway, the condom broke and I'm on my way to get a morning-after pill—I just don't want to go back in there and *ask* for one." I sigh. "What about you, you seem very busy. I don't think the tied woman will appreciate staying tied while you hear about my evening."

I hear a muffled, "Untie her and show yourselves to the door," and then his voice sounds close to the speaker. "I'll be right over."

"What? No!"

He hangs up.

I text him.

I'm not even home!
Where are you?

I hesitate, then give him the name of the hospital.

I'm pacing as I wait. The tires of his car screech soon afterward on the hospital driveway, and he swings open the passenger door from the inside.

And he's so good-looking—he looks especially perfect tonight—I purse my lips, humiliated all over again, and at the same time, relieved.

I don't know why I called him out of all the people in my contacts list. I don't know why I bolted so fast out of my apartment, refusing to even look at Trent or ask him to come with me.

Somewhere in the back of my mind, as I was going through the uncomfortable and humiliating moment of spreading my legs open so a gloved hand could retrieve the condom, I found comfort in the thought of Tahoe. I used him to distract myself, to keep from feeling dirty and alone. And now here I am, standing in the hospital driveway while he leans across the passenger seat and waits for me to move.

"Get in," he says, all lowered brows, his eyes glimmering with protectiveness and concern.

I do, shutting the door to find myself enclosed in the confined space of his white Ghost.

The scent of leather and pine trees hits me, a scent I associate strongly with him.

There's a silence as I sit in the passenger seat, and he sits there, his hands gripping the wheel, his jaw set as he inhales.

And I realize I must smell awful, like a hospital, like antiseptic and maybe even sex. He turns around as if to say something.

"Don't give me shit," I warn angrily.

He scowls. "I'm not."

I scoff.

He shifts gears and pulls into traffic and laughs darkly.

He's pissed off as he drives, I can tell.

"I'm upset on your behalf. What kind of moth—"

"It was an accident, okay?"

He growls under his breath, "Bullshit," then eyes me, his voice painfully tender as he reaches out to take my chin and draw my gaze to his. "Hey. Gina. You okay?"

His touch could break me right now. My eyes water and I glance out the window. He drops his hand and puts it back on the gearshift.

"So he's not perfect," I blurt, throwing my arms in the air. "Sometimes the guys you're dating never are. You start to wonder why you even bother…" I glare out the window. "But then you think of the cuddling, and just having someone's warmth in bed, and who cares about perfection?"

Silence.

I glare defensively and cross my arms tightly over my chest. "Why am I telling you this? You wouldn't even know. I doubt you've slept with a woman after…you know."

"That's right, Gina. I just use them then kick them out the door," he says sarcastically, almost with self-loathing.

We end up at the pharmacy, buying me a morning-after pill. Just in case.

He adds a pack of Trident bubblegum, then fishes out his card and pays for everything.

"Thank you," I whisper as I pull out his gum, hand it over, and carry the bag to his car. "I've never taken one of these but Wynn has and she says she felt absolutely awful, crampy and like shit," I complain as he opens the car door for me.

He climbs behind the wheel, and he's dead silent and unnervingly thoughtful as he drives me to my place. He parks the car, and as I say thank you and get out, he turns off the ignition and follows me into my apartment.

Silence up the elevator.

He takes the key when I fish it out and opens the door, then he waits for me to pass. I've never had Tahoe in my apartment. It's a little jarring to see him step inside. He throws his jacket aside, rolls up the sleeves of his navy-blue sweater, and settles on the couch.

"What are you doing?" I ask.

I don't know why, but the sight of Tahoe invading my apartment and taking up my couch makes me feel vulnerable. The situation strangely intimate.

He kicks off his shoes.

"You're not planning to stay here, are you?"

He raises a brow and grabs the remote from the coffee table. "In case you don't feel well. Get crampy and shit." He quotes me, smirking.

I frown.

He turns on the TV. And the last show I had been watching, *Vikings*, flares on the screen.

Reluctantly I admire the man on the screen, and then the man on the couch in my apartment. Both so raw, so blond, so virile. One of them—the one in my apartment—wreaking havoc with my lungs.

"You look like him, you know," I say in a bit of an accusatory tone. "Ragnar. That hunting look in your eyes. You don't look polished even in your business suits. You look like you belong somewhere outside." *Wild and untamed.* "Like a Neanderthal."

He frowns back, then pats the couch. "Come here."

"I'm not a dog, don't tell me 'come here.'"

But I go anyway, kicking my shoes off and dropping at his side. He wraps his arm around me and I feel myself stiffen. His chest is like a wall. He smooths his hand down my arm and chuckles softly. "Come on, relax," he whispers, his smile accidentally grazing my ear.

It feels insanely good just to be held—no expectations, no sexy times ahead, just being held. My eyes flutter closed, relaxation seeping into my bones.

"I can't afford this apartment anymore," I tell him. "I'm not renewing my lease. Wynn is moving in with Emmett, and I really don't feel like acquiring a roommate. I'm going to look for a new place, a small one, just for me."

I hadn't realized I was stroking his chest. He's watching me with a heavy-lidded gaze. The air thickens with awareness.

Our eyes hold.

His expression is so hungry, and inside that gaze is that primitive look, so intense it borders on pain.

"I should go," he says softly.

"You should," I say just as softly.

He releases me reluctantly, then grabs his jacket and leaves without another word.

Minutes later, Tahoe stands in my doorway with his jacket still in hand, his other hand shoved into the pocket of his dark-wash jeans, that navy-blue sweater draped sexily over his chest.

"Your doorman let me back in."

I feel myself stand like a sleepwalker, getting sucked into his gaze. "I can see that."

He shuts the door behind him. "I'm spending the night."

"You are? I mean…no, really, you're not."

He walks back in and throws his jacket on the couch we'd been sitting on and starts to prowl my place like some beast on the loose. "Where's your bedroom?"

"There—" I point down the hall, stunned when he immediately heads in that direction. "But what are you doing?"

"Look, I've probably got a shit-ton of girls still back at my place. I really don't feel like playing the player tonight."

"I don't care what you feel like. I don't feel like having you—"

He lies on my bed.

"—lie on my bed and—"

He takes off his shoes, wearing no socks; his feet are sexy.

"—and putting your feet on my—"

He puts his feet up and jerks off his sweater, and he's suddenly bare-chested and I struggle to talk.

"—on my, on my… No! Don't get under the covers!"

He gets under the covers, barefoot, bare-chested, in his jeans. And then he smirks and shoves one muscled arm under the sheets, and then I see him toss his jeans into the corner.

I grab a pillow and sigh, dropping onto the other side of the bed.

"Get under," he says, no-nonsense.

"Wait, what?"

"Get under the sheets. You'll have a warm bed tonight, Regina."

I open my mouth to speak, but no words come out.

Cuddling and a warm bed…friends do that, too, right?

I swallow, head to my bathroom, close the door, brush my teeth, and look at my face in the mirror. I still have my makeup on, but not as perfectly as I'd like. I find myself retouching, my hands trembling and I don't know why. I certainly don't plan to sleep with him. Ever.

He had his chance.

We had our chance.

We're friends now.

I head out and jerk off my dress, slip into a T-shirt, feeling him watch me as I remove my bra from under my shirt. I toss it aside and climb onto the bed. It squeaks as I lift the covers and slide in.

He opens his arm, smiling a harmless smile, but the look in his eyes… God, that's as harmless as the look of a demon. Even when I see all sorts of things lurking there—darkly in his gaze—I am tempted to trust him. Trust that despite his male reactions to me, he's more determined to be friends.

But I don't want to be haunted by what it feels like to lie in those arms with veined muscles popping out, so I shake my head. "Don't get touchy-touchy on me, alright? I like my space."

"Your space?" He chuckles and smirks. "I happen to be in your space, Regina. I thought you liked cuddling and warm beds?"

"Beds warmed by lovers, not by guy friends. By the way, I'm really glad we're friends," I admit as I get settled under the blanket but make sure our bodies don't touch. I get a glimpse of black tight boxers and long male legs and instantly jerk my gaze away when I feel a pinch between my legs.

He laughs quietly, almost incredulously.

I lift my head, frowning, all the warm, fuzzy feelings I was feeling toward him gone. "What? We're not?" I accuse.

"I'm zipping it." He zips his mouth with a fingertip.

"No. Really. You don't want to be friends with me? So that I don't call and interrupt your fun times?"

"Regina. I'm glad we're friends."

I feel myself frown, but relax a little because his smile is all over his face, even in his eyes, and it has this effect on me. "I owe you one."

He grabs the remote from my nightstand. "Don't worry, I'll collect."

"You've only been in my apartment for an hour and you're already taking over both my TVs." I scowl.

I plump my pillow and make certain there are enough inches separating us, head to toe.

"Just stay on that side of the bed."

TRENCH COAT

He spooned me.

I'm at work the next day, organizing the makeup drawers, remembering the pitch black of my bedroom when we lay there falling asleep.

Him shifting in bed. His eyes finding mine in the dark. His hand splaying over my stomach. Pulling me closer. My back flattening against the front of his body.

Neither of us said a word about it the next morning as we had coffee and pancakes. He didn't even kiss my cheek when he left for work; he was late to some meeting and in a rush to go. He just lifted two fingers in a peace sign and shut the door behind him.

I call Wynn during my break.

"Why would he spoon you?" Wynn's voice sounds dubious over the phone.

"I don't know."

"Go over there and bang him."

The urge to do just *that* burns so fiercely inside me that I can't think straight. No rationalizations can quell the fierce little fire burning in me now.

That evening when my shift is over, I put on a trench coat with nothing but a pink thong underneath. I head to his place. I've been here a couple of times, and the thing about Tahoe Roth is, his doormen know he's a total player. They seem to allow all his girls free access. The uniformed man in the elevator only nods formally when you tell him you're going to the penthouse, which requires him to slide in a special access card.

He wears a gold name tag that says Ernest.

He's still stoic when we reach Tahoe's floor and I thank him under my breath.

I wander inside his apartment and spot his blue and yellow Van Gogh on the fireplace mantel in his study. There's music in the background. "Walk" by Kwabs. A total make-out song; a total *everything* song. I wander into the living room...and then see the two women surrounding that blond head of his. He's standing in nothing but ripped muscles and naturally gold skin, and they're also naked.

I catch my breath. He moves out of my vision as he urges one to lie down on the couch.

I peer over the back of the couch and he's bent over one. His ass flexing, his body moving powerfully. "Ladies first," he's telling the woman as she starts to come.

I hurry back down the hall as fast as my noisy heels allow without drawing attention, and suddenly I don't know what to do with myself. I don't even have words to describe what I saw to Wynn.

Ladies first...

Oh my god.

He's such a...

I've been closed off for years, but lately feeling like I should give men another chance. Why I'm obsessed with this one is beyond my comprehension. He's worse than Paul.

Beast. Stud. He's hot. Irreverent. Insatiable. Incorrigible. Pure I, I, *I*—cause he's selfish too, and he'll never care for anyone more than he cares about *Tahoe*.

I hurry back to the elevator and press the down arrow repeatedly until it *tings*.

Too bad the elevator tings just when the Kwabs song ends and the room falls silent. Which means that, very likely, he *heard*.

I board quickly and hit the lobby button, riding with another elevator man. Richard.

I stare anxiously at the numbers as we descend, step briskly out into the massive lobby and am heading straight for the revolving doors when I hear another elevator ting—

Then, in a familiar light Texan drawl, "Regina."

I stop in my tracks, knot my sash tighter.

"Thanks, Ernest," I hear Tahoe say, his drawl still a little noticeable.

I turn to face him and nearly buckle when my eyes meet his puzzled blue ones.

"Hey," I say.

His brows rise questioningly.

"I came to visit my client and totally messed up my floors," I hastily explain as he walks over in an open white shirt, his lips raw, his eyes raw, his hair mussed, so beautiful. It hurts that he's so out of my reach.

I turn to leave but he takes a step. "Why are you leaving then?"

"Oh, because I realized I have a message. A message she's canceling, and I didn't know. So."

Realizing I'm madly waving my phone in the air like a nitwit, I tuck it into my pocket and turn away quickly.

Then he reaches out and puts his hand on the back of my trench coat, turning me a little toward him. I'm careening on my axis, my senses out of control at the unexpected touch. I don't understand it.

He runs the back of one finger down my cheek, and the touch sparks fire.

"Did you hear me?" he asks.

His eyes glimmer dangerously with something.

"No. What did you say?"

Once again, I'm starstruck by those eyes, deep as oceans. "I asked if you want me to take you home."

As he speaks, the words ripple through my body in delicious little waves.

His gaze lifts all of a sudden and stares intently past my forehead. "What's with the hair?"

"I combed it."

Two blunt fingers take my chin, hiking it up an inch as he studies me with an interested expression. "So you did. You look very nice. You should comb it more often."

I feel that familiar stomach pain I felt when we talked at my place and he was in my bed. When he looks down at me again, I feel like he's peeling me open. Like he's seeing what I came here for, what I want, something I'm afraid for him to see. "I'm fine taking a cab," I say, suddenly too eager to be in that cab right now. "I have somewhere I need to go."

I'm desperate to leave so why am I still standing here, facing him?

I like spending time with him more than I've enjoyed spending time with any other guy. I wake up and crave his company.

"Thank you for offering, by the way," I add. "You're a great friend. Loyal."

"So are you."

"So why can't you be loyal in relationships?"

I don't know why I ask this now, but for some reason I just can't hold it back. He's been a great friend to me; he's equally loyal to Saint and Callan. I don't understand how someone can be so loyal to his friends and so bad at relationships.

"You can't have such poor control over your anatomy."

"I can handle my anatomy just fine, Gina." He laughs in amused disbelief and then smirks. "I was loyal once." His voice sounds dark and somber.

"What happened?"

The look in his eyes turns cynical and cold. He sounds part angry and part resigned. "What else, Regina? Life."

Was he betrayed?

Why would a girl betray *him*, the epitome of beastly manhood?

We stand there, looking at each other. The doormen pretending not to look at us. I realize I have to leave, but he isn't leaving either.

He hikes his thumb and points upward, in the direction of the floors above. "Sorry you had to see that."

I wave dismissively, determined for him never to know how much it hurts that he's good enough for others and not for me. "Oh, not at all, just the thing to get a girl in the mood."

He frowns at that.

I smile and say, "Well, bye." I lean up and kiss his jaw, close my eyes and inhale his scent, then wave as I step outside.

His eyes are tender as he crosses his arms and watches me with great interest, as if he knows I was lying through my teeth.

I sit in the back of the cab, wanting him. Wanting to be the girl beneath him. I don't remember wanting anything this much except once, when I desperately wanted Paul to take back the words *I don't love you.*

I call Rachel.

Get voicemail.

She's traveling to Timbuktu or I don't know where, and she's sent me a few emails and texts. She probably steals a moment, connects with all of us, and goes back to being Mrs. Saint on her honeymoon.

I stand, in my panties and my trench coat, on the sidewalk just in front of my building. I call Trent.

"Hey, is there somewhere we can meet so we can properly finish what we started?"

We meet the next day at a club that Rachel has mentioned is the new "it" spot.

"I was glad you called. I'm sorry I freaked out," he says sheepishly, rubbing his freckles.

"At least I learned one new thing about you. Never to trust you putting on the condom."

He laughs. "Try me once more," he begs.

And I take his sweet face and kiss his lips and whisper, "Maybe tonight." I bite my lip at the look of excitement in his eyes, laughing softly.

I'm happy—happy that I called Trent—when Tahoe arrives with Callan and another guy I don't know. He looks at me from across a roomful of people, the music at full blast, and then he looks at Trent.

He looks so thoughtful all of a sudden, scowling a little bit.

I'm breathless and I finish off my drink to try to hide it. Someone slaps his back, drawing his attention.

"What's his problem?" Trent complains. "He thinks he's king of the world, man. Hate guys like him."

"You were happy last weekend when he paid for our dinner, and before that when you went to his party."

"Sorry, it's just that…I don't like the way he looks at you. Can I get you another drink?"

"Sure. Thanks."

He heads off when "All We Need" by Odesza starts playing. Tahoe stares at me. I stare back at him, my heart pounding when he starts making his way toward me.

He walks the walk, this guy. It feels like the crowd parts to let him pass.

His lips start curling. A foot away, he extends his arm a little mockingly and opens his big palm. "I believe this is our song," he says, flat and no-nonsense, very unlike the socially playful Tahoe I normally see at the club.

I want to laugh but he looks serious.

"It is, isn't it?" I say, playing along.

He's lying. We have no song. But I'm bored and it looks like he is too. I give him my hand like a lady, laughing, and let him draw me onto the dance floor. He smiles and looks down at me as he finds us a spot and leans in close, his body heat crackling all around me.

"He the one?"

I nod, lift my arms and lock my wrists over my head, and start moving to the music.

He moves sinuously, like a wildcat, and as he does, he looks at me again, longer this time. "So how are you?"

"I'm good."

It's hard to concentrate when my body is so close to his.

Shivers run down my spine and I think he feels it because he drags a hand across the back of my neck and down my back. "Why are you even giving him the time of day?"

"He's my booty call."

His eyebrows pull into a frown and mischief sparks inside his eyes. "Getting a condom stuck inside you not enough of a cockblock for you two?"

He takes my wrist in his grip and leads me off the dance floor, and I'm puzzled as I follow him. "Where are we going?"

"Anywhere else."

He leads me to the elevators, ushers me into the first one that opens, and pushes the *T* button, where the word *Terrace* is engraved beside it.

I'm not prepared for the view. It's spectacular. Wind slaps us as we step outside, and I'm surprised to find speakers on the terrace, playing the same music that had been playing down-stairs. Several empty seating areas are scattered beneath the night sky. I suppose during the summer people like coming up here, but we're heading into the holiday season and Chicago has been cold for weeks.

Sam Smith's "Like I Can" starts playing, and he says, as we take one of the empty lounge seats, "Maybe that's his song for you. Think he likes you like that?" He shifts forward and props his elbows on his knees as he studies me.

Sam Smith sings, *"He'll never love you like I can..."*

"Oh, no." I laugh, reaching up and trying to control my hair.

He's still thoughtful. "Why so certain?"

"Because nobody can like me like that." My smile fades. I can't believe I said that.

We stare at each other for a long moment. Not a breath leaves me, not a sound. It's as if I'm absorbing every part of this moment—the song lyrics, the shade of his blue eyes, the line of his jaw and the slits of light caused by the angle of the moonlight.

His stare generates a heat in my stomach that's so hard to bear.

"So this Paul," he says, stretching an arm over the back of the lounge seat, his hand dangerously close to my nape. "What does he do?"

"I don't know. But I hope he's eating shit and busy dying."

He chuckles—the sound low but resonant enough that it reaches deep inside me—and the corners of his lips hike up. "You don't keep tabs on him?"

"No, I'm not interested in the daily life of cow dung."

He laughs, and I grin, and he shifts a little and I shiver.

He starts to remove his jacket.

I open my mouth to protest but when I'm engulfed in it, I can't talk. I duck my head when I feel myself go red and I don't want him to see it.

"Thanks," I mumble, tugging it closer.

I burrow deeper into the warmth and stare out at the city. "He sent me a letter, a few months ago. I tucked it into my underwear drawer and decided not to open it. The guy didn't get that when I said I didn't want to hear from him ever again, it included the written word."

"Let's go open it."

"Excuse me? I don't want to open it."

"Yeah you do." He pokes my tummy with a finger, and I hold it.

"Really." I squeeze his finger.

He extracts his finger and this time touches his fingertip to my nose. "Liar."

I open my mouth and bite his finger before he can pull it away.

"Whoa. Hungry little cat, are we?"

I let go, laughing.

"What are you doing with this guy Trent, Regina?"

"What?"

"What are you doing with him?"

I stare. "I feel like getting laid very hard."

"No, you don't." He smiles at me. "You feel like being made love to. There's a difference." He looks at me, eyes sparkling. "Candlelight, soft sheets beneath you…"

"No! Where's your sense of adventure? Against a wall is fine."

"Your hair spread over the pillow, every stitch of you naked…"

"No, I just want hard sex, partially clothed. I don't like being naked when I'm having sex, it makes me wonder if I look okay, and I don't like wondering."

He lifts his brow. "Really."

"Fact. You can ask the members of my club."

He looks pissed off. "The members of your club don't seem to do a very good job of making you forget yourself."

"Well, not all of them get to have as much experience as you."

He doesn't laugh, only eyes me.

"Not even with putting on a condom?"

I laugh. "God, don't remind me." I shrug. "Maybe I *do* want to be made love to. I deserve it."

He pulls one curl of hair from behind my ear, smirking. "That very much makes me want to be him tonight."

"GINA?"

Startled, I look up and struggle to my feet when I see Trent stepping off the elevator with my drink in his hand. "Someone saw you two come up here."

I glance apologetically at Trent, then at Tahoe. "I've got to go."

Tahoe purses his lips and clamps his jaw, shoving his hands into his pockets as he stands and watches me leave. I'm smiling as I board, as he stands and just looks at me with a slow smile that flashes just for me, and when I tell Trent we may need a rain check for a make-out after all, I'm still smiling when I get home. Did he really mean what he said?

Do I want him to mean it?

Do I want to do anything about it?

I hit the bed and pull out my iPod, play some music with headphones, wondering if I have the courage to do anything about it or if keeping the status quo would be best. Hours later I stand up and go to my drawers, opening the top right one and peering under the clothes to the bottom, where I set Paul's letter months ago. I didn't even tell Rachel about it because, luckily, I was the one who retrieved the mail every day while she was busy falling for ex-manwhore Saint.

Yeah, it's still there.

I slam the drawer shut. Because I won't give the asshole the satisfaction of reading it.

NOVEMBER

The first weekend of November I get a call from Rachel. She sounds so happy and so far away. As we say how much we miss each other and I ask her about her honeymoon and she tells me all about the places they've gone, I wonder if I'll ever even leave Chicago. Or better yet, leave Chicago with a guy, just because we're each other's best person to spend time with on Earth.

She asks me if I'll be going to Wynn's gallery exhibition this weekend.

I tell her I can't go, that I'm working overtime, which is partly true. She drills me for more information, so I say I'm making house calls now, and that I spent all Halloween doing monster faces, which was fun.

"Have you seen Tahoe and Callan? What are those two up to now that my guy is gone?"

"Mischief," I say. "Tahoe keeps asking me to one of his lacrosse games."

"Yeah, he told Saint he can't wear you down. He really wants you to go!" She laughs.

We talk a bit more, and I hang up the phone, increasingly unhappy about not going to his games, not feeling the relief I thought I'd feel by avoiding him. Instead I'm dissatisfied and curious, wondering what he'd say or do if I showed up.

For the past three weeks, Trent has been asking me out every Saturday. I hesitated at first but I finally decided I want to see where this leads, so I've said yes all three times.

I glance around my apartment while Trent snores in my bed.

We could work out.

For the first time in a long time, I think I have a shot.

I pull my knees to my chest and stare at him. I feel much more relaxed now about us and the sex. It was good. I get up and hurry to make breakfast, trying to make the tray as pretty as I can, the breakfast as perfect as I can.

I suppose I could chalk it up to the smidge of guilt I felt last night when occasionally I got distracted during sex and thought of…well. You know.

I wish my best friend were in town, so she could remind me of all the things she knows from Saint about Tahoe that bug me. There are so many things but right now I cannot name any except one: the girls he always hangs out with.

Again, I wonder why he's good enough for them, but not for me.

"Back in bed, Regina," Trent yells from the bedroom as I finish fixing up the tray.

I bring it over. "I hope you like eggs."

"Ahhh, no, I'm vegan." He frowns. "Haven't you noticed?" I look down at the tray I made and want to just drop it and dip my face in a tub of water out of pure embarrassment. I've been going out with him for a few weeks and I hadn't noticed he never ordered meat or dairy?

I hate admitting it but I thought it was because he's a bit of a pinchpenny, to the point I've started ordering only appetizers as main dishes too.

"No worries, come here. Let's have another go." He lifts the sheets.

"I'd like that. Yes." I set the tray aside grudgingly, trying to work up the enthusiasm for morning sex.

"I'm one hundred percent sure I'm not messing up with the condom this time either," he says sheepishly.

"Good, 'cause I don't want to go through that again."

He asks me to the movies that weekend. After a full day of work, I'm starving as we walk into the movie theater. I order a medium popcorn and a Coke, and then I follow Trent into the theater and settle next to him to watch the movie. We end up sharing the popcorn as we watch the film, and I realize I haven't had a nice evening like this in a long time.

THE SAINTS

I focus on work the following week. The streets are cold and we get our first consecutive days of nonstop rain. It's really dreary to be alone in my apartment so during the day, I hardly go there anymore. I have lunch with colleagues or friends—even Rachel's friend Valentine. I've also been working nonstop, putting in extra shifts and adding more house calls to my schedule.

I get a call from Rachel one morning while at work.

"Gina!! We're flying back to Chicago as we speak! Oh my god, when am I gonna see you? Are you free tonight? *Wait.* I need to unpack."

"That's not even an issue, I'll head over to your place and I'll help you unpack."

I'm excited to see Rachel.

That evening, I head over to the Saints' new penthouse. Wynn has another gallery opening tonight, so it's just me.

Rachel and I spend the first hour just talking while she unpacks. She tells me about their honeymoon. Their new penthouse is so grand and beautiful, I get easily distracted.

I hear male voices out in the living area for a moment. They're combined with several sets of long, heavy male footsteps, then they fade away. I keep wanting to ask her if Saint is seeing his friends tonight. But I don't want to feed my curiosity, and decide that if I tell her anything about my life, it should be about Trent.

"Bali was so wonderful I wanted to stay there forever. We went to Bora Bora, Dubai, then Saint had some business in Berlin...oh, but it's nice to be home."

"Rachel, I could get lost in this apartment."

"I know. It feels so big for just us two. But tell me about you!"

"What is this?" I fish out a lovely velvet box from Rachel's suitcase.

She comes over and flips it open to reveal a pair of gorgeous, irregular gray pearl earrings.

"Some black pearls we snatched on the streets of Papeete. Saint was like: 'I can get you a pair a thousand times better than these,' but I insisted on these ones. They were right there, the moment we were, and I like that they're flawed, see?"

She puts them on and then pulls out a T-shirt from her suitcase. "So, I brought you this. I saw it in Harrods and it reminded me of you."

It's a white T-shirt with Marilyn Monroe on it. In pink italics: *Beneath the makeup and behind the smile, I am just a girl who wishes for the world.*

I clutch it to my chest. "It's perfect. I love it. Thank you, Rache."

"What are you up to? Did Wynn move in?"

"Not exactly. I might move out."

"What?! There is *no way* you are moving out."

"The apartment is too big for just me."

"Gina! Malcolm will take care of the rent. I know he'll *insist* on it. Here, let's go ask and I'll show you the pics. They're on his phone."

"I am *not* going to let anyone pay my rent, Rachel," I hiss as I follow her to the library. "I'll kill you if you tell Saint about it, do you hear me? I am not taking anyone's charity and I've got this under control," I continue. The sound of male conversation reaches us as we walk up to the half-open door.

"I'm seeing someone," I whisper to distract her.

She pivots around to face me. First thing that Rachel asks when she digests this information is, "What? Gina! When do I meet him and how come I didn't know?"

I groan. "You were on your honeymoon! And I didn't know where it was going, so…"

"Well. Where *is* it going? Tell me about him!"

I hesitate because, compared to her whirlwind relationship with Saint, my relationship with Trent seems so…simple. But simple is good for me. "You'll get to meet him soon, I guess," I say.

She looks stunned, and it just feels so great to have my friend back, that I can't help but smile at her confusion. I motion toward the door and quickly change topics. "Anyway, show me the pictures."

She frowns at me. "I'm hearing all about it before you leave, Gina," she warns.

I nod, laughing, and push her toward the door.

"No hair off my balls, right?" Callan is saying inside the room, followed by male laughter.

Rachel pushes the door wider and breezes into a library fit for a whole state. "Malcolm, Gina doesn't have a roommate."

Well, I guess my attempt at distraction didn't work.

Her husband is leaning against the bookshelves with his arms crossed and immediately spreads out one arm to hug her to him. "Well that just won't do," he says as Rachel sets a kiss on his jaw. "Hi, Gina."

"Hi, Saint. I've got my situation under control so please don't even think about it." I shoot Rachel a disgusted look when she flashes an unapologetic smile at me.

Although I had sensed Tahoe in the room, I don't spot him until I dare to turn around. I watch him rise to his feet and come to his full intimidating height. Our eyes meet—his blue ones striking me like a Taser—as he pulls his hand out of his jeans pocket, and I feel his stare travel to deep, dark places in my body.

"Hey, Gina," Callan Carmichael says sweetly from his seat.

Rachel and I say hello to Callan, and then Rachel casually says, "Hi, Tahoe," and I'm suddenly facing him and only him—and if Malcolm Saint is some sort of Zeus, then Tahoe Roth is a blond Hades—and I'm forcing my tongue to move as I stare into his face.

"Hey, stranger," I say.

His sudden smile electrifies. "Hey, back."

He may look like an Adonis, but there's a darkness in his gaze. Sometimes I wonder if I'm the only one who sees it. I see it now as I stare at his gorgeous, haunting face, with a shadow of a beard and full pink lips that I continue to see in my dreams.

He continues to smile, but his eyes are somber, blue pools of darkness sucking me in.

"Saint, I want to show Gina the pics of our Bali house and all those castles we went to."

Saint signals to Tahoe, who, with a raise of his hand, confirms that he has Saint's phone. He doesn't hand it over, but merely watches me as he takes a seat on a long brown leather couch and continues looking at me, as if waiting for me to come and see them with him.

I sit on the couch beside him, and as I lean over and peer into the screen, his scent reaches me. He smells like pine trees. I love the scent of pine trees. It's exotic to me. Like a vacation.

He uses his big thumb to scroll through the images as we both take in the pictures. Images of lush greenery and the most fantastic landscapes I've ever seen, like the Saints' massive modern house in Bali and a lovely gray castle with a moat sitting in paradise.

"That's my new place." I reach around his arm and tap the picture of the gray castle.

"Nah…" He backtracks and shows me a picture of Versailles. "That's the one."

I set my chin on his shoulder and stare at it longingly. "That's delightful…When do we leave?"

I nudge his elbow with mine, and he nudges me back with a twinkle in his eyes. "Whenever you want…perks of having a private jet."

"Jackass. Should I pack a swimsuit?"

He smirks mischievously and nods at me slowly. "If you want to, but it's certainly not required."

"You're not seriously alluding to skinny-dipping? You know I only do that drunk and at weddings."

"I'm just saying, fortune favors the bold." He looks at me with a raised eyebrow and that lone dimple of his.

"The bold, not the nude."

He laughs—deep, rich male laughter—and I have never felt someone's laugh course through my skin like a shiver.

"Hey, guys?"

I start at Rachel's voice and only then realize that Tahoe and I are sitting so close we could be one. One of my breasts is basically pressed up against the back of his arm, nearly flat against his triceps muscle, and my chin is resting on his shoulder as I peer at the pics.

Rachel and Saint stand at the door. Rachel looks at me with curiosity, and Saint's expression is unreadable.

"We're starved and our kitchen won't be stocked until tomorrow. Want to get something across the street?" Saint asks, looking at Tahoe meaningfully.

I stand slowly on rubbery knees and Tahoe says, "Saint," and tosses his phone in the air.

We end up heading across the street to have dinner at a small café. Wynn joins us after the gallery opening, and because it's so crowded and the restaurant only offers tables that seat up to four, the guys sit at the bar while Rachel, Wynn and I sit at one of the small tables.

The guys are causing quite the stir. Several women who were originally seated at tables are now moving to wait for seats at the bar, hovering near the guys and hoping to catch their attention. Saint ignores them, Callan chats them up, and Tahoe simply charms their socks off as they pant all over him.

Curious to hear what he's telling the girls to make them look all googly-eyed, I decide to refill my glass at the bar. I'm surprised to realize he's telling them about lacrosse. I would have thought the conversation to be a lot more lewd and crass.

They ask him all sorts of questions, but while he absent-mindedly answers, he watches me. He's still flirting and smiling, but his eyes are on me.

The *feel* of him watching makes me so nervous I trip on the leg of his stool on the way back to my table. He reaches out and steadies me, his fingers tightly grasping my arm. I recuperate quickly and mumble, "I got it."

But actually, it's Tahoe who's definitely *got it*. He's got his hands full with two women and somehow the guy still manages to get one of those hands on me!

I take my seat, and Rachel continues drilling me about Trent.

Trying to keep my eyes off the bar, I tell her more details about how we met, but I avoid mentioning the condom issue. Nobody knows about that but T-Rex and I want it to stay that way. And speaking of him, I'm also thankful that Wynn doesn't jump in and tell Rachel that just the other night, Tahoe spooned me.

I tell Rachel that Trent is red-haired and good-looking in a non-overwhelming way. As I say that, I glance at Tahoe— the danger symbol and the complete opposite of Trent—and I notice that he's moving like a blond panther toward our table. And he is looking directly at me. God help me, his dimple is showing.

"Regina," he takes my arm to help me to my feet, "can I see you for a minute?" There's laughter in his voice, and it makes me curious to know why, as well as want to share in that laughter for some reason.

"Yeah, sure." I immediately stand and let him guide me to the door. "What's up?" I ask, narrowing my eyes suspiciously, feeling myself smile because he's smiling so hard.

He squints up at the clouds crowding the night sky, that Cheshire grin still on his face. "Too cold out here, let's go sit in my car for a bit."

We walk to his car, which is parked in the lot beneath the Saints' building.

He opens the door for me then climbs behind the wheel. It's warmer inside, but I rub my hands together and blow into them anyway.

"What is it?" I insist. "Come on, I'm freezing. And your floozies are probably dying after two minutes without you now."

"They'll be fine," he cockily assures as he looks at me, his lips tilted, his dimple still showing.

"What is it?" I ask again. "I'm seriously starving and you're interrupting my dinner, Roth."

"*I'm* interrupting?" He laughs richly at that. "You, sending a little present to me, was not interrupting?" He pulls out what takes me a moment to discern are a pair of red lace panties.

"Those aren't mine."

He looks at them closely.

"Those damn panties aren't mine. God, you're disgusting!" I laugh.

"These aren't yours?" He studies them again, then grins and stares at me. "I figured you for a red lace kind of girl."

"Never."

He opens the glove compartment, which has a shit-ton more panties.

"God, you're disgusting, Tahoe!"

He shuts it after tucking the red panties in there, and he is wickedly sexy and shameless about it.

"What's your kind then?" he asks, reaching out to my backrest and leaning forward into my seat a little bit.

"What?" His hand on the back of my seat makes me start for a second.

"Your kind? Men can tell a whole lot about a woman based on her underwear." He nods knowingly.

"You totally flatter yourselves. You only think it says a lot but all they hint at is the mood we're in."

"Really."

"Umm, yep. Really." I nod knowingly too.

"So what mood are you in?" His voice drops a little bit as he looks down at me.

"I'm hungry," I say flatly, aware of my stomach rumbling.

"Hunger is not a mood."

"Right now it's a state of being. I'm super hungry and I get moody when I'm hungry." I glare at the glove compartment. "Now what woman on Earth would want to add her panties to that pile? Huh?"

"Someone fun and naughty," he says.

I meet his gaze, and he meets mine back, so very blue and so very taunting.

I pull my eyes away and stare out the window, feeling a little bit provoked. It's nothing unusual, really, but tonight it feels worse, I can hardly stand it.

The night is cold; winter is coming to Chicago already. The windows are fogging up with our body heat. He alone is hot enough to fog any window; his body feels like a furnace. I can feel the warmth he emanates all the way to my seat and it takes effort not to draw closer.

I'm feeling reckless, crazy reckless. Determined to show him that I can be wild, fun, and unpredictable too. *Fucker.*

I turn my body so that he can't see, then reach beneath my skirt and slowly start to ease off my panties.

He's narrowing his eyes and smiling in disbelief, and I toss him a mischievous smirk as I ball them up and toss them into the glove compartment.

"Did you just take your panties off for me, you wicked girl?" he croons.

I nod slowly, inwardly feeling more disbelief than he. "If you can figure out which ones are mine, I'll give you an A-plus and a gold star," I say, trying not to sound breathless as I reach out to pat his stubbled cheek three times. Then, without another word, I get out of the car.

As I close the door, I see him grab all of the panties before getting out and following me. He shuts the door and locks the car with a beep, and as we head back to the sidewalk, he throws all of the panties into the first huge trash can that we see with the exception of one pair, which he keeps tightly fisted in his hand.

"You just threw away your entire collection? You could have totally thrown out mine!"

"We'll see." A confident smirk graces his lips.

He guides me back inside and takes his seat at the bar, while I return to the table with my friends.

From across the room, I watch as he reaches one thick finger into the right pocket of his leather jacket and pulls out an inch of fabric.

Peeking out at me, I see the navy-blue stripes of my little sailor boy shorts.

It should be funny, I mean, I was just joking around. Instead, all the dormant feelings and longing this man stirs in me are heightened as I think about him possessing something as personal as my pair of panties. And when I think of the collection he already had, I want to hit him nearly as hard as I want to take his goddamned beastly handsome face and kiss him.

I'm relieved and a little guilty when I get a call from Trent. I pick up and cover my free ear so that I can hear him better.

"Still with your friend?" he asks.

"Rachel, yes. We're having dinner."

"Where at?"

I tell him the name of the café.

"I'll stop by on my way home, pick you up?"

I glance at Tahoe and notice there's a girl talking to him and a part of me wonders if she's the one who slipped her red panties into his pocket—panties that he thought were mine.

"Sure," I whisper.

When Trent arrives in a cab twenty minutes later, I introduce him, "Trent, this is Rachel. Rachel, Trent."

"Trent, I've been back less than a couple of hours and I haven't stopped hearing about you," Rachel says warmly as she greets him.

I lead Trent to the bar to introduce him to Saint and tell them all that we're leaving.

Tahoe, who's talking to some blonde, watches Trent narrowly while Saint shakes his hand.

As we say our goodbyes, Tahoe kisses the blonde on the cheek and comes to his feet. "I'm on my way out, I'll drive you." He looks directly at Trent as he fishes out a hundred-dollar bill to set on the bar.

I start at the offer, but Trent is already pumping his hand in greeting. "If you don't mind, we appreciate it. Thanks, man."

I ride shotgun in his Ghost, while Trent rides in the back, whistling appreciatively over the fine interior of Tahoe's vehicle. "Great wheels, man. Spectacular."

"She's a smooth ride, isn't she?" Tahoe's voice is low and *so* intimate as he looks sideways at me that I feel naughty just hearing it. "A bit temperamental but I like her just like that."

Trent laughs, but I'm scowling.

There's silence before I once again hear Tahoe's raspy voice. I notice his drawl is more evident.

"Hey, Regina, can you store this in my glove compartment? Some gorgeous cupcake left this in my possession and I want to be sure it's in pristine condition when she wants it back."

He smirks at me, his eyes dark and challenging.

I shove my navy-striped panties into the glove compartment, gritting my teeth, stealing a glance over my shoulder to see if Trent is watching. He isn't...he's preoccupied with the smooth leather and gadgets of the car.

When Tahoe finally drops us off at Trent's building, I follow Trent out only to make an excuse and walk back. I swing open the passenger door of Tahoe's car, lean in, and say in a demanding tone, "What are you doing?"

He looks at me, his eyes wild and untamed.

"Do you want him to break up with me? He *likes* me. He's going to think you and I..."

I exhale, fighting very hard to recover my patience and self-control. I'm mad, but I don't want to make a big deal out of it and alert Trent that something is up, so I open the glove compartment in an effort to retrieve my panties.

He reaches them first. He pockets them again, his expression unapologetic, a muscle working in his jaw. Then he nods at Trent, who's looking at me. "Your prince charming awaits."

THANKSGIVING

I tell no one about the panties and throw all my energy into the Thanksgiving holiday—I want it to be special since it's the first holiday I'm spending with Trent. I ask him over for dinner at my place—and he's "looking forward to it."

It's a bit complicated, having a vegan boyfriend. I spent the whole day yesterday trying to figure out what to cook for us. I researched online and end up trying a quinoa recipe and a cranberry sauce. We have a nice dinner at my apartment, and thankfully Trent seems to enjoy the meal. He brought wine and lifts his glass.

"I'm thankful for you this Thanksgiving, Gina," he says.

"I'm thankful for you too." I smile. We kiss a little, but I tell him I need to go to bed early, so he reluctantly goes home.

I want to get a good night's rest so I'm ready for the Black Friday sales tomorrow. It's one of the busiest days of the year at the department store. But even after going to bed early, I still have a restless sleep and spend an extra twenty minutes on my makeup the next day, trying to cover the bags under my eyes as I head to the store at 5 a.m.

THE PERFECT GIFT

It's the first week of December, and I don't know why I'm surprised that my parents can't make it for Christmas. They can never make it. It almost feels like they would rather spend Christmas anywhere in the world, with any other person, than with their only daughter.

"I hope you make plans with one of your friends," my mother says over the phone. "I don't want you spending the time alone in your apartment. And I'm very sorry about the loan, but with all this traveling, we really can't afford the expense."

"Don't worry, Mom, I'll figure something out."

I knew it was a stretch to ask them for a loan, but a part of me is still loath to leave my apartment.

I have the first half of next year to figure out my new situation, and although I've been working overtime to pay my rent, I still need to buy Trent a Christmas gift.

I schedule a shoot with a photographer for the first week of December, and on the second week, I go pick up my pictures. Since Trent left a few days ago to visit his family, he's taking a little longer to answer my texts.

Peering into the manila envelope with the pictures, I sit and ponder what to do.

I call Tahoe's cell phone. I don't know why it's his opinion I want, why he's the first one I'm going to show these to, but I tell myself it's because he's the player that I'm closest to and maybe I also want to start our friendship back up.

"Hey. Hi. It's Gina. Hey, could I come over to your place today?"

"Yeah, sure, Regina. Everything alright?" I imagine him frowning.

"Oh yes. No…hospitalizations." I laugh at my own joke. "I just wanted to make sure you're not busy. *You know*, doing…"

He chuckles a low, lazy chuckle, catching my meaning. "Come by my office, I'll be here for a while."

"Okay, I'll see you there. I won't really take up much of your time. Oh and hey." I pause. "Thank you."

His office is in the corporate building that handles most of his enterprises, a massive forty-floor skyscraper that could not be more modern had it been built a hundred years into the future. After being allowed inside by the receptionists in the lobby, I take the elevators to the executive floor.

I introduce myself to a young, handsome guy who is probably Tahoe's PA. He greets me cordially and shows me down a hall with dozens of black-and-white photographs of oil rigs. The floors are dark wood and the furniture light in color; the combination simple and powerful.

"Miss Wylde is here, Mr. Roth," his assistant says as he opens a massive brass door.

He keeps it wide open and there sits the dark prince of the playboys. The blond beast in his cave.

Tahoe Roth knows how to rock his suits. But every time he wears one, I'm struck by the ruggedness that still seeps through, like he's more of an outdoors kind of guy —an adrenaline junkie and a nature lover, one who hit a gold mine when he struck oil and invested well. There's smarts and pride behind those eyes. He owns the suit but it looks like his cage; the beast is prowling within.

His blue eyes flare when he sees me. His lips curve up in a smile as he stands. He moves like a lazy feline, stretching his muscles after a long nap.

I'm massively impressed as I head inside. "Nice cave," I say appreciatively.

"Nice dress," he drawls back softly.

I feel myself warm as he looks at me in a long cashmere dress that hugs my body and reaches my ankles, but for the most part I try to ignore his compliment—maybe he was teasing me—as I head to his desk and watch him take a seat behind it. My eye is drawn to a frame holding a picture of an older woman and man smiling at each other.

"Who are they?" I ask as I lift the frame and study the black-and-white photograph.

"My parents."

"You must be close, to have their picture on your desk. Do you go visit them?"

I try to remember if I've ever heard him mention that he's going home to see them, and I can't remember an instance.

He leans back in his office chair and links his hands behind his head. "Only when I have to. They're always on my case." He smirks.

"Are you going for Christmas?" I ask.

"I don't think so. Too much to do."

I set the frame down on his desk. The quality of the photograph is incredible.

I feel like my pictures are even lamer now than I imagined. But although my budget was limited, my intentions were good. I slowly start peeling open the top of my manila envelope. "Okay so I'm trying to figure out what to give Trent. It's not like I can give him a car, and he's a vegan and sells produce so I can't even give him a fruit basket. Plus he doesn't wear ties. And he's been away and I feel like he isn't thinking about me—"

"Why do you say that?"

"Because his texts take forever."

"That doesn't mean he's not thinking of you."

"Well, I thought this was a good reminder, and something easy and cheap to ship to him by Christmas day." I pull out the eight pictures and clutch them to my chest. "So, you're a connoisseur about this. I really want your opinion on these."

If you're a big-butt girl, nobody made you feel it was alright to have a big butt better than J. Lo. So when I booked this shoot, I was inspired by the pics she took for Ben Affleck, except I didn't go that far. I'm wearing white boy shorts with a lacy behind, and my back is bare, with my dark hair loose and curly and reaching to the small of my back, and I'm mostly in profile except for one shot where I turned to ask something of the photographer and she snapped the camera.

I don't like that one, I look unaware and…naked. Even with my boy shorts.

I don't think I look that sexy, but I've spent all my Black Friday commissions on the shoot.

"Which one would a guy react to more strongly?" I ask him as I spread them out.

He scans them all with a quick sweep of his gaze, looking thoughtful. "Just one?"

"Yup."

Frowning, he points toward all of them with a motion of his hand. "I'm supposed to like one better?"

"Yes! Don't be obtuse. Oh, but not this one." I push it aside. It's the picture that included my face. I'm not photogenic. I don't like pictures of my face.

Stroking his chin, he looks at me carefully. He picks up each photo and studies it for a long moment. His eyes have never looked so blue.

"Who took these?"

"Taylor Watts."

His voice is oddly textured. "That a guy or a girl?"

I'm confused. *Does it matter?* "Girl."

His face is unreadable, but almost imperceptibly, he relaxes his shoulders as he studies the pictures again. "This one."

The one I'm most covered in?

"Are you certain?"

"Dead certain." He taps it with his finger. "This one."

"But it's not the one in which I look sexiest, in my opinion."

He just looks at me as if I'm stupid. "You look like sheet-clawing sex in all of them."

His comment is so forthright and matter-of-fact, my knees nearly buckle.

"So what is he getting you?" he asks.

"What do you mean?" It isn't until I speak that I realize my voice came out a little too wispy.

He nods at the pictures. "You're giving him a gorgeous picture of yourself, what's he giving you?"

"I told him chocolate."

"Chocolate," he says flatly. "Really."

"Yup. Anything chocolate totally wins me over."

I gather the pics and carefully slip them back into the envelope.

"He hasn't answered my calls," I whisper.

"He doesn't deserve you," he whispers back.

I glance up at him in confusion. "I feel like I'm screwing it up, Tahoe. Like there's something about me that just can't...make it work with a guy."

"You're not screwing it up. How can you, Regina? You're too good for the guy."

"Relationships take effort! Which is why you choose not to be in one, am I right? Cause you can't be bothered."

"Pass me the phone, I'll have words with him." His hand comes down over mine as he tries to take my phone.

I draw back, instinctively leaping at the electricity his touch provoked. "Haha, what kind of words?"

"Like he needs to call you, or he'll have to deal with me. I'll tell him if I wanted you to get all fucked up over a guy, you'd be dating me."

"You don't date, remember? You're a ladies' man. Of many ladies, and you don't think you can stop or else you'd at least try to get serious with one."

"I have nothing to offer her. I'm not what a one-man woman needs."

Silence.

He stretches out his hand. "Give me the phone, I'm calling him."

"You are doing no such thing."

"Tell me one good thing that you see in him and I won't call."

"He's not a ladies' man." I grin as I gather my pictures and head to the door. "Thanks, T-Rex."

I arrive at my apartment shortly afterward and head straight for the fridge to make myself a sandwich. As I take my first bite, I turn over the manila envelope and skim the pictures again. Only seven pictures slide onto my kitchen counter.

I tap the envelope against the edge, then lower my sandwich and peer inside. Empty.

I call Tahoe's cell. "Did I lose a pic at your office?"

"Negative," he says lazily, as if he's got his feet up on his desk or on the couch or somewhere.

The news doesn't make me happy.

"It must have fallen out," I groan, then thank him and hang up. I have a momentary panic when I think about that picture appearing somewhere on some playboy site. My worst pic, too—somewhere out there. Then I shake the thought aside, pray that it won't fall into the wrong hands, and turn over the picture Tahoe suggested I send to Trent. With a red magic marker, I scribble on the back,

Merry Christmas, xo, Regina.

I package it in a pre-paid envelope, then head downstairs to ship it off.

CHRISTMAS

Rachel invited me to tag along with her and Saint on Christmas Eve to dinner and the poshest club in the city, but I'm exhausted after all the selling. My feet are killing me and my body is starving for a full meal after all the rapid-fire snacking during work breaks. I settle for Skyping with Trent that evening and having the turkey microwave dinner I picked up for myself. He sent me a text this last week.

Thank you for the gift. Going up in a frame soon! I guess I better send you those chocolates soon. Skype?

I'm happy and relieved that he liked the photo. It makes me think of Tahoe—and how his eyes looked so blue when he looked at the pictures. I've been wondering what he thought of them, if he really liked them. I've even been wondering if a part of me wanted him to see them, see me, feminine and lovely. Or at least trying to be.

I attribute these thoughts to my exhaustion, but I'm still thinking of him after Trent and I Skype and he hangs up to have dinner with his family. I settle down to watch Netflix and heat myself the microwave turkey dinner—there was no way I was going to cook a turkey just for me. I don't think Rachel and I were ever even able to fit one into our tiny oven.

As the amusing little movie *How the Grinch Stole Christmas* plays and I fork pieces of turkey and rice into my mouth, I want to wish my T-Rex happy holidays but I don't want to do it too directly, so I grab my phone and tweet him.

Merry Christmas @tahoeroth

My landline rings less than ten minutes later. I pick up and swallow the last bit of turkey in my mouth before answering.

"Hey." I hear Tahoe's familiar baritone on the other end of the line. "Merry Christmas to you too."

I clutch the receiver tightly, totally not expecting his voice in my ear. "Hey. What are you up to?"

"Hitting this club with Carmichael and a few other friends. Want to come?"

I regretfully look down at my flannel checkered pajamas. "No, thanks."

"Yeah, I didn't think so. Well. Rachel said you were busy. Goodbye, Regina."

"'Bye." I hang up, and whisper, "T-Rex."

I'm still watching the movie at midnight when I hear noise outside my apartment. If I were five, I'd leap to the window thinking it's Santa Claus, but instead I blame the neighbors for the noise.

I ignore it for a minute, but I hear it again. I mute the Grinch and head over to the door and stand up on tiptoes to peer through the peephole. My breath seizes when I see a tall man outside.

I swing the door open and Tahoe stands on the other side. He's dressed for the club in a black turtleneck and dark-wash jeans, his blond hair wet from a recent shower. He looks so delicious my mouth waters.

He smirks, but his blue eyes look a little stormy. "Got lost on my way to the club."

I shake my head, a little breathless.

Yeah. Like this guy would get lost *anywhere*.

He walks in. "Actually, I didn't like the idea of you here all by yourself." He shuts the door behind him.

"I'm not by myself. I'm with the Grinch."

"I'm comforted then. Hey, I got you something." He reaches into the back pocket of his jeans with a wicked look in his eyes as he hands me an envelope.

I stare at it.

"It's a tour of the Blommer Chocolate factory. I thought you might enjoy it," he says.

"Tahoe."

He smiles at me, but his eyes still look stormy. "She likes it," he says.

"She loves it." I frown. "But I didn't get *you* anything."

He takes a seat on my couch, and I sit down next to him.

"Yeah, you did," he says.

"Uh, no. I did not."

He looks at me, his tone low but firm, unapologetic. "Your picture. You didn't lose it, I took it. You looked lovely and I took it."

"Wait. What? *Why?*"

Heat blooms all across my body, and I hate thinking that I'm blushing head to toe.

"You collect those too?" I ask when he doesn't reply.

He frowns darkly as if he dislikes me thinking this of him and continues looking at me with those tumultuous eyes, then he playfully purses his lips and pokes the tip of his finger into my tummy. "Not yet."

"Yeah well, knowing you, you're about to start."

I rib him, frowning; he ribs me back, laughing for real at last. "What are we watching?" he asks.

"Your twin, the Grinch, whose heart will grow by the end of the film. Watch and learn."

I motion to the TV and look down at his gift and I want to say thank you again but I can't trust my voice to speak. It's my first Christmas gift this year. My parents send me a $50 gift card every Christmas but it hasn't arrived yet, and this is the first gift that someone actually took the time to choose for me.

So I just hold the envelope on my lap while Tahoe looks at me with blue eyes that look clear now, and I look back into his eyes and smile.

NEW YEAR'S

Trent gave me a box of chocolates when he got back from Atlanta and I've limited myself to enjoying only one a day, not because they don't taste like heaven, but because I plan to look good tonight. I'm determined to spend New Year's Eve the way I want to spend the entire year.

Wynn said that's what everyone should do, while she, Rachel and I had our regular weekly brunch. She and Rachel insist that New Year's Eve sets the tone for the year and whatever it is you start the New Year with, that's what your focus for the New Year will be.

So I've told myself I'm going to be sublimely happy tonight. But since I sometimes seem to require a little help loosening up, I have a few glasses of wine as I mingle with the crowd.

I'm dressed in an emerald green sweater dress and brown leather boots that reach just below my knees, my hair held back in a high ponytail. My ponytail doesn't manage to tame my curls, but at least it helps keep them off my face.

We're at a posh New Year's Eve party, the most decadent in the city. It's being held in a five-star hotel. The ballroom is aglow with trickling champagne fountains and sparkly trays. Conversation is flowing as well as the alcohol.

Trent and I have mingled together all evening, but when he gets a phone call with bad news about one of his produce trucks being stolen during transport, he excuses himself to go talk outside.

Tahoe arrives very late. Tahoe's girl is a strawberry-blonde with locks that fall all the way to her waist—the most gorgeous hair I've ever seen. I feel a pang of envy as he leads her over, followed by Callan Carmichael and his date.

"Someone introduce me to this gorgeous lady," Carmichael says in reference to me.

"Haha. Hi, Callan."

Tahoe looks at me quietly. "He's right, you look gorgeous tonight."

His words make my pulse skip a little but I roll my eyes and look at the blonde hooked on his arm. "Gina," I introduce myself.

"Stephanie." She smiles tartly at me.

Tahoe tugs on my ponytail playfully and, as he leads his date away, whispers in my ear, "Don't eat all the chocolates."

"It's my life's purpose, no matter what you say!" I yell out with my hands on the sides of my mouth so that my voice carries to him as he walks away.

Later that night, I go in search of Trent. I'm worried about his stolen delivery truck, but aren't all holidays a playground for thieves? I'm winding through the crowd when I spot Tahoe heading back toward the group with his date's drink.

Our paths inevitably cross and our eyes latch when we try to pass each other. I go left and as we move accidentally in the same direction, we laugh.

He stops smiling, opening his mouth to say something, but what he's saying is suddenly drowned out by the chorus of the crowd.

"Ten! Nine! Eight! Seven! Six! Five! Four! Three! Two! One!"

Claps and cheers erupt. I shake myself from my laughter and Tahoe trails off from whatever it is he was starting to tell me.

"I'm wasted," I hear myself say. "Wait, is it twelve?! OMG, it's twelve."

Tahoe looks at the drink in his hand with a wry smile, tosses half back, and then extends it to me. I take it and toss the rest back, then set it on the nearest table.

We look at each other with the realization that we are going to kiss each other this New Year's Eve.

The thought makes me nervous and excited and anticipatory—more than I ever would have expected. As people kiss left and right, time feels slow in the space where we stand. Flashes of color and movement appear in the corner of my eye but he is the only clear thing, the sounds muting until I only hear my heart as we both gravitate to one another and get closer.

I grip his hair and I do *not* want to let him go, ever. His hands open on my back and they're so big they cover nearly all of it.

"Happy New Year," he says.

He gives me a peck on the lips as a friendly New Year's kiss. He eases back an inch and returns to give me another.

As his lips press onto mine, my toes curl unexpectedly. My mind spins in a thousand directions. I replay things Rachel has said about him, which I have mulled over consistently in private.

That he called me *succulent.*

That he's a lacrosse fan and would have gone pro if he hadn't literally struck oil, big time, becoming a multimillionaire overnight—a billionaire within years.

That Saint respects him and has invested in helping him through the volatility of this market because he believes in Tahoe's business sense.

The three friends' public personas aren't necessarily true. But what *is* true for Tahoe Roth? He is the embodiment of *sex.* He also has a gentleman ingrained in his bones due to his southern upbringing. You can tell a lot about a person by how well they treat others, and he is playful but honest, and always himself.

You can tell a lot about a man by how he kisses, and nobody has ever sparked me up the way his strong, firm lips do.

We ease back and stare at each other.

Tonight Tahoe is in jeans and a soft white V-neck sweater, and he looks delicious. His blue eyes are so achingly familiar on me they're like a shot to the heart...as he reaches out and takes my hand, and kisses the back of it.

He doesn't smirk, he doesn't smile, he just kisses the back of my hand, all while looking into my eyes, his gaze possessive and raw.

"Happy New Year, babe!" Trent cries, pulling me to him. His mouth covers mine, and by the time I'm able to peel away, I glance frantically around the room.

At midnight, I was with Tahoe Roth. Is it true that's where I should focus?

I then catch a glimpse of him crossing the room, leading the blonde he came to the party with out the door.

START WITH A BANG

I overslept. Or actually didn't sleep. At the department store, we're open from 10 a.m. to 6 p.m. on New Year's Day, and while I'm standing looking pretty and trying to be helpful behind the Chanel cosmetics counter, I replay it.

Yeah, not a good idea.

Every time I replay last night, Tahoe's eyes seem a little darker and his gaze seems to trek over my face a little more slowly. His arms feel a little stronger and a little tighter around me. And his smell is a little fiercer and manlier.

I want to text him something funny and ludicrous. To make last night seem what it was, just another New Year's Eve kissing the first person who passed. It could have been Rachel. Or Wynn. Or even Valentine.

But none of them would have looked at me the way Tahoe Roth did last night.

I don't know what to text, but I fiddle with my phone and scan my Twitter to distract myself. To keep from texting him. Or maybe to stalk him. Fuck.

He posted:

Not a bad morning.

Okay Tahoe, speak in English buddy. What the hell does that mean?

I'm sure he's referring to the strawberry-blonde he took home. *Is* he? But what if he isn't? What if he, too, remembers the kiss…? The mere thought of him remembering it gives me palpitations.

It's already been on my mind every minute since last night.

I know we're just friends and that he can't be monogamous and doesn't even want to. At least he's never hinted that he wants to, and even if he did, I have no reason to believe he'd choose me as the girl he'd want to be monogamous with. The staring contests, the panties, the tour of the chocolate factory, last night—they don't mean anything but friendship.

Even that kiss was a friendly one.

It wasn't wet, or hungry; it was tender almost…curious. All of that equals *friendly*.

The toe curling wasn't his fault, that was all mine, and I have to move on with the knowledge that my closest guy friend is a sex god and my body reacts to him. So what?

Still, I'm so haunted I can't stop thinking about it. Trent has been sweet to me. Last night he told me he'd been waiting for a girl like me his whole life, that I'm funny and not frivolous. After being lied to for two years by your ex, it's almost surreal to hear nice things and realize how much you want to believe them. I really like being around him, and I want to see how far we can go.

So I'm extra reluctant when I get a text from T-Rex:

Game tomorrow night. Come?

Shit! I nearly drop my phone.

I set it down and hurry to the customer who just sat to get her makeup done. I start with the foundation and silently work to enhance the best of her features.

She peers into the oval handheld mirror on the counter while we're in the process. "Do you think it's too much blush?" she asks.

"Hmm?"

I ease back from her face. Shit. She's got red suns on her cheeks.

"We'll get that fixed," I say.

Thanks, Roth.

"And too much eye shadow? It's a daytime event," she says worriedly.

Brown rainbows over her eyes, um, yes, a tad too much.

"Right, uh…" I hurriedly dab with a cotton ball. "There. You'll look great in the pictures."

"There won't be pictures."

I look at her. Then dab at her face with more cotton balls. "I'm sorry, let me fix this."

"Boy trouble?"

I purse my lips. I won't discuss Tahoe with anyone. He's my dirty secret, like a fantasy.

"Nah, just thinking about a friend," I finally say.

"I have never gotten *that* color on my face except with a brush. Not a friend."

I smile and wave at the lights above us. "These lights fluster anyone."

I run away to get a good shade of lipstick to match the mess I made on her face, and I roll my eyes at myself and get back to finish her up, wondering what to say about the game.

That night from my landline, while on a conference call re-hashing the party, Wynn and Rachel make fun of me because they saw me kiss Tahoe at midnight.

"What does that say, Gina?" Wynn insists as I check on the vegan pizza I'm cooking for Trent and me.

"That I was drunk?"

"No, really," Wynn says. "What *does* it say?"

The fact that Wynn is so insistent makes me pause in the middle of my kitchen.

I pull out my cell and read his text, so determined for things not to mean *anything at all*, I finally answer:

Can't. But drinks are on me if you win!

There.

Just what any buddy would answer.

"Emmett told me Tahoe spent quite a substantial amount of time last night questioning him about Trent. What he does. Last name. Family origins."

"What?" I ask, surprised.

Rachel is quiet on the other end of the line.

And I fall just as quiet with this bit of information. But then I remind myself it *doesn't mean anything at all.*

"He's ape man like that, we're friends, you guys know," I finally say.

"Guys…" Rachel begins. "I'm four weeks pregnant."

The news completely wipes away any other thoughts from my mind, which is probably a good thing. I tell Trent all about it when he arrives at my place, and I tell him we're invited over to the Saints' tomorrow night for a mini celebration.

"I wish I could, babe, but I have a dinner with a possible new client tomorrow. How about I meet you there?"

We talk a little while after dining on my pizza, but when I kiss him good night as he leaves and I finally go to bed, I keep staring at the ceiling, thinking of Rachel with a little *baby* in her arms.

Wynn and Emmett pick me up on their way to the party the next evening, and we all talk about it in the car.

"Huge step," Emmett says. "Huge."

"Emmett, I know, but isn't it exciting?'" Wynn presses.

I'm basically sitting quietly in the back of the car—nervous and excited for Rachel. Rachel has always been so career-oriented that Wynn and I simply cannot believe our closest friend is having a baby in September.

As soon as we arrive, hugs and congratulations are exchanged, and then the men and the women separate. The girls sit in the sumptuous, modern living area while Saint, Emmett, and Callan hang out by the bar. The guys rib Saint about payback for all the mischief he caused when he was young.

I know that Tahoe had a game tonight, but I keep glancing at the time on my mobile, wondering when and if he'll show up. I've grown so used to seeing him whenever there's any Saint event, I hadn't expected to miss the sight of him. I need to see him to confirm that nothing changed after New Year's.

Absolutely *nothing* at all.

Wynn is on a roll with the baby talk, even more than Rachel, unbelievably. Though Rachel told us they'd already been trying, and that when she found out she was pregnant, she didn't tell Saint for three days. "I first rush-ordered a little baby tee from a customization store online that said 'Daddy's little Saint,' and one night when he came from work, I set it right on his side of the bed over his pillow. Oh guys! You should've seen his face when we finally retired for the night and he saw that tiny little tee. His face went from disbelief, to total shock, to this gorgeous laugh and a hug so tight I thought he'd break my bones."

"Awwwwww!" Wynn says.

I laugh happily, feel warm even though I'm still at the shocked stage myself.

Even when Rachel goes to check up on the snacks, Wynn continues to talk to me about babies.

"You know, after that pregnancy scare at Rachel and Saint's wedding, I haven't been able to stop thinking of babies. I see them *everywhere*. I have never seen so many babies in my life. They're in the soup, I tell you. I keep wondering if Emmet is the kind of father I want for my kids. Am I the kind of mother I want for my kids…"

"Wynn," I say drolly, "you have no other choice on that one."

"I have a choice in self-improvement, though," she counters. "Obviously for change to work you need to be aware of the problem, accept that it needs fixing, and then, actively try to fix it. Like I'm disorganized, but now that I've moved in with Emmet, I'm trying not to be so messy—though it's nice for my flaws not to matter that much to him, I guess."

"Oh noooo." I laughingly shake my head. "I'll be dead before I'm seen without makeup. I sleep with it on if a guy stays over. I set the alarm and put on makeup before Trent wakes, that's how much it needs to be on my face."

"Speaking of, I like that Cleopatra look."

"Thank you. I worked hours on it." I grin and wink as I edge closer to her. "Do you think the eyeliner was too much?"

"Why is it so important?"

Tahoe Roth steps off the elevator, and it's hard not to notice the *wow* look on Wynn's face when she sees him in his casual jeans and comfy sweater.

"I do this for a living. It's my presentation card," I tell her. "Nobody wants a fat dietician or a clown-faced makeup artist."

"There's your buddy Tahoe." She points, wiggling her eyebrows.

I ignore her (and him) but I shiver when I hear his voice, greeting Rachel's husband and congratulating him.

Their laughs fill the room. Tahoe has this easy laugh, it's almost contagious. It sounds delicious and it makes you want to have such a delicious time. I find myself smiling because of it when he heads over and greets Wynn, then he looks at me.

"Hey. What's up with you?" He drops down beside me.

"Nothing's up. What's up with you?" I counter.

He looks really cozy in a draping, heavy-knitted ivory sweater, warm and inviting. That familiar irresistible grin lights his face as he looks at me. He leans back and folds his arms behind his head. "A whole lot of nothing." He leans closer to me. "Why didn't you come to my game?"

"Why you assume I'll ever want to is amusing. That beard is getting long, by the way."

"We're in a bad streak."

"Right. You loser."

He laughs and caresses his jaw, smiling ruefully, the dimple showing. "I used to be luckier. I've still got what it takes though. If you'd only come watch, I'd be happy to show you."

"I don't cheer for losers." I stick my tongue out at him.

"Tsk, Regina," he drawls, "I would no longer *be* a loser if you came to cheer for me."

He's teasing, and we both laugh, but when our eyes connect again, a shock runs through my system.

Did you like that kiss even a fraction of how much I liked it?

I shake the thought aside and look at my martini on the coffee table. He's a womanizer, he seduces women, this is what they see in him—confidence, a bit of an alpha nature, those wicked teasing words of his, that rebel streak, the laugh, the good times, the money he spends so easily, the lips, the body, I'm not even going to think about the rest but I can tell by the wear of his jeans that he's as well-endowed there as everywhere else.

Don't they say everything is bigger in Texas? Well, he was born there. Enough said.

The drawl is not always noticeable. I wonder what it is that makes it come out, like now?

Wynn heads over to hang with Rachel and Emmett, and we're alone now and silent as we watch them.

"Babies, huh," Tahoe says softly.

"Babies."

He lifts my martini, sips from it then hands it over so I can take a sip as well.

We're both thoughtful and puzzled. Stunned. We're both at the moment you realize your closest friends are growing, leaping forward, charging ahead, and you're still the same, you still aren't really sure where to go from here and if you're happy where you are at all. I can't assume Tahoe is really happy, or why would he want to hang out with me?

"While the Saints play house and your friend Wynn over there maneuvers to get an engagement ring on her finger, you're probably going to be stuck with me," he says sardonically as he watches me set down my near-empty martini glass.

A smile appears on my lips and I guess it appeared quickly enough to amuse him, because his eyes start twinkling as he smiles at me too.

BURNING

A blizzard hits the city two weeks later, and I have to re-schedule some of my house calls. I spend a lot of time in my apartment whenever I'm off work, watching movies with Trent.

By the time the blizzard stops a few days later, I've had a lot of things to mull through. I stare around my apartment when I arrive after a particularly exhausting day at work. My lonely apartment. Which I can no longer afford.

I feel unsatisfied and restless, but I don't know why. It's almost as if I can't seem to find my place in the world. Rachel is expecting, Wynn has moved in with Emmett, while I'm barely in the beginning stages of a relationship, and about to have to leave my apartment.

So I decide I want to try to buy my own place rather than rent. Set down some roots. To do that, I need a boost of income, enough for me to save up for a small down payment. I really need to be earning more if I hope to buy my own place—one where I won't be getting kicked out. Ever. I boot up the computer and spend all night searching Monster.com and the classifieds, and end up making a few queries.

Two days later, I get a call and land a huge gig.

The gig requires me to wear a black waitress uniform with a cute little white apron. I'm serving at some sort of investors' get-together, where would-be investors can learn the how-to's of investing.

I'm there early that evening, helping set up the kitchen and uncork the wine and fill the glasses. Soon a live band is playing in the main room, and groups of men are scattered throughout the space that's big enough to sit two hundred guests. I walk past tables with a tray of wine glasses containing a crimson-red cabernet, heading toward the area my boss told me I would be responsible for.

I have never waitressed before and although my uniform fits me all wrong, I am completely focused on not spilling the tray of glasses as I head to the nearest table and start setting down drinks when a familiar voice reaches me.

"Gina?"

I cringe, but force myself to turn.

Paul is standing only feet away, sharply dressed in a tailored suit with cuff links and an expensive but simple tie clip, surrounded by similarly dressed executive types. And I stand here in an ill-fitting waitress outfit with an empty tray in my hand, instead of a toothbrush.

He runs his gaze down my body in disbelief. I can see it in his eyes: *Wow, you're a waitress?*

He looks at my attire with quickly growing scorn, and I want to throw my tray at him while, at the same time, wanting to hide behind it. I guess I knew, deep down, that I'd one day bump into him again. I always imagined I would look successful, have an incredibly hot guy on my arm, and be wearing my best dress. I always imagined I'd lift my nose at him, like the scum that he is.

I didn't expect it to hurt, still. After all this time. For the sight of him to rip off the Band-Aid I've worn for years and make me bleed again.

I don't love you...

I want to yell. I want to hide. And I hate hate hate that what I really want to do is cry, as if I haven't cried enough for him already.

But all I can do is turn away and charge across the room, almost stumbling to get away, until I finally reach the kitchen. My eyes burn and I hate that they burn. I feel small and I hate that I feel small. I set down the tray, fumble through my pockets, and take out my phone.

Me: So Paul is at this gig I'm working...

Rachel: NOOOO! Gina, breathe. Don't talk to him, don't even look at him!!!

Me: I'm his waitress!

I wait for her reply, and it takes nearly a minute to appear on my screen.

Rachel: Gina...don't be upset but, I told Saint I wanted to leave our event early to go support you, and guess who punched the table and shot out the door?

"Gina? What are you doing in here? Go back out there, please," my boss snaps.

Hastily I tuck my phone away and hurry to refill my tray. With every glass I fill, I brace myself to go out there again. I fantasize about walking out and dumping the tray accidentally on Paul's lap. Then I picture walking out with my best smile and...and what?

I exhale, balance the tray in one hand, and head to the main room.

I scan the area for Paul. I need to know where he is just to avoid him, but my gaze pauses on a tall man in the entrance, talking to my boss.

Shoulders a mile wide that taper down to a narrow waist and, as if that weren't enough to stop you in your tracks, add to that a butt that seems to be held up by angels.

I take in the back of his full mane of blond hair and I know, my body knows—my heart leaps a little, my stomach tumbles, my skin pricks—that it's Tahoe even before he shifts and lets me see his profile.

He's in a crisp black evening suit. Dark black slacks, white button-down shirt, sharp gray tie. His lips look moist, and stained red. As if he was messing with someone not long ago. His blue eyes flare when he sees me and for the briefest instant, they flash protectively.

The event manager walks over to him. "Mr. Roth, we were told you were too busy to lead the gentlemen's conference but it's an absolute honor, please—"

"I'm not staying," he growls, dismissing him.

Clearly this event was not as good as the other one Tahoe was attending with the Saints tonight.

Then I feel fingers on the small of my back, undoing the knot at the back of my apron. He speaks close to my ear. "You're done here." He lifts my apron off over my head, sets it aside, takes my tray and sets it down, and won't heed any of my protests as he leads me out the door.

We're in his car, heading to my place, and I'm barely holding myself together. I'm acting like it's nothing. "Pretty arrangements, though not my color of choice for a gentlemen's event."

Tahoe has been silent the entire ride, letting me bluff it out as he stews a little bit too.

He jerks the gearshift almost angrily as he parks in my building's underground lot, and I leap out of the car, surprised when I hear a second car door slam shut. Tahoe is at my heels boarding the elevator, walking—more like stalking—by my side as I head to my apartment door.

"Oh, wait! My keys. Ha!" I pull them out and jingle them noisily. I open the door, step inside and flip on the light switch. "Home sweet home. Ahh."

I turn to fake-smile at him, but when I meet his concerned, furious blue eyes, my smile starts to tremble. The knot in my throat doubles in size, and I don't know what it is about this man, I don't know why seeing Paul made me feel so little and so unworthy, I don't know why seeing Tahoe's anger and frustration on my behalf makes my cheeks grow wet. One second I'm fine and the next, the tears are spilling.

He shuts the door behind him, his voice gruff with tenderness. "Come here," he says.

He seizes my face and draws me close and his thumbs streak across my cheeks.

"He's such an asshole," I sniffle as he swipes my tears away. "Even now he acts like he was too—too—too good for me."

He presses his lips together in anger and looks deeply into my eyes. His face grows blurry as the tears keep streaming. He leaves me for a moment to head into the kitchen, run the faucet to dampen a small clean towel, and head back to me.

"What are you…?" I protest as he runs the towel gently over my eyes. "You're smearing my makeup—"

"No." He cuts me off with a sly smirk and violently concerned eyes. "Your tears are." He wipes my cheeks and under my eyes.

I fall still as the tears stop, and I notice the look of harsh tenderness on his face. "Did I…were you busy right now?" I croak.

"Yeah. Some event I was only too glad to get away from, trust me."

It makes me realize his life is full of obligations as well, even if he's rich.

He tosses the towel aside and just when I'm thankful he left on my lipstick, he starts wiping it off with his thumbs. One thumb scrapes over my lips to the right, the other thumb to the left. The knot in my throat starts burning with some new emotion, something other than pain, something I don't understand amidst my panic of being completely makeup-less.

But I can feel the lipstick smearing over my cheeks as he gets it off my lips, and with every stroke, he seems to look more deeply into my eyes until I can feel the bareness of my lips.

I'm bare—more self-conscious about my face than I am about my body. My plump lips and wide, expressive eyes. And right now, Tahoe Roth is taking it all in.

Taking all of me in.

I've never been seen like this, since Paul. I've never allowed people to see me like this. Not a man, not anyone. I'm not even comfortable looking at myself like this.

Tahoe is oblivious to that, and he stares at my face for a long time. He stares with such searing intensity I could burn to ash.

His blue eyes look and feel intense on my face, his hands still on my jaw. I raise my hands up to his as he leans forward, exhaling, and he kisses my cheek. His beard scrapes over my skin, and I don't move a muscle. My eyes shut, and when I open them again, I start to caress his face. He's studying me. Still holding my jaw.

I run my fingers over his beard. "It's past the prickly part. It's soft now," I croak.

He laughs softly and rubs the knuckle of his thumb over my lipstick-less lips, his eyes a little heavy looking. "My beard isn't soft; *these* are soft," he contradicts.

I trail my fingertips over his beard, and then, impulsively, over his lips.

He opens his lips as though he means to taste me. He seems to catch himself, taking my wrist in one hand and lowering my arm.

His vexation over Paul is evident in his voice. "Where is it?"

"What?"

"The shit letter he sent you. Where is it?"

More than be affronted at the anger in his voice, I'm surprised by the intensity in his tone as I look up. I sense that he's not mad at me, but for me, frustrated that he can't help me.

"I...*you remember that*?" When he only looks at me with a black look, I go to my room then open the drawer. "Under all my...stuff..."

He reaches through dozens of panties, feeling through my drawer. His hand is big and my panties look so flimsy as he burrows among them up to his thick wrist. He finds the letter, tucks it in his back pocket, and closes my drawer.

"Let's go do something. We're going to make this disappear, and then we're going to chill, and not for one second will you be thinking of him."

He leads me across my apartment and opens the door, and as I pass, he warns me with a determined look, "That's the last time you cry for some motherfucker."

We're at Navy Pier, sitting on the dock with our feet hanging over the water. The rides and shops are quiet. Tahoe called Saint on the drive over, and apparently he knew someone who let us in.

It's a dream here. A nearly finished six-pack of beers sits to my right, Tahoe to my left. It's freezing, so we sit as close as we can get. The sounds of night surround us, so distant they could be a memory. I take a deep breath, finally relaxed.

Ten minutes ago, Tahoe handed me the letter along with his lighter. He asked me if I wanted to read it first. I didn't. I was ready to let go, and I didn't care to know. I didn't hesitate. I lit that sucker on fire, watched it burn for a few seconds, then dropped the burning letter and watched the ashes dissolve into the water.

We toasted with beers, me on my first, T-Rex on his third.

"I love that you drink beer straight from the bottle," I say.

"Why?"

"You can blend with the posh, and you can fit in with average guys." I shrug. "I don't know. I just like it. You're like a tamed beast."

He's momentarily speechless, then he scoffs and shakes his head incredulously. "You did not just call me a tamed beast, Regina."

"I did." I giggle.

I watch him put his lips on the beer bottle and take a slow swig.

I can barely stand the physicality of him, the reaction I have to him, and I'm aware that I want to have sex right now. Or maybe I just want to be close to someone. Maybe *he's* the one who always makes me aware that I want to be close to someone.

He looks at me with his blue eyes. "I like that you drink beer…like a guy," he teases as he nudges me.

"Wow, thanks! I feel so womanly."

His smile never falters, but his voice lowers. "You are. You put on a fierce face, but I've never bought it." He takes another sip, his Adam's apple bobbing as he swallows.

"Yeah? I totally buy yours."

He laughs and then sobers up, crossing his arms. "No one is the way they seem. We all hide little pieces, either because we don't want to be judged, or because we don't think we'll be understood, or simply because we don't want those pieces of us to belong to anyone but us." He lifts his beer and drinks, and I drink too.

As he lowers the bottle to his side, I look at his moist lips for an extra second.

Tahoe has never bought into the image I put out, and I don't understand why—even before we became friends, he seemed to see right through me.

A part of me has also always understood that the person the world sees—the lazy, laughing, easy-going Tahoe—is a front for a far deeper, more complex man beneath.

We all hide little pieces of ourselves. He's right. The teacher who told you that you'd never be good enough marked you in more ways than one. The birthday your parents forgot. Tiny little details that add up to your sense of inadequacy, of simply not being *enough*. So you stop wanting to please the teacher, stop expecting anything for your birthday; you stop putting out your good stuff because you don't want the world to crap on it. Where does that stuff go? Is it there lingering, waiting to come out?

He smiles at me, and there is the tiger in me, wanting to pounce on…him.

I've tucked things about me so far deep I had forgotten they were even there. That I used to be a giver, and I loved to take care of Paul. That I really liked being home—in all the homes I've had. That I worry too much about my friends because I don't want them to be hurt.

But see, that's the thing. How far will I let these things, things people did to me and then went about their lives like normal, affect my life? Even today, Paul hurts me. His betrayal hurts me.

He hurts my belief in men, my ability to connect with one.

I've reserved the good things about me for those who live inside the wall with me, and the rest has been kept from the world—because I don't want to be judged, or because I don't think I'll be understood, or I simply don't want those pieces to be abused by someone else.

I'm such a coward, and that's the truth.

Afraid to just be myself.

Afraid to trust, to love, to give myself another chance.

But I find myself reaching out to this guy, I find myself constantly drawn to this guy. "So what's your secret, T-Rex?"

"If I told you, it wouldn't be a secret," he says with a wink.

He glances at my mouth, then at a spot past my shoulder, as if he's been drawn back into some bleak memory. "Besides, it's in the past. No sense in wasting time with it when there's nothing you can change. Is there?"

"Absolutely," I agree.

His eyes trap mine again, and I want to say something snarky. But he looks raw, and I can't.

"Thank you," I finally say. "I was not very happy when I heard you were coming over, but when I saw you, I felt so relieved. Thank you."

He looks at me with a half-smile and devil eyes. "For destroying his letter?"

"Yes. I feel…better."

He's thoughtful in the silence that settles between us. It's so easy with you, I think. So easy and also so exciting with you.

"Any other letters from any club or non-club members we must destroy?" He narrows his eyes threateningly as he looks at me.

"No!" I laugh and shove both my hands in my pockets to warm them.

He laughs too, and when we stop laughing, our eyes meet, and I feel myself heat up so hard and so fast that I need to drop my gaze.

He remains studying me in silence. "So only Paul. Who was the founding member? Let's talk about him for a second."

"Roderick? Not Roderick! Or Vince...no, not him. They were both just...part of growing up."

"Paul? Part of growing up too?"

"I guess. And you? All your flings?" I nudge him.

He nudges me back. "What about them?"

"Well, were they part of growing up?"

"They're part of what's become my life, I guess."

"And what is this life? Is it everything you wanted? More?"

He pokes the tip of my nose with a fingertip. "I actually didn't plan this life for myself."

I wrinkle my nose and pretend I'm going to bite his finger when he removes it. "Really. What was it then? An accident?"

He laughs and scrapes his hand across his bearded jaw. "Yeah."

I feel warm under his regard; it sends my pulse spinning.

"How was the one you planned? Better?" I'm starting to get confused, and I think it shows on my face.

"Yeah, better." He stares away. "Different."

"How different?"

"I didn't plan to leave home, for starters."

"Why did you?"

"It was tough to stay. Is yours what you pictured it to be?"

"Nope. But do you ever think of correcting paths?"

"Nah. There are no what ifs for me. What was was, and what is is."

"I do. I think back to what I wanted before him, who I was before I got lost in him, what I wanted, and I want it back. Trent is my do over."

He looks at me, and something like raw truth shines in his eyes.

"Good for you, Gina." He reaches out and skims his fore-finger over my nose. I shiver.

"What about yours? Your first?"

"Her name's Lisa."

"Wow, you remember her name."

"I actually remember plenty about her." A muscle twitch-es along his jaw, and he sets his beer aside and takes my arm. "Come on, let's take you home."

"No," I groan, "not home."

"Yes. Home. Now."

"My apartment is so lonely and ominous…so quiet. Take me to Trent's. I told him I'd be there by midnight, when I was done at my gig."

He clenches his jaw thoughtfully.

"Come on, take me to Trent's." I nudge him.

He just keeps clenching his jaw, grabs the back of my neck and steers me toward his car.

We're silent on the drive over, and I'm close to dozing in my seat, feeling safe and comfortable and warm.

I groan when I need to stand and walk toward Trent's building, but I lean on Tahoe for support all the way to the 5th floor. He deposits me right at Trent's door, and when Trent opens, Tahoe's drawl is thicker than ever. "Take care of her," he says, and walks away.

"I saw my ex today," I tell Trent as I cross his small apartment and head straight to his bed.

"Oh no. Don't you just hate that?" He embraces me gently.

"Hate that," I agree, burying my nose in his throat. All I notice is the fact that he doesn't smell like pine trees. And that his jaw is so…smooth. So beardless. "His name was Paul. I'm so over him I didn't want to tell you about it. He cheated on me. You're not the kind of guy who'd ever do that to a girl you like, are you?"

"No, shit, of course not. That's so low. You're more than I can handle, Regina," he assures me sheepishly.

"I'm enough?" I ask, eyes widening happily. It feels good to be enough.

"More than enough."

I frown thoughtfully. "*More* than enough? Trent, don't say that! I want to be *just right*, not more, not less," I complain, but I drift off, exhausted.

I have nightmares about Paul, dumping me, but Paul somehow morphs into Tahoe. I wake up the next morning too early for a Saturday, guilty about dreaming of Tahoe as I notice Trent soundly sleeping in bed beside me.

HUNTING

Aside from burying myself in work during the rest of February, I also start looking for apartments. Trent suggests that I look at vacancies in his building but although his place is okay in terms of transportation to work, I don't want to limit myself to only one neighborhood.

So I spend all my time either working or looking for apartments, all while also trying not to worry overly much about my living situation. Every night I remind myself that I've got this and that taking this step will be worth it.

I'm scouring the classifieds late one night, disappointed that Trent spared only a minimal look at the options I showed him before he headed to my bedroom and to bed.

I feel restless and crave company.

I even call my parents but I get voicemail so I leave them a message.

"Hey, Mom and Dad. I guess I just wanted to touch base, see how you were. Things are well over here. I'm working overtime and looking for a new place. And, well, I'm seeing a guy. I also went to see a new apartment yesterday and although

I haven't found the ideal one, I hope to soon. I miss you. I...I love you. 'Bye."

I hang up and stare at my phone, almost willing them to instantly call me back.

By midnight, I've found one promising prospect and I find myself taking a picture of the ad and texting it to Tahoe with this message:

Versailles is unavailable. But how about one-bedroom cozy chic?

The pic shows that some renovations are in order but the plus is, I can *afford* it.

He texts me back two words.

Him: Rotund no.

Me: Hey that's my line!

Him: That's right. I claimed it ;)

Me: Naughty boy

Him: Naughty possessive little girl.

My phone falls silent for a good twenty minutes.

I'm busy scanning more options in the dark. My eyes are starting to ache from the meager reading light when the phone buzzes. Sitting upright, I turn my phone around and see his name again. I swear to god I feel my heart practically leap out of my chest and the biggest smile spreads across my face.

I press the little green button and, next thing I know, Tahoe's chocolaty, deep voice is rumbling in my ear, "Hey, I'm downstairs. Ring me up?"

I freeze.

Aware of Trent sleeping in my bedroom, I hurry to ring him up.

I open the door just in time to watch him step out of the elevator. He's wearing a white shirt, a brown leather jacket, and dark-wash jeans, a half-grin on his face. The one that makes that lone dimple say hello in that endearing way.

I cross my arms and frown a bit mockingly. "Couldn't bribe my new doorman?"

His wink seems very confident. "I'll wear him down."

We both stare at each other for a long, quiet minute, almost as if we'd never seen each other before. As if we weren't at the Pier only recently, drinking beer and talking about Paul and his…Lisa.

"What are you doing here at this hour? It's the middle of the night and Trent is asleep in my bed." I'm near whispering as I try to keep my voice down.

He scrapes a hand over his head, all five fingers running over the top of his wind-mussed hair all the way to the back of his neck. Then he lets his hand drop and sighs, leaning into the doorframe with a cocky gleam in his eye. "Just wanted to see you, that's all."

"What…why?"

He shrugs devilishly. "Make sure you don't move out of the country, I guess. Purely selfish reasons," he smirks.

Then scans my features with his eyes again.

"You okay?" I ask suspiciously.

He's looking at me as if he can't get enough. His eyes as blue as they looked when I showed him my J. Lo pictures.

"Yeah."

"Come in, don't make noise." He comes in, and I close the door and usher him to the pitch-black living room. "Are you drunk? What? You couldn't find a floozie available to go out tonight?"

"You could say I was more interested in your apartments tonight." He walks into my kitchen, also unlit. "Anything to eat?" He opens the fridge, and for a moment he is all I see. A big, hulking figure illuminated by the interior fridge lights.

"I've got a salad I picked up and didn't eat. You can have it," I say.

He pulls it out of the fridge while I get a fork from a drawer and hand it over to him.

I don't want to turn on the lights and wake up Trent, but we somehow manage to make our way to the round table in the small dining area.

I don't really understand Tahoe's reason for visiting to-night but sometimes I wonder if he doesn't simply want some-one to talk to that he doesn't have to seduce or be fun with all the time. Maybe he enjoys my company like I do his. Maybe I calm him like he sometimes calms me. Except for the few moments when his looks quicken my pulse—like a little bit right now—he's the one person I seem to always crave being with lately. At any hour, even in the mornings, when I'm a bit grumpy.

I sense my mood would improve in the mornings simply knowing this blond beast was around.

We sit on opposite ends of the table. He forks a few pieces of salad but keeps staring at me through the shadows. "Turn on the light," he says.

"I don't want to wake up Trent," I hedge.

But the dark makes his voice feel even more hypnotic than usual.

"Turn on the lights."

"What for?"

"I want to see what I'm eating, for starters." Pause. "And I want to see you."

"I'm sort of…indisposed, wearing sexy pajamas."

"I've seen sexy pajamas before."

But not on me, you cocky jerk.

Sighing though, I go and turn on a living room lamp and come back to my seat. His eyes turn extra blue as he takes me in in a spaghetti-strapped baby doll.

He frowns then, and reaches across the table. "You sleep with this on?" He reaches out and pinches a bit of material, tugging it a little.

"Yep. I don't sleep naked, thank you very much."

He frowns when he studies my face. "That too?"

"My makeup? Yes, I like to look pretty."

"You look pretty anyway," he says.

I'm helpless not to flush and I'm grateful when he lowers his gaze to finish his salad. He then gets some water from the kitchen.

I settle on a living room couch and watch him return. "How's your week been? I'm excited to go to one of your games. Have you made an appointment with your barber yet?"

"Nah, I don't want to jinx my win."

"You're superstitious? Why are all athletes superstitious?"

A smile touches his eyes as he sits by me. "That's for me to know and for you to ponder."

"Come on."

I punch his shoulder.

He stops my second punch by opening his palm to catch it.

"Gina?" a voice calls from the bedroom.

Tahoe looks at me ruefully, raising his brows.

I giggle and go tiptoe up the hall and close the bedroom door, not before apologetically whispering, "We'll be out here talking, okay? Tahoe just stopped by for a snack."

"Fine. Don't wake me please, babe."

I shut the door and pad back into the living room. "He's grumpy when he's tired." I drop back on the couch. "I'm glad you're here, I actually couldn't sleep. I've been circling advertisements as much as possible."

"What have we got here? Humboldt Park?" He scans all of my circled classifieds but keeps his finger on the Humboldt Park option that has a double circle around it. "There's no way you're living there."

"I don't know, Roth, it's starting to appeal. Maybe it'll keep *you* from visiting at ungodly hours."

"But it won't keep the rapists, killers, and gangsters away." He lifts his brows.

"You're so picky. What do you think of this one?" I show him another.

He laughs sardonically. "No way in hell you're living there alone, Regina. Let's find you something in the Loop."

"I live near the Loop already, it's a bit more expensive."

He doesn't listen as he grabs my pen and starts circling some other places. "Bring your laptop, let's get a look at some pics," he says, patting my butt fondly as I get up.

I swear it burns for the whole hour afterward with the imprint of his hand.

We end up spending the next couple hours looking for good places for me to live. For the first time since the Pier, I feel like I'm actually talking—really talking—again with someone. I feel a little more alive than I was before he stepped through my door.

"Want to know something, Regina?" He leans back and crosses his arms behind his head with a thoughtful look on his face. "A friend of mine owns a prime piece of property at the best location in the Loop. They're demolishing it to rebuild new apartment complexes but permits could take up to a year. I bet he'd let you rent something for pennies in the meantime."

My heart stops from the excitement. "You think so?"

"Hell, I know so." He rumples my hair and flashes his pearly whites, which look extra white against his scruffy blond beard. "You'll be set up for at least a year. Gives you time to figure out exactly where you want to go."

"You'd call him for me?" I ask dubiously.

He presses a button on his cell. "I just did." He winks and lifts his phone to his ear, then proceeds to leave a message, his voice low.

Smiling, I shut my laptop and fold the newspapers neatly into a pile, exhaling a sigh of relief. I never realized I was starting to feel homeless until now, when the real possibility of finding a new home has come up.

Less than an hour after he leaves, after I've showered and am ready to hit the bed, I get a text from him saying that it's all set and that his friend William Blackstone will show me the apartment as soon as I'm ready.

Me: Thank you, amazing T-Rex!!!!!!

Him: Don't make plans next Friday afternoon. You're coming to my game.

GAME

I missed the game, and I am haunted by it. The same day of Tahoe's lacrosse match, Martha needed me to cover for one of my coworkers. I'm so mad about that. Because the reality is that he is always there for me. And I want to be there for him. So half a week after the missed game, I lie in bed, sleepless, and glance at my "missed calls" screen, where his name is written next to a (2). I decide to stop avoiding the issue, put on my big girl panties and call him.

"I can't sleep," I say immediately after he answers.

There's a long silence, as if he's taken aback by my call. At this hour.

"Why can't you sleep?" His voice is raspy, as if I caught *him* sleeping, or maybe even having sex.

"I want to go to your next game."

Another silence. "You're messing with me." His voice sounds completely disbelieving.

"No! Why? What? I'm not invited anymore?" I prod.

"I'm not in the city," I hear a squeak as if he gets out of bed, a soft moaning protest, and then a door shut, and silence, "but I'll be there for this weekend's game."

"Cool." I grin happily.

"I'll text you the time. On one condition." There's a warning in his voice.

I groan in dread.

"You've got to paint my number on your cheek," he says next.

"Um, no?" I say.

"Well then, it was nice saying hi."

My heart stops when I realize he's about to hang up. "Fine! What is it? Sixty-nine?" I ask with mock boredom.

"Double zero."

"Fitting, 'cause you're a whole lot of nothing," I say drolly.

"You're a mean girl, Regina." There's a smile in his voice. "Now sleep."

"I'll sleep when you do." I hang up, smiling down at the phone.

I'm still thinking about him when I finally turn off the lights. I'm still thinking about him in the middle of the night when I wonder where he is and who he's with. Some girl he thinks he's good enough for, even when he thinks he's not good enough for me.

Well she's welcome to him, really. I have Trent, who makes me happy, and who I'm good enough for. Trent only needs me, not a battalion of women like Tahoe does.

I'm sitting in the second row of bleachers at the large lacrosse field of Tahoe's men's league when the players shuffle out onto the field. I spot him instantly. Double zero. One of the tallest, largest forms out there. He wears a white jersey with red numbers. Cleats, shorts, shoulder pads, thick white gloves, elbow pads, and a helmet streaked in red and white. He's wearing a helmet with a facemask—all the players are. But Tahoe also wears a visor underneath the facemask. It's a swirl of colors, starting with red at the center, fanning out to orange to yellow to blue. I can't see his eyes; but I can feel his stare as he looks up at the stands.

He looks as intimidating as shit as he heads straight to the middle of the field. He faces off against his opponent, hunches forward. They're nearly nose to nose, their lacrosse sticks down on the ground.

He glances in my direction. My heart flips in my chest. Nervousness fills me for him, for the game or for some other reason, I don't know, but I squirm a little in my seat.

"About to face off," a voice through the speakers says.

I'm holding my breath by the time the whistle sounds.

It all happens so fast. Lacrosse is so quick, it's hard to keep up as a spectator, hard to understand without prior knowledge. Muscled guys in uniforms run around the field, swinging their sticks. But I actually googled the game before so I know a little bit about what's happening now.

The men hold their lacrosse sticks; they call them shafts or handles as well. They're alloy metal or titanium, with a pocket that holds the ball. This ball is their ultimate possession. This ball is what Tahoe just scooped up, and the announcer yells, "Possession Red! Pinch and sweep, and he's off!"

He moved so fast, the opponent fell, face flat to the ground.

He holds the stick low to his chest as he charges forward at full speed. Defense moves in; he stutter-steps and then split-dodges to the left, fooling the defense, and then throws over his head.

"Score Red!" the voice calls.

I try to catch my breath, but once again they're facing off. Tahoe hunches low, glancing in my direction for just a second. It's only a second, but it's enough to make me suppress another squirm. He's very menacing. No emotion on his face as he turns his head just a fraction, his colored visor flashing with the move.

Each team has ten players. The goalie, three defenses, three midfield men, three attackers—then two referees. Tahoe is the center midfield man, the one who faces off and fights for possession of the ball every time a game begins or a goal is scored.

He's super quick, muscular in form and as athletic as a pro.

On his second face-off, he makes a fast break—claiming the ball with a flick of his wrist, a run, and a perfect pass. His team member catches and throws, and when team Black's defense steps in to scoop up the ball, Tahoe charges forward.

"Check him, check him!" someone cries beside me.

Tahoe checks him by slapping his stick into the other guy, throwing checks left and right as he fights to recover possession. Before I know it, he's not only scooped up the ball, but immediately passed it to a team member a foot away from the goal.

"Score Red!"

I can tell he's comfortable with both hands, even his off hand. I can also tell he's an aggressive, no-nonsense player. If anyone has the ball, he wants it, and he'll check and use his speed, his wits, his everything to get it.

During the third face-off, he looks at me again. I came alone, am sitting here surrounded by strangers, but I don't feel alone simply because he keeps turning his head to look at me in a way that makes me feel as if I'm with him.

His head remains tilted in my direction—they face off.

"Possession Black!"

His opponent runs with it; Tahoe gets so mad he charges forward and trucks him to the ground. "Unnecessary roughness," the announcer says. "Illegal procedure number zero-zero, penalty box, thirty seconds."

"Oh, that always happens," someone beside me tells his friend. "He plays so aggressive, he always gets a penalty."

I watch Tahoe grip his stick angrily as he storms to the box, seething as he drops down on one knee, his head canted up at the clock, waiting impatiently. A trainer approaches to offer him water, and he declines with a shake of his head.

The backup does the face-off, and the announcer soon calls, "Score Black!"

As the teams position at the center of the field again, Tahoe charges out of the penalty box.

He leans forward, in position to face off. He's seething testosterone as he scoops up the ball and runs with it, so powerful that he throws the ball from far away. The ball blows upfield and the goalie sweeps to the right, but the ball hits the top shelf, right at the bar, then bounces inside.

"Outside shot, score Red!"

I can feel the energy in the stands increasing, people excited that this is going to be a big-scoring game.

They face off again. Eye to eye—his head turning a fraction.

God, will he stop looking at me?

I watch him intently, noting how he puts his head over the ball, pitches it upward with his wrist, swiftly scoops it up, and runs like the devil. Defense charges forward; Tahoe fakes it, and when they fall for it, he takes two more steps and puts it in. "Score Red!"

"Score Red!"

"Score Red!"

"Holy shit, that was a 105-mile-per-hour shot!" someone near my seat cries.

During halftime he's the only player who doesn't remove his helmet or take water. He's ready to go out again, eager to play.

I cannot take my eyes off him when he's back on the field. I hardly know what's happening with the other players because I'm watching only him. I wonder why he wanted me here. Why he wanted me to see how he possesses that ball, how strong he is, athletic he is, how fucking hot he looks with that visor. Passing fast, facing off, possessing the ball, time and again, shooting high to high, high to low, shooting into the ground at an angle that bounces in front of the goal and goes in.

The game lasts about two hours. Red wins 20-1, completely squashing their competitors.

The crowd cheers and whistles as their victory is declared. The players shuffle out, but rather than leave, I watch with accumulated nervous energy and excitement as zero-zero heads toward the stands.

He jerks off his sweaty jersey with one gloved fist. His visor tips upward in my direction.

He balls the fabric and in one powerful throw, just like the ones he did on the field, he throws his dirty, sweaty jersey directly onto my lap.

My seat neighbor reaches out to catch it with a thrilled, hungry little gasp.

"Nope," I tell her, yanking it free from her hands.

I frown when I realize how possessive I sounded but, thankfully, double zero is already striding toward the lockers. Thank god he didn't see me get territorial.

I can smell the testosterone on his shirt as I head down the stands and into a sheltered hall with exits to the parking lot.

"Hey! You with Roth?"

A guy from the Red team is looking at me questioningly.

I nod.

"Get over here." He motions me to follow him, then leads me farther down the hall and straight into the men's locker room.

I follow him, a little bit uncomfortable at all the men in nude and semi-nude states.

"So fucking cold today, you get hit with a metal stick and it hurts like hell," some guy says.

"Don't play on off-season then," another retorts.

"T, swear to god, you're the only lacrosse player who whips ass and likes baseball too. *Real* men play lacrosse. Hell, you almost killed someone today. All baseball guys do is stand there and hit the ball."

Following the voice coming from the second row of lockers, I head down and around the corner. I spot a pair of white custom gloves with *Roth* embroidered on the wrists on a wood bench. The guy who had been speaking presses ice against a burn on his thigh, and I notice the long, tanned, muscular arms of Tahoe bearing the same burns.

I glance upward, and he's in a towel, his chest bare.

I try not to notice the damp rivulets trailing down his torso, dipping into the dents between the squares of his abs.

He senses me and turns. Seeing his blue eyes without the visor sends a shock of electricity through me. His face breaks into a smile, and he's so amped up I can feel his energy.

"My lucky charm," he drawls.

He lifts me up and twirls me so fast I get dizzy. I hear him chuckle and it makes me laugh, then I punch his shoulder so he'll put me down.

His eyes darken a little when he lowers me to my feet.

"Always this noisy in the locker room?" I ask, not knowing why I'm whispering.

"That's the sound of victory." He takes me in as if he's thrilled to see me, then he turns back to his locker and pulls out a clean long-sleeved crewneck and shoves his head and arms inside. "It's dead quiet after a bad game," he says with a wink.

"Really?"

I glance around. The players are hyped up, slamming doors and slapping each other's shoulders with good energy all around.

The coach walks in with two other coaches flanking him. One clap from him, and the players fall silent.

"That was good, but keep working on your shit—no more of the streak we were in. Got it?" He scans the players, all nodding happily, then locks his gaze on Tahoe. "Good work, Roth." Respect and admiration echo in his voice.

"*Good work*, Coach?" a player yells after him. "We fucking destroyed the other team! Fucking smothered them." He laughs and comes to slap Tahoe on the back, already dressed and ready to go. "Plus no one got injured."

He walks away, and once again, I notice the burn mark streaking across the back of Tahoe's hand.

"No injuries? What's *that*?"

"Nothing. That comes with the turf." He grins and turns around, whips off his towel, bare-ass naked, and eases into his jeans.

I turn away, my cheeks heating to a thousand and one degrees from the sight of the most perfect freaking male butt I've ever seen. It's as tanned as the rest of him, which only confirms this guy sunbathes *in the buff.*

While I do anything but look at Tahoe, another player walks up to him.

"Twenty to one—that's demoralizing. Just what my ego needed after our losing streak." His eyes fall to me in appreciation. "Is this the lady I need to thank for your excellent performance, Roth?" the guy asks.

Tahoe smirks but slams the door of his locker. "Yeah, but you can thank her another day," he says. His gaze falls on the sweaty jersey I'm holding against my chest. "You caught my jersey."

It's just him and me now in the aisle.

"I kind of had no other choice, it was either catch it or let it fall on my lovely face."

"Ahh, we can't have that, can we?" He laughs and pokes the tip of my nose with his fingertip.

I scrunch my nose up and pretend I'll bite his finger if he touches me again. "I'm not putting it on. But it'll be great to dry my dishes with."

"Hey, a wash and it'll be good as new." He pats me on the butt.

"A wash? This needs to be burned, T. Roth. *Burned*," I say.

"So where's the fire?" He lifts his brows in challenge. His eyes sparkle. Is it possible that up close and smiling, this man looks even more intimidating than he did out there, wearing that threateningly mysterious visor?

"I..."

The fire is inside me.

In places you will never know.

"Let's do a crazy ceremony—we're burning your sweaty jersey before it stains my closet," I tell him.

It seems like a good idea not to hang on to his jersey. Soon I'll be sleeping in his shirt like Rachel did with Saint's— and that did nothing to help her stop thinking about him. I don't need to think of Tahoe for another second, *especially* at night. I have all I need in Trent. I do. I *do*.

He shifts close, his thigh against mine as he toes my shoes with his bare foot. "Should I bring the matches?" He's smirk- ing as he sits down on the bench to slip on his loafers.

"I've got plenty of matches."

As he stands, he tucks a strand of hair behind my ear. "That's right, you do." He looks briefly at my lips, then he grabs his duffel so we can leave. "Let's get you home."

He leads me out and drives me home.

On our way there, we talk about the game—his goals— and the fact that they won.

He tells me the history of lacrosse. It started with Native Americans. When a boy was ready to become a man, he would play a game of lacrosse. But it would be played across eight or nine miles, where, once gaining possession of the ball, the boy would have to run like hell mile after mile, never knowing when he would be attacked and fought for the ball.

"Fastest-growing sport in America," he finishes.

"Well it was about time people caught up. I declare myself a fan. I'm a lacrosse groupie."

He grins at that then shakes his head. "You could never be a groupie."

"Excuse me?" I scoff. "Because I didn't paint two zeros on my cheek? I like my makeup to make me look better, not worse."

He shoots me a doubtful look and then parks his car in an empty spot outside my building. He turns to me. "Hey, thanks for coming today. I liked seeing you up there."

The car feels warm all of a sudden.

I try to shrug casually. "I liked seeing you play."

"Yeah?"

"Yeah." It has to be 200 degrees in here. "And you know it, Tahoe! You're like a star for your entire team."

"My team and I have been training for years."

"You really love the game, don't you?"

He nods. He uses his hands to create the long rectangle shape of the field before him. "I stand there, in the middle of the field. Behind me is my goal. Before me, my opponent's goal and my attackers. My defense is behind me, my wings to my right, all I need is to get the ball and put it in that goal. That's it. Simple. Nothing else in life is that fucking simple."

The passion in his eyes makes me feel…happy. Giddy almost. And so very warm.

We're still parked in the same spot. I wonder if we're prolonging the moment here. In his car.

"What else are you this passionate about, besides scoring?"

"I live for scoring." A devil's light sparks in his eyes and suddenly I can't take the heat anymore.

I force myself to open the door. "Don't get out, I'm fine."

He gets out, locks the car, and follows me inside. "So what's in line for tonight?" he asks me in the quiet elevator as we ride up to my floor.

"Bed."

He stares at the elevator numbers as they climb. "Alone?" His eyes slide to mine, and he quirks a brow, but his gaze is intense.

"No," I admit with a shrug.

"Davis?" He almost sneers the word.

"Wait. How do you know his name is Trent Davis?"

"I asked."

"Well, stop asking. And it's not Trent, it's Wynn. Emmett is out of town and we're having a girls' sleepover."

"Ahh." He smirks.

I point at his beard.

"You should celebrate by visiting your barber. That beard!" I cluck and shake my head.

His lips look extra pink next to the beard as he flashes his smile and follows me to my door. "Regina." His voice stops me before I walk inside, his gaze as happy as I felt downstairs when he told me about the game. "I appreciate you coming to the game."

He looks as if he wants to lift me in the air and throw me or something.

"I might have enjoyed it if the team I was rooting for hadn't lost," I bait him.

"We didn't lose," he says, still grinning.

He leans over and kisses my cheek, his smile brushing my skin.

"Have fun with Wynn tonight."

Pine trees linger in my nose as he walks toward the elevator. He hops on board, gives me a peace sign and his highest-megawatt smile, and the doors close and take him away.

I clutch his jersey to my chest and step into my apartment to find a note from my landlord, reminding me that my rent was due today. I sigh and drop onto the couch.

I look at his shirt then I go dump it in the washer and go have a bite to eat.

Forty minutes later, I switch it to the drier and feel myself smile as I watch his shirt go round and round.

Wynn arrives soon and we're watching *Tequila Sunrise* but I can't really focus on the movie because my mind keeps returning to Tahoe. There is so much more to Tahoe Roth than meets the eye and I'm pretty certain not a lot of people get to know the man on a deep level. Seeing his passion for lacrosse only brought to the surface my own excitement about it, and I'm stunned that he can have such a powerful effect on me. I keep wondering what he's doing now as I watch the movie on my bed with Wynn and pretend I'm really paying attention to Michelle Pfeiffer and Mel Gibson.

Wynn puts the movie on pause. "Gina, you're way too quiet and I'm the only one eating popcorn. Maybe you haven't noticed but I have." She eyes me probingly. "Do you want to talk about it?"

I look at her. I was ready for bed by the time she arrived. I'd already taken Tahoe's shirt out of the drier and shoved it under my bed skirt because I simply didn't want questions that I didn't have the answers to.

So I give her a chiding frown, as if it's all in her head, and say, "There's nothing to talk about."

"Isn't there? How are you and Trent?"

"We're good."

"You're lost in outer space and you're smiling when there's nothing funny happening in the movie. You think I don't notice? What's up?" She narrows her eyes. "You're also wearing less makeup. You look so good! And so sweet! What's up with that little change? Are you *in love*?"

My eyes flare wide at that. "No! Wynn…Trent and I are dating. We're getting to know each other still."

I start laughing out of pure nervousness because I'm not ready to fall in love. It's too soon to fall in love. I'm too wary and distrustful of love.

"Hmm," she says thoughtfully, a sly little grin on her lips. "I'm here if you ever want to talk about it, Gina."

"Thank you," I say, then grab the remote and press Play.

The TV and one tiny lamp on my side of the bed are the only lights in the room as we continue watching the movie and I continue to find my mind wandering back to the jersey with the double zeroes that lies under my bed skirt.

SPRING BREAK

April arrives with the promise of spring break, and the girls begin making plans.

"Callan's invited us all to his Miami beach house. Trent too, Gina. We have to make the effort to go, spend time together," Rachel says over brunch.

"I'd kill for a tan right now." Wynn looks at her white hands. "And a manicure."

I've been working double shifts at the department store. I've also managed to land some steady clients who want their makeup done during the weekends, plus a few gigs at children's parties where the kids want their faces painted like their favorite animals. It leaves very little time for Trent and me to see each other. Sometimes I only get to see him once or twice a week. Work has also been getting in the way of my usual Thursday date nights with the girls.

So when, this Sunday during brunch, they begin making plans for spring break and tell me we're all invited with our partners to spend a long weekend at Callan's Miami house, I'm too work-tired to decline and desperately looking forward to some fun times.

Trent, however, is not that excited about the expense. I convince him to use his airplane miles, but when it turns out he doesn't have enough miles, I end up using all of my saved credit card miles and splurge on both of our tickets.

I know that his business has put a strain on his finances. I also know that I'm saving for an apartment and can't afford frivolous spending. But I'm excited about spending time with him out of the city. Between my busy work schedule and his, we don't spend as much time as we should together. I want to remedy that this spring break.

I end up packing last minute on the very same day we leave for Miami. Trent is already at my place, all his stuff packed in a tiny black carry-on duffel. Men. There is no way I can fit all of my things in even a bag double that size.

I rummage through my closet and I hold up a bikini that I got as a birthday present from Rachel two years ago.

"What do you think about me packing this bikini, as well as my one-piece?"

He eyes the bikini thoughtfully, scratches one of his freckles with a sheepish look, and then looks at me. "Are you going to fix your hair?"

"What do you mean? Of course I'm fixing my hair." I tug the careless ponytail I'm wearing and roll my eyes.

"Then I like it." He grins.

I continue packing, suddenly shooting him a sideways frown. I like that he's honest, I prefer honesty over the pure bullshit I got from Paul. But I love wearing my ponytail when I'm relaxing or when I'm having a bad hair day. A ponytail is so much easier than spending hours with the flat iron.

"I better shower and get ready to leave," I say when I notice the time. Our flight leaves in three hours.

Trent glances at the time too and nods at me with a wink, looking cute in a baseball cap and a blue tee as he helps me zip up my luggage.

I check my phone and see a text from my mother.

Heard your message, Gina! Glad things are going well, we miss you and hope to come home for Christmas this year and meet this boy of yours! Love from Mom and Dad

"My parents want to meet you," I say.

"Wow. I'm so ready for that," he says, stunned but obviously happy.

I purse my lips thoughtfully, then realize I will never be able to change my parents. I know that they love me in their own quirky way, but they never really loved spending time with me more than they enjoyed spending time with each other.

I will never come first.

They will never rush to answer my phone calls, my texts, my messages.

But they want to meet my boyfriend now, and I'm grateful that they're even moderately interested.

"You know what?" I say thoughtfully. "Me too. I feel so good about this trip, Trent, I really want to spend time with you."

Aiming to prove to him how much I mean it, I spend half an hour after showering to flat-iron my hair, determined for him to drool over me the entire long weekend.

BEACH HOUSE

We arrive in Florida at 3 p.m. The humidity is so high that my hair starts curling within minutes of standing out on the airport sidewalk while waiting for a taxi. I end up having to pull my hair back in a ponytail and "I really like you with your hair down best" Trent pouts sadly.

"Complain to the humidity." I realize I sound cross and this is not how I wanted our vacation to go, so I force myself to lighten up and nudge him. "Come on, it's still me."

He frowns. "Why are you hitting me?"

I pause and straighten. "Hit you? I was just...*nudging* you...whatever." I shake my head and laugh to myself.

My stomach sinks a little. I remember all the things about myself I had once tried to change to please Paul. Does every relationship require that to work? Do you need to change stuff you like or do simply to deserve being wanted and loved?

I push my dark thoughts aside when the cab halts at a massive wrought-iron gate with a *CC* emblem at its center.

Once we're allowed to pass, the cab pulls over before an *Architectural Digest*-worthy Mediterranean mansion that consists of a pristine white building plus ten villas spread across the beach. Every villa is facing the waves and sand. Callan greets us when we arrive, hair mussed and sexy as only he and his gang of playboy friends can look. His date is a petite brunette—Sandy—who's trying to prove to the elusive billionaire how good a hostess she is by offering drinks every couple of minutes to anyone who crosses her path.

She shows us to our room and I fall in love instantly with the simple, sophisticated décor. Everything is done in neutral tones with the exception of colorful pillows strewn on the bed and patterned art deco curtains on the massive glass doors that lead to the terrace. The terrace has an outdoor shower and a private pool.

Trent and I get settled in record time then meet up with everybody at the main pool. Drinks and conversation flow as Rachel, Wynn, and I lie on deep orange chaise lounges and the men sip drinks in the pool. Saint playfully leaps out of the pool to join Rachel, stroking his hand up and down her tiny, nearly four-month-pregnant belly. The adoration in his eyes is heartwarming and I can't help but feel a flood of happiness for them, for my best friend.

But as the hours pass and the sky starts casting a pinkorange glow across the horizon, I realize I'm not having as much fun as I expected as I would.

Maybe because I can't help but notice that everyone is here…

Everyone but Tahoe.

Even after a full day at the pool and a tray full of margaritas, I can't sleep that night. I find myself wandering out onto the terrace. I'm wearing a flimsy camisole and shorts and I'm enjoying the way the warm spring Florida night feels on my skin. I take one of the terrace lounge chairs and stare out at the waves. The sky is pitch black with only a sliver of moon, one of the few lights I can see.

My eyes are drawn to the only other light nearby, flooding out of the villa next door.

Its windows are open, and the gauzy drapes billow softly with the wind.

The villa was vacant, as far as I knew, because I heard it was supposed to be Tahoe's. Did he finally arrive? I expect to hear moans and groans at any moment now.

Instead there's movement, and as my eyes adjust to the shadows, I realize there's a man sitting outside too. His blue eyes glimmer in the dark, and there's a light smile curving his lips as he lifts his fingers in a peace sign.

My stomach, my heart, my whole body seems to clutch and spasm in reaction.

Tahoe is sitting alone. How long had he been watching me?

His chest is bare. But he's wearing some sort of drawstring pajama pants that are light in color and possibly linen. He looks like a god in the moonlight. And the sudden thought of a woman being inside that villa with him causes a dull thud of jealousy right in my center.

I'm suddenly too aware of how flimsy my camisole is, and how very much my nipples are poking into the material as the wind presses it against my skin.

I know Tahoe notices.

He's too observant a man not to notice, too perceptive.

He must be wondering why I'm not in my room, in my boyfriend's arms.

I wonder why too.

Behind me, my boyfriend is warm, asleep in bed, but my mind is stuck on Tahoe and how he makes me feel. Why does it feel like my life is moving, but I'm stuck at a standstill, just waiting for glimpses of *him*?

Him and that slowly curving smile appearing now.

Soon I find myself smiling back at him.

I'm really happy to see him.

I CANNOT TAKE MY EYES OFF HIM

I wake up late and alone the next morning, a little disoriented. When the fog clears, I remember that I'm at the beach, in the loveliest villa I could imagine, with my boyfriend and friends, and a smile lights my face.

I get up, brush my teeth, fix my face, and notice on the pillow next to mine a note from Trent. It says he's having breakfast at the main house with everyone and that he'll meet me at the beach.

I change into my one-piece black swimsuit, wrap a pareo around my waist, and slip into my sandals. I'm heading down the beach path toward the main house when I hear the sound of running water coming from Tahoe's villa.

I stop to peer through the palm trees. My jaw drops as I stare at the most primal thing I've ever seen. Tahoe stands alone in the outdoor shower, muscles glistening with water and sunlight. His head cast up to the shower spray.

He's pumping his hips, his thick erection in his fist.

He is such a beautiful man I could probably come by just staring at his body. Just by staring at him like this. *Oh god.*

He's ripped, and cut. As for his beautifully proportionate cock...

He's uncut. And he's fully extended. Raw, glorious. My throat feels thick, I have trouble swallowing.

Tahoe Roth.

My guy friend. And THE SEXIEST THING ON THE PLANET.

My body reacts so violently I feel pain at the tips of my nipples, between my legs, in my chest, all across my skin.

My skin that suddenly wants those big hands to be stroking...me.

I think I make a sound, and he turns his head to look at me. For an awkward second we both stare. He leans his free arm on a nearby tree branch that I suppose is meant to shelter him from view.

Which it doesn't. Not one bit.

And I cannot take my eyes off him.

His eyes are so wild, they look almost unholy. "Join me."

"You..." I shake my head.

He releases his cock and steps forward. Naked and unashamed. I'm wet between my legs, and my stomach is full of stupid butterflies.

I take a step back. "There's no way I'm joining you."

He pauses, and I take in every line of muscle on his chest and his dark nipples. Rivulets of water trail down to the squares of his abs and down the *V* of muscle on his hips and he's...*so very huge and so very hard!*

He's looking at me so casually, as if he takes showers with his female friends all the time.

I turn around and flee.

The main house is empty, but a huge buffet remains set up for latecomers. I grab a plate with shaky hands, struggling to rid my mind of Tahoe's body.

When Tahoe appears, I almost drop the plate, flustered as I set it down.

His hair is wet from his shower and a pair of navy swim trunks hang low on his hips, a *V* of muscle visible just above the drawstring. He heads straight toward me, tugs me behind a thick stone column and smiles. "Hey."

I'm struggling not to sound breathless. "I didn't see that."

"Yeah, you did. You couldn't get enough."

"Not true." I glance downward at my sandals.

He chuckles.

"Hey," he tips my chin, "nothing wrong with that."

"I know."

"So…"

"So I can't unsee it, that's what."

"I don't want you to unsee it."

"Tahoe," I grit, "someone is going to hear you and I don't want to deal with questions I don't have the answers to."

"I like you flustered."

"You can't get me flustered. I won't let you."

"Why not?"

"Because."

"You aren't flustered right now?" he dares, taunting me.

"No. I'm embarrassed because I shouldn't have seen that."

"And yet you couldn't stop looking. I really like how naughty you are."

"I…" I push him.

He laughs.

I kick his ankles, trying to hide how flustered I am with mock anger.

He kicks me back playfully, dropping onto a nearby lounge seat, stretching back and crossing his arms.

Giving up the act and knowing he's too smart not to know that he seriously affected me, I sit down next to him and sigh.

He tugs on my ponytail. "I like this. You look cute," he says.

I pry my ponytail free. "Trent likes my hair down and flat-ironed," I say.

I think I sound bitter because Tahoe frowns, his eyes becoming stormy in an instant.

"Do you want breakfast?" I ask, distracting him.

He eyes the buffet table with a mischievous glimmer in his eye. "Let's do it."

He pats my butt to get me going, and he follows close, standing right behind me as we both help ourselves to the offerings. He starts to playfully take some of my pieces.

"There's a million croissants in the basket, why do you want mine?" I chide.

"Because it has my name written on it." He steals another pastry from my plate. So I steal something from his in return.

"That's my apple, Regina. Do you want a bite of my apple?" His eyes twinkle even when he scowls down at me.

"Only because you stole my croissant."

We do this all along the length of the buffet until we each end up with basically a plate full of what the other had chosen.

We end up breakfasting on warm croissants, fruit, and sugary churros.

I can't help the queasy feeling in my stomach as we eat in comfortable silence.

When I say comfortable, I'm of course excluding the queasy feeling in my stomach. And the occasional thoughts of how beautiful he looks and how beautiful he looked just now, my T-Rex in the wild.

We munch on churros and seem to lick our lips far more than usual to get all the specks of sugar outside our mouths.

The queasy feeling is still there as we head to the beach and I drop down to tan next to Trent and Rachel. Tahoe disappears for a few minutes, then comes back wearing a wet suit that hugs every muscle and plane, and hops on one of the WaveRunners.

"Trent? Want to join?" Saint asks. "There's gear in the shed and a jet ski just for you."

Trent leaps to his feet and heads out with the guys, leaving us girls to tan. I notice Tahoe actually starts showing Trent how to use the WaveRunner.

He towers over Trent unashamedly, and Trent is obviously a bit awkward with the WaveRunner when he climbs on top, but Tahoe is being patient and easygoing, treating Trent like just one of the guys.

When Tahoe says something that sends Trent into a roar of laughter, the queasy feeling returns full force.

The fact that Tahoe is man enough to show my boyfriend the ropes, even when I sense he doesn't like him much, makes my admiration for T-Rex grow.

QUEASY FEELING
OF RECOGNITION

B y the next day, I recognize the queasy feeling in my stomach. The same one I felt when I stood staring at Paul with my toothbrush in my mouth. It's the sensation of caring too much about a guy and fearing that not only can he hurt you, but he *is* going to.

That he's already hurting you.

That he's standing right in the middle of you and a nice guy who you could have something real with. So when we all sit down for breakfast, I avoid him by sitting in the seat farthest away. Then when everyone heads to the pool, I play a game of staying out of the water whenever he goes in, and taking a dip as soon as he gets out.

Finally he catches me that afternoon in the sunlit library as I sit on a window bench with a book.

"What's up with you?" He fills the doorway completely and he sounds vaguely puzzled.

"Nothing."

"Nothing's up with you, so why aren't you out with us?" He seems genuinely confused.

"I'm reading."

He wants to know what I'm reading. *The Nightingale*, by Kristin Hannah. We start arguing over why I thought it was a good idea to read now.

"Are you avoiding me, Regina?"

"Wha—" I sputter and set the book down. "*No*, absolutely *not*. In fact, I was going to hit some balls at the tennis court just now." I leap out of my window seat and take advantage of him having walked into the room, unblocking the exit, to breeze through the doorway.

He follows me to the mudroom and scoops up a tennis racket after I do, smacking it gently on my rump. "Let's go."

CLUBBING

I didn't beat him in tennis, but the exercise helped release some of the sexual tension that has been building in me since I saw him shower. He didn't get tired like I did, but he seemed to enjoy teasing me and making me run after the ball—watching me with a half a smirk on his face and thoughtful eyes.

We ended up playing four sets, and then I went back to shower. The thought of him naked in the shower was replaced with thoughts of him smashing the hell out of the tennis ball—which is somehow equally disturbingly sexy. But at least the knot in my stomach lessened some. Because we laughed and teased again—friendly, as usual.

We're supposed to meet everyone at a club downtown.

As Trent and I arrive and give our names to the bouncer, we're allowed inside and we both head toward a large VIP area at the back that consists of four booths facing each other.

I instantly spot Tahoe.

Tahoe's smile freezes when he sees me. His eyes run over me in my red cocktail dress, once, twice, three times, and then a woman taps his shoulder. He takes a quick swig of his beer and turns, ducking his head to listen to something she has to say, scraping a restless hand over his jaw.

I've seen him with women a thousand times, so I don't understand why this time makes me uncomfortable. I especially don't understand it when Trent is so sweetly holding my hand.

"Roth," Trent interrupts and greets him.

"Davis." Tahoe doesn't look at me as he grabs and shakes Trent's hand.

His lips curl the barest fraction as he glances in my direction, but his stare is dark and he's deathly quiet, not speaking a word to me at all.

What's going on?

Are we not friends anymore?

What did I do wrong?

"Come on, let's get you something to drink." Trent leads me to the bar and we watch as the server makes me a cocktail. We sit at the bar with our drinks, avoiding the crowded dance floor, but past my shoulders, I keep looking at Tahoe with an awful feeling in my chest. He didn't tease me. He didn't even say *hi*.

Through the corner of my eye, I watch Tahoe move to join Saint, Callan, and Emmett in their booth. A bottle of beer in his hand, his features scrunched into a thoughtful frown as he stares at the liquid. He alternates between taking a swig of his beer, and staring into the bottle as if it holds the answer to the most pressing mystery.

Tahoe is always the guy who's laughing. But tonight I notice the absence of his laughter.

Our eyes meet again, and his eyes are dark and stormy and I feel the storms raging inside me too. I remember the Pier.

Until this moment I hadn't realized how much I missed that with him. How I kind of wish I was over there, just so I could tease him or talk to him. How I kind of want to be sure that we're still as close as I thought we were yesterday. But there's this huge feeling of restlessness in me, as if things are changing and I don't know how to change them back.

Wasn't this trip supposed to be about me getting closer to Trent? a little voice inside my head asks.

But now all I can think of is why Tahoe isn't smiling and why he's not even trying to tease me. He's so....hard to read. Tahoe can be smiling, but his eyes can be SO dark you could get lost in that gaze. I find myself always thinking of him and the shadows that I see, as well as the smiles he flashes that make the shadows vanish completely.

I've often sensed that his public persona is meant to keep anyone from looking too closely. I'm the only one who really looks. No, not true, many people look. He's this beast of a modern Viking, of course everyone looks. But am I the only one who really sees that behind the smile there is something more?

And yet tonight he's not even bothering with the smile, he's not even trying to have fun. It's as if he's not interested.

Did I do something wrong?

As if reading my mind, I watch Tahoe studiously take in Trent before he takes me in next, his Nordic-blue eyes looking up and down my red dress again, and beads of sweat form on my neck under his gaze and I run a hand through my hair, self-conscious.

The same girl taps his shoulder once more and they begin to chat, and I see his mouth flip into a smile.

Again I wish I was over there standing with him, listening to whatever it is he's saying to her that finally made his dimple show. I can still see his profile and a smile linger on his lips, but I wonder if his eyes are a part of that smile or if they remained dark and mysteriously thoughtful, like they just were with me.

I shake the thought away, finish my drink, and ask Trent to dance with me.

I dance all my confusions and frustrations of the night away, never once looking at anyone else, worrying about anyone else, just letting myself get lost in me.

I'm relieved when we take a break and decide to sit down at the bar, and as if the alcohol has broken whatever barrier stood between us, Tahoe comes to sit beside me while Trent chats up Tahoe's redhead. The moment Tahoe sits, we're inundated with waiters, all offering us drinks and anything that we want.

I can tell that Callan's date is delighted with Tahoe. She tells him he has the smile of a lady-killer and that she likes his dimple.

Tahoe laughs and tells her that his mother dropped him on a rock when he was very young.

I kick his ankles, telling him he's shameless.

He kicks mine back and says that I love it.

Sandy goes back to Callan, but not before shooting Tahoe an air kiss.

"You totally charmed her," I say, playfully chiding.

He winks mischievously, which fills me with happiness and relief that everything is fine and perhaps the tension between us was all in my head, then he reclaims his drink from my hands and smiles as he leans back.

When his date comes to his side, I find I can't stand to watch her cuddle up to him. I mingle all night until my feet start killing me and the alcohol starts messing with my motor skills.

I guess I know that I should stop drinking, but I'm finally starting to relax and I'm too determined to have fun tonight to stop myself.

I wake up disoriented a couple of hours later and realize that I'm lying on a couch in a room with open windows that allow the moonlight inside. The clock on my cell says 4:14 a.m. I have no idea when I fell asleep, but I quickly realize that someone brought me into the main building of the Carmichael house.

There's a platinum watch on the coffee table. An eerily familiar cell phone.

I move, and some sort of coverlet rustles over me. Panic seizes me because I don't know how I got here. I leap off the couch, search for my shoes—which I find nearby—and slip them on. It's quiet outside so I assume everyone is gone, but as I peer out the windows to the terrace, I realize it's not in fact completely silent. I hear a female voice, and the low rumble of a man's voice outside.

It's Tahoe's voice, Tahoe and some…girl. His date.

I should've known he couldn't stay away from floozies too long. A woman sits by his side on a long ivory couch. The last thing I want is to see them make out so I guess alerting them to my presence is best.

"Hey," I say awkwardly.

Tahoe's head turns at the sound of my voice.

"Hey," he says, concerned. He unwinds his arms from the back of the couch and slowly rises to full height. "You were pretty wasted back there. You feeling alright?"

I don't know…

Because his black shirt is partly unbuttoned, revealing a good patch of smooth, tanned muscle. His lips are a little swollen, and for some reason my eyes leap to the woman's face simply to verify that it's probably a hint of her lipstick that he's wearing.

I swallow thickly, wondering if sadness is a side effect of alcohol.

I run my hand over my hair, trying to tame it. I haven't checked my makeup but since the woman facing me is so perfect, I wish I had.

The woman follows him to his feet, asking curiously, "Are we having a second, Tah?"

"She's a friend. Her boyfriend asked me to bring her home when she passed out in the booth and he wanted to stay for another round."

I search my memory to confirm his explanation, but it's blank. But that same little feeling of rejection that I sometimes get from my parents, as if I'm not good enough to waste time on, drops like a dull little stone in my gut.

"I'm ready to go to my villa," I whisper.

Tahoe briskly reaches out to the coffee table for his cell phone and watch. "I'll take you."

"I'll go too," the girl chirps.

The redhead walks with us down the sand, and although I try to hang back, Tahoe won't let me. He wraps a gentle arm around my waist to keep me steady. I keep looking at his face as he stares down at me too. His blue eyes are clear, so I guess he's not drunk, but he looks intensely thoughtful. His face is bronzed by the sun, and I can't stop staring at how the scruff of his beard gives him an even manlier look.

The redhead puts her hand on his other shoulder. "So how did you two meet?" she asks, trying to get his attention.

"Long time ago," Tahoe says.

"We met through the Saints," I say.

I unwind myself from his comforting arms and point to my villa. "This is me."

"I'll walk you." He holds my waist again and leads me up to the terrace doors. I check to see that they're unlocked, and they are. I slide one open only an inch, then whirl around and hear myself slurredly beg him, "Stay. Stay and talk to me."

He looks at me in the moonlight, studying my face as if I just punched him.

I laugh, then shake my head. "I'm sorry, I'm…drunk. I think."

He leans me against the window firmly, raising his brows in warning. "Let me let her in the room. I'll meet you out here, all right?"

I nod happily.

I watch him walk the redhead back down the beach, noticing the woman is annoyed.

It feels like forever until he comes back. Our eyes hold in silence. He hands me a bottle of water he seems to have fetched from his villa, and I appreciate him not saying anything about my drunkenness. I appreciate him knowing I'm not too proud of my current situation. I sit in a chaise, and he sits down next to me, and I take a sip, then stare at my feet and all the specks of sands that got into my sandals.

I'm so selfish, I realize. I'm so selfish to ask him to stay when he clearly had something better to do. Someone else to do. "I just sometimes want to be with you. I'm sorry," I blurt out.

"Hey," he laughs. "Don't apologize. I like it best when I'm with you. Come here. Have some more water. It will help with tomorrow's headache." He unscrews the water bottle for me to drink, but I decline.

"No. No. I just…I thought you were mad at me."

"I'm not mad."

"Distant. I don't like it. I couldn't…" I wave my hands and shake my head. "I couldn't breathe right when I felt you were being distant."

"You couldn't breathe right?" he asks roughly. "Woman, I thought I was hit by a bulldozer."

"Why?"

"Why? Regina." He laughs again gruffly, then glares out at the sea before he turns back to me. "I know every delineation of your curves by memory. I know your every smile, every tiny shade in your eyes. I know when you're happy and when you're sad and when you're feeling sexy. I see you with that guy and you're none of that, you're none of that with him and it frustrates the shit out of me."

"I'm trying, Tahoe!"

"You shouldn't have to try. It's either there or it isn't." He takes my hand and laces his fingers through mine, fire streaks through my whole body. "It's there or it isn't." He eases his hand away, and I'm drunk enough that I'm not thinking right. But I still say, "Don't sleep with her tonight. Are you going to sleep with her tonight, Tahoe?"

"Yes, Regina, I'm going to sleep with her tonight."

I want to scream, *Why? What does she have that I don't? What do they all have that I don't?*

Instead I stand up and shove him. Hard. He doesn't budge.

He slowly comes to his feet and watches me with a puzzled frown, and when I'm tired of lifting my arms and pushing the unmovable mass that is Tahoe, I sigh. Too weak, I let him carry me inside and tuck me into bed.

HUNG OVER

I wake up certain that I dreamed the night before, uncertain of what really happened and what didn't. Whether Tahoe kissed my cheek or my chin or my nose before he finally went to his villa. And whether it was, in fact, sex noises I heard coming through the thin walls. Or if my mind is confusing the noises for the sounds of Trent stumbling back from the club about the same time the sun rose.

The hangover beats heavy in my brain as I shove all my things into my suitcase and hurry to make it to the airport. Trent needed to work, so last night was our last night hanging out with everybody. Our flight leaves early today. Everyone is still snoozing by the time Trent and I call a cab to take us to the airport.

We fly back to Chicago with the kind of silence that comes after a very intense weekend, and although he declares this weekend was his best trip ever, I can't summon the enthusiasm to say the same.

"Did you change something?" Trent asks me after hours of silence and the plane begins to descend.

"Hmm?" I ask as I stare out the window, eager for a glimpse of Chicago below.

"Did you do something to your face?"

I lift my head and blink, then touch my fingers to my face. "I'm hung over. I didn't have time to…I'm just wearing less makeup." I stare at him thoughtfully. "You don't like it?"

He shrugs. "You look different."

"Different good or different bad?" I'm frowning now.

"Just different."

I turn back to the window, fishing my sunglasses out of my bag and slipping them on to keep the glare of the sun out of my eyes.

Although being hung over isn't the best time to make decisions, I know that the man I want to be with wouldn't have asked another guy to take me back home—drunk—because he wanted to stay and have some more fun on his own. I know that the guy I want will like my hair flat and/or curly and my face with any color I choose to put on it. I know that Trent genuinely likes me but I also know that the guy I want is not flying back in this airplane with me.

Tahoe and I would never work, but that doesn't mean that Trent deserves a lukewarm relationship like this either.

I also…want *more*.

So when we get to my apartment, I tell Trent the truth.

That I am utterly and completely confused.

That I want us to work, but that I need some time to think.

We have a big but short Talk—and we decide to take a break for a month or two, to see if we're really what each other wants.

"Take all the time you need, Gina," he says confidently, squeezing my hand as he stands at my apartment door. "But I will *still* call. I'm wooing you so there are no more doubts in your mind."

MAY

Aside from packing boxes nonstop when I return from spring break, I continue working overtime. I'll be moving into another apartment for a year, but I've still got my eye on buying one for myself. So I spend all my time either working or looking for apartments and also trying to forget all the memories of Tahoe that keep coming back to me from spring break.

Trent has continued calling, and sometimes I agree to see him—on friendly terms and with definitely no hand holding, no kissing, and no sex.

I think he understands that I need to think things through and he's mostly giving me space, which I appreciate.

One Thursday during our usual cocktail night, I tell Rachel and Wynn in confidence that Trent and I are taking a break and are thinking things through.

"Good for you, Gina," Rachel says.

I'm actually surprised by how *un*surprised they both are.

"We don't want to see you get hurt again and you need to be sure you're with THE guy," Wynn insists.

"Thanks." I sip my drink, suddenly wondering if, like them, there is even "THE" guy for me out there. "Just please don't say anything yet, we may actually end up working things out."

Wynn, Emmett and I are clubbing one night and I'm trying to get my mind off work when I spot Tahoe in the club and a prick shoots right through the center of my chest. I haven't seen him for a while. He hasn't texted me to invite me to another practice game, and although I know lacrosse is already in season right now, I've wondered if there's another reason he hasn't invited me. Maybe he simply doesn't want me to go and watch him anymore. Not after spring break.

Whatever the reason, I'm breathless when I see him winding through the crowd toward me as my group and I try to locate our reserved table.

"Hey, Regina."

Tahoe's lips curl tenderly as he looks at me.

"Hey, T-Rex."

"I could've used some of my lucky charm the other day at practice." His voice lowers as he steps over, a hand in his pocket, the other one covered by a black jacket draped around his forearm. He's ludicrously sexy. His smile as deadly as the tip of a knife poking into my breast.

"Send me an invite and I'll do my best."

He pulls his hand out of his pocket and squeezes my elbow and looks at me with a rueful smile I don't quite understand.

It seems only a few seconds after we stare at each other that he notices Emmett and Wynn, and I notice Callan and the blonde who might be either Callan or Tahoe's date. It feels like I'm coming back to Earth and I can almost hear the regret in Tahoe's voice when he greets my friends.

Callan calls for Tahoe.

The things I'm feeling from seeing Tahoe again are too overwhelming to suppress.

"Would you like to sit with us, Regina?"

My startled brown eyes fly up to find a pair of Nordic blues staring back. I feel like there's no air inside the room when he's in it, an unbelievable mix of sophistication and primalness.

I suck in a calming breath, but he's still big and manly and beautiful and smelling delicious and with that mouth.

As his eyes keep staring into mine, there's a crack in the shields, and I see an incredible force and power simmering underneath. I suppress a shiver. Breathless, I give him a slight shake of my head. He smiles a sad, rueful smile, and says, "Come over if you change your mind. 'Bye, Regina," and just like that, he walks away.

A dozen women catch up with him.

It isn't until I have breakfast with the girls the next day that Rachel mentions the cast.

"What cast?"

"He was wearing a cast at the club this weekend, didn't you see?" Wynn says.

"He broke his wrist in practice," Rachel says as she bites into her croissant.

"What?"

His comment about needing his lucky charm at practice finally makes sense. I'm a little bit angry with myself because, had I not been too excited and unexpectedly affected by seeing him again, maybe I'd have had enough working brain cells to notice?

I excuse myself from the table, step outside the restaurant to the sidewalk, and call him. Whatever went on that weekend in Florida, I'm sure he understands that I was drunk and not thinking clearly. He still called me his lucky charm even though I doubt that I am one for anyone.

"Is that why you haven't invited me to one of your games?" I ask when he answers, shocked.

"So you've missed me," he says. He sounds deeply satisfied.

"*No.* Yes. I mean… Are you injured?"

"Yeah, I fucked up in practice," he rumbles ruefully. I can hear the frustration in his voice. "Haven't played."

"God, Tahoe. I want to know these things, we're friends. You were at the hospital for me, I want to be there for you."

"I'm fine, Regina." He laces his voice with a bit of un-characteristic tenderness, and then he sounds amused. "I could've definitely used spooning though."

I laugh. Then I check the time. In mere seconds, I calculate how much time I would spend baking a pecan pie and come to a decision. "I'm coming over tonight," I say, and hang up.

I hardly notice the silence at the table when I return to the girls, or how they're sharing questioning looks between themselves until I glance up from my plate.

"What?" I ask.

Wynn says, "I didn't say anything."

Rachel just looks at me with that concerned look of wanting to tell something to your best friend but don't know how to do it without riling her up. So I decide there's no point in discussing anything, and I bring the topic back to Rachel's upcoming ultrasound and whether or not she and Saint will finally learn the sex of their baby.

I ride the elevator up to Tahoe's floor a little after 8 p.m. I'm dressed casually in jeans and a sweater I bought with my special employee discount. It's emerald green and warm enough that I didn't need a jacket.

I'm more nervous than I expected to be, my heart pounding as I step off the elevator. I've been here before, first with Rachel and Saint, then when I dropped by unexpectedly, but I'm not used to his apartment. The place is so immense and *bold*, I don't think I'll ever get used to it. Wood floors, leather furniture, stone-covered walls with Expressionist and Impressionist paintings scattered all over. Every painting on his wall is old. The frames are old, gold and carved. They contrast greatly with the modern furniture, creating a very complex, manly, elegant look.

The most impressive piece is the Van Gogh above the fireplace mantel. Van Gogh, a man so lonely and tortured and passionate, he chopped off his ear for love. He worked his whole life without selling a painting, save for one. I don't have much appreciation for art, but I've gone to exhibitions with Rachel and the only painter I've truly gotten, and will never forget the story of, is Van Gogh.

And sitting with a pile of papers strewn all around him is Tahoe. I knew that he expected me, but it's always still a surprise to see him alone, no floozie clinging to his shoulders, no woman draped over him.

He looks so good like that, all male, solitary. It somehow fits him. He was reading something in one hand and his injured arm is spread along the back of the couch, casually lazy, the lights above shining on his blond mane.

I feel like I haven't seen him in years.

Except for last night at the club, I haven't seen him since I got drunk and punched him.

Ohmygod, I'm such a lousy drunk!

"I brought you something."

I extend the pie as some sort of olive branch.

His eyes shine as he takes me in with a sweep of his gaze and smiles at me. "Wow. Food." He slowly comes to his feet, then reaches out with his good hand and rumples my hair.

I feel…warm.

But my eyes wander down his chest and the length of his arm, to the thick white cast around his wrist. I don't like seeing him with a cast. I can't imagine what it means to him to miss his games and practice sessions.

"Just don't eat the aluminum, okay?" I stick my tongue out at him and set the pie on the coffee table next to his pile of papers.

He lounges back down with that lazy grace of his and watches me with a peculiar frown, one that almost seems to wonder why I'm still standing. "Aren't you going to stay and feed it to me?" he teases.

"What?"

He holds his arm upward and glances at his cast. "It's difficult to eat with a retired right hand," he says.

"I'm not feeding you pie." I scowl, but lower myself down next to him anyway. I nudge him for being shameless enough to ask. "You're spoiled. Who spoiled you? Your first? Lisa?"

"Not really."

"You loved her?"

"I worshipped her." He glances at me with his most somber expression, the one that makes his face look extra chiseled. "Do you love Trent?" he asks.

He looks so intently at me you'd think that discovering my answer is his reason for living.

"I don't know, I mean it takes a while to love someone like that. I really like him. I want to love him." I'm tempted to tell him that Trent and I are on a break, but I don't want him to ask any questions, so I don't.

"Does he love you?"

"How am I supposed to know?"

"You know because he tells you that he does."

"He hasn't told me." I turn my face away and glance at the Van Gogh over the limestone mantel. "What are the words worth, anyway? Paul told me a million times, until he added *don't* before the *L* word."

His voice flattens with displeasure. "But we're not going to talk or even think about that motherfucker anymore. He's... fish food."

I laugh. "Oh, Tahoe." I sigh and drop my head back and stare at his ceiling as he does the same. "Were you unfaithful to her?"

There's a frown in his voice, and a bit of a scoff too. "Yeah, Regina, 'cause that's what you do to a woman you worship."

Neither of us lift our heads as we continue staring at the ceiling—a beautiful ceiling with thick wood beams. "Tahoe, come on. You can't keep it in your pants, you have too much testosterone."

"I keep it in my pants with you."

The comment makes me too aware of what he has in his pants. And I sense him turn his head to look at my profile.

I swallow. "Because I have a boyfriend, and we're friends, and there's Rachel and Saint."

I turn my gaze to his, and he eyes me. He's so close that I can see the light blue flecks inside the darker color of his eyes. "I don't think you love Davis," he says.

"Why?"

"You wouldn't have kissed me like you did on New Year's."

"We were both drunk."

He laughs. "I wasn't that drunk."

I sit up and scowl. "You weren't?"

He sits up too, and shakes his head.

The sudden mix of honesty and raw hunger in his eyes hits me somewhere in my chest, and I feel suddenly vulnerable.

"I'm going to get some water. Do you want some?"

I don't wait for a reply. I don't know where exactly the kitchen is, but I don't really care. I need to get away.

I walk around, trying to locate it. I navigate my way through the apartment until I find the kitchen. I find a water glass after looking through all twenty cabinets.

I'm unsettled.

Just knowing I'm here, the place where he sleeps, works, showers. Just knowing he is close to me right now... here, in this decadent guy cave, does some serious things to me.

I shudder and return to my water.

I grab the glass and head to the faucet to fill it, then start taking a long gulp when I see a dark figure to my left.

I was so lost in thought and I'm so startled, I hear glass shatter, a dark rumbling voice telling me not to move, and the beat of my heart.

"God, T-Rex—!" I start.

"My fault," he interjects, eyeing me cautiously. "I shouldn't have snuck up on you."

I want to say that it was my fault until I realize I did nothing wrong, so instead I laugh and say, "Yeah. It was."

He looks at me and smiles. "Go get a fresh shirt from my closet, I'll clean this up."

I hesitate only a second before deciding I don't want to stay soaked and therefore I head out of the kitchen, down the hall in search of his bedroom.

I pause at the threshold and peer inside, taking in the massive bed and modern decor. It's dark outside, only the lights of the city illuminating the room, and the moon casting a gray-blue light on Tahoe's bed.

Unwillingly I picture him lying there—lying there beautiful and naked—and I instantly chide my brain for coming up with the image in the first place, especially when I have never imagined Trent like that.

I search the drawers and then settle for a long-sleeved White Sox T-shirt, and when I slip it on, something on one of the twin nightstands catches my eye.

It's my photograph, right next to his watch and his wallet. The one where I'm looking at the camera, looking vulnerable and caught by surprise.

I try to ignore the hot little clench in my stomach as I force myself to head back to the kitchen.

Tahoe stands by the kitchen window, staring at the Chicago skyline with a clenched jaw, as if he's trying to control some inner frustration.

Every sharp angle and smooth curve of his face is beautifully outlined in the dark. His blue eyes practically glow when he turns and sees me in his White Sox T-shirt. Something raw and hot flashes in his gaze for the briefest second before he quells it. I can't breathe.

I gulp and try to distract myself and him. "I was getting us some water."

"I know," he says, not interested in my thirst.

He looks into my eyes for a long moment before trailing his down my body. I stand there and let him.

I let him look at me.

In *his* shirt.

Though he doesn't say anything about the shirt I chose to wear, he's looking at me as if he thinks I look gorgeous in it. I don't think a man has ever looked at me this possessively before. He clenches his jaw. His dark voice breaks through the air. "I'll get you some water."

He reaches for a plastic cup and pours water in it.

I defiantly stare at the little plastic sippy cup, quirking my brow at him.

He smirks. "I have a little cousin." He looks into my eyes again. "Besides, I think we've already established we can't trust you with sharp or delicate objects."

I laugh and roll my eyes. "Shut up." And I open my hand. "Give me my sippy cup."

He laughs and hands me the cup, taking me by the arm and leading me to the study. He plops down on the white couch and pats the seat next to him. He turns up the fireplace, and as I sit down beside him, I notice he's cleaned up all of his papers.

I'm clutching onto my sippy cup for dear life, afraid to move.

After a few long, dragging, crackling minutes, I hear a low rasp. "Hey, come here for a bit." And he reaches out his arm and draws me into his chest. "I like that you came over," he whispers, brushing my hair behind my cheek.

I swallow. "Well. Someone has to watch out for you, I guess."

"I guess," he agrees, looking into my eyes.

We stay there silent for a while but I don't make a move to leave his arms.

Knowing I shouldn't get comfortable, I eventually force myself to sit up straight and put a little distance between us.

He drags his hand lazily down my spine then drops it. "What's up?"

I shrug then glance at a thick vintage car book on the coffee table. "Are you as passionate about cars as you are about lacrosse?"

"My grandfather restored vintage pieces. The one on the cover is mine." He smirks and spreads his arm on the back of the couch again. "They used to build things to last in those days," he says.

"Really? Hmm. It's lovely."

"I'll drive you around in it someday."

He rests his head on the back of the couch and stares at the ceiling again.

The exhaustion of the past few weeks from hard work and apartment hunting start weighing on me, so I place my cheek on the back of the couch, facing him. He tells me about his grandfather and his collection of cars, and the museum in Texas in his memory, and I focus on the sound of his delicious voice, lulling me to a near sleep.

The exotic smell of his soap and skin makes me feel like I am on vacation and nothing else exists but this. Him. Him him him, god, *HIM.*

"I'm comfortable around you," I whisper, as quietly as a confession.

He turns his head to me, his eyes half-mast. "Does your boyfriend make you feel as comfortable as I do?"

Some fiery warmth in his eyes makes me want to admit, *I started dating him because you've always implied that I can't be with you.*

His pupils enlarge, as if he can read the answer in my eyes.

"He doesn't," I admit. "But…does that matter? So what if I'm more comfortable with you? Maybe you're just good with the ladies." I smirk, trying to lighten the thick-as-tar air between us. "Ladies are your specialty."

He scowls. "Hell, I never said that."

"Then what are we doing here discussing... What are we even discussing?"

He sits up and looks at me, shifting his body as he does, his expression deadly somber as he rests his elbows on his knees and grabs his cast with his good hand as if it suddenly hurts. "Just because I'm not with you, doesn't mean I don't think about it." He raises his brows, challenging me as he slowly adds a bad boy smile and lets me register what he said.

I blink, flabbergasted.

"Are you teasing me?" I narrow my eyes, straightening too.

"Why would I tease you, Regina?" He tugs on a strand of my hair, smiling with a sparkle in his eyes.

"Tahoe Roth, the infamous player, would be monogamous all of a sudden? What? Do you want a girlfriend now?" I ask, pushing at his chest, laughing at the thought.

He laughs too. "I'm too old for a girlfriend," he says, catching my wrist before I can retrieve it and squeezing it gently in his warm palm.

"So what do you want? Do you want me to be a permanent groupie? And what, you promise not to break my heart, you shameless heartbreaker?"

He smirks as he holds my wrist in his hands, squeezing it gently—and in that moment I feel like he's squeezing my heart.

He smirks again, but his voice is low and husky, as is the look in his eyes. "You'd need to give it to me for me to break it."

"In your wildest dreams, Roth." I sound breathless. I am breathless. I pry my wrist free of his hold. "Look, I like being with you, so what? And maybe you drop my defenses, so what? I got drunk and said some things at the beach house. That's what this is coming from, right? It's no big deal."

He leans back and spreads out his arms, and his dimple is still showing even when his eyes swirl like storms. "It's a big deal to me."

"It's *not* a big deal." I straighten in my seat and tug down his shirt primly. Nervously.

"Alright then, it's no big deal." He smirks, cants his head and links his hands behind his head, looking at me as he waits for a reaction.

I exhale. "You told me yourself you had nothing to offer me. It's taken me a while to see you were right, Tahoe."

Ever so slowly, he lowers his arms back to rest his elbows on his knees and leans forward. He clenches his jaw in frustration, his eyes losing their shine. God, they're almost black, they're so dark and stormy.

He looks at me, all of his energy muted, as if he's coiling it all within himself for control. "You're not yourself when you're with him, Regina. The girl right here with me now," he runs his eyes over me with a slow, meaningful nod, "the girl with me, is the Regina I know. The girl I see with Davis is a shadow of her. You can do so much better than that motherfucker and you know it."

All the confusions about my relationship with Trent rise to the forefront, and I hate him for bringing them here.

"He's good, Tahoe," I say lamely.

"Is he good, Regina?" He raises his brows, and if I didn't know better, I'd swear that beneath the playful, devilish glint in his eyes, there's a jealous fire brewing there too. "Do you give your boyfriend your panties too?"

"No." I bristle at the reminder and poke his chest angrily. "By the way, I want those back."

"That would be a no as well." He catches my finger, caresses it between his thumb and forefinger before I pry it free.

I fold my finger back into my palm; it burns a little. "Why not?"

"'Cause I like the way they look," he says with a shameless glint in his eye, "I like the way they smell, and I like the way they feel between my fingers."

The color rises up my cheeks and neck and body.

Heat floods between my legs.

My heart feels like a volcano, pumping nothing but lava into my veins.

"I don't think you love him," he continues. "You're not happy with him. It's like you're forcing yourself to be whatever you think he wants you to be. If he's with you, he should want *you*, just you, period." He glares in confusion and frustration and anger on my behalf. "Baby," he exclaims, shaking his head in bewilderment, "why would any woman want to be anything else when they are *you*, huh?" He grabs my face and looks into my eyes, frustrated. "Huh, Gina?" he demands, searching my face.

His eyes bore into me.

His jaw is clenched so tight I think he'll break his molars.

"What if that motherfucker is the best I can do?" I challenge back, just a breath.

He laughs softly and caresses his thumbs over my cheekbones before releasing me.

He falls back on the seat, shaking his head.

"That's not true, you can do so much better," he softly assures. He reaches out and touches my hair, gently tweaks my nose, and leans over. He sniffs me as he says, "You're gorgeous, girl. You're authentic. You smell like heaven." He eases back, his smile so honest and adorable. "Your presence is like a sparkling firework that never goes out. You bake pie. And your smile is an absolute addiction."

Scoffing, I nudge him to try to hide my blush. "You're a jackass! Come *on*."

He chuckles, still smiling as he swears, "Regina, this is no joking matter." He nudges me back. "I love that smile of yours. Show me that smile of yours." He ducks closer and peers into my face.

I raise my chin and fake a flat, hard smile.

He frowns instantly. "Yeah, um, a little less purse of the lips." His thumbs gently force my lips to curl upward. "There," he murmurs, raising his playful eyes to mine.

I feel his thumb remain on the corner of my lips for a second.

I see his smile fade just a fraction as our stares hold.

And all I can think of right now is that I want his lips. I want his hands all over me. Under his shirt that I'm wearing. Between my legs and inside of me.

We stare at each other, and he looks at my mouth like it is all that exists for him right now.

My heart starts pounding.

I'm scared.

His stare is frightening—it's so blue, so clear, so expectant. So fucking hungry, this guy would eat me up alive and leave no bones to bury.

Slowly…his thumb brushes my lips, removing a little of my lipstick.

My heart almost leaps out of my chest and toward him when I realize he wants my mouth. He wants my mouth bare—with nothing but me.

But I'm so scared I'm trembling. I think of Trent. Of us, on this break.

Finally there's a good guy who likes me, who might love me. And here is this guy who can have everything he wants and who can take it all away. Who is already such a threat between me and Trent, between me and *any* other guy.

I cannot get on the Tahoe rollercoaster. Maybe before, when it would be a one-night stand, it was an option.

Now I *like* him.

Now I care more about him than I care about makeup, jobs, apartments, friends, *chocolate.*

He's funny and I think of him often and he's generous and protective and cocky. And he makes me feel alive. And more than anything—a revelation, really, because a year ago I never thought it possible that we could grow to be this close—I'm too scared to lose his friendship too.

I push myself to my feet, my voice thick with unwanted lust. "I have to go."

He catches my wrist. "Hey. *Stay.*"

His blue eyes bore into me, something fiery crackling in their depths that some hidden part of me fiercely responds to with a hot, tight little ache.

Something about the look in his eyes transports me to the Saints' wedding.

That same rawness is there, that same quiet demand, that same hunger.

When he asked me if I wanted him and I said no.

This moment if he asked me again, I don't know if my answer would be the same. But then what? Then I'd lose his friendship, and still have the pleasure of watching him womanize his way across the continent?

Thank you, but I deserve better than that. Even Trent is better than that.

"I really have to go." I pull my wrist free of his grasp and head to the elevators.

I'm already repeatedly pressing the elevator button when he calls my name.

I turn. He's standing with his legs spread and a look of determination and undiluted frustration on his face. "Do you think about us at all, Regina?"

"Yes."

His eyes sparkle menacingly.

"But that doesn't mean I'll ever do anything about it. You want other things, and I want what you can't give. So...eat your pie and...get well soon," I hurry to say as I board the elevator and then turn.

We keep staring all the way until the doors close. And even when the doors close, I hear him slam something hard and growl, "Jesus goddammit fuck!!"

And my throat swells with emotion when I am pretty sure that he threw my pie at the wall.

HOME

The next few weeks feel as if I have shoved the entire contents of my life inside a blender and pressed spin. I've moved several times in my life, but this time it feels a bit more nerve-wracking because I'm moving to the first apartment meant just for me.

In winter, the birds sense a change, and they migrate in groups, all looking to improve their situation. After Rachel got married and Wynn moved in with Emmett, it seemed *I* was the only bird not migrating with the others. But that changed this summer when I met with Tahoe's friend, William Blackstone, who showed me a beautiful apartment, the perfect size for me and in the perfect Loop location that I adore. It's a one-bedroom, with a bedroom twice the size of my current one, views to die for, and a closet that I could probably never fill up.

It's time to fly the coop.

Now, my last days here, I glance around my old apartment and to the pile of boxes I've begun to tape closed. The apartment Rachel and I shared for years. I know the creak of my bedroom door no matter how much I oil it. I know the noisy hours, and know that I'll wake up when our neighbors turn on the shower on the other side of my bedroom wall. My *other* wall was where I could always hear my best friend and her now-husband heatedly fucking on the other side. I know this apartment, every detail of it, and what it's been through (like leaks and cracks in the mirrors) for the past few years. But now my lease is up and I have to leave.

So it's Friday night, and it's just me and these boxes.

I take a sip of wine and wonder why it looks so spacious without my clutter, and why it also looks so worn without the little details that enhanced it—sort of like makeup?

I have a thousand good memories here. Some bad too, like the death of our neighbor. But despite my sadness, there's a feeling of certainty that there is nothing more for me here. I'm making a change. A positive change. Turning a new page. Changing my scenery.

This one-year lease will give me time to save up more money to buy my own place. I want to lay down roots and I want to make a home without waiting for someone else to want to be in it *with* me.

I want to be happy. I want to feel complete.

After all those weeks packing boxes, I finally move into my new building on a hot July day.

It's said that home is where the heart is, and the big window facing the west and the spacious closet just for me have already made my heart soar.

I walk into my new apartment, blinded by the sunlight streaming through the windows, hardly believing this incredible place is mine. I stalk to the window and stare at the view I will stare out at on many future mornings. Beautiful neighboring buildings, clean streets, flying flags at the foot of a school and a park. The nearby Loop. I head to the closet and admire the numerous racks, empty and waiting for my shoes, accessories, and clothes. A sense of incredible amazement permeates every pore in my body as I look around, seriously happy and lightheaded.

Ohmigod! I'm home.

Home for now.

Rachel sent Saint's two corporate drivers to help load, transport, and unload the boxes. By 5 p.m., my friends have helped me open most of them, and I've even made my bed.

I get a call from Trent. Although we're still on a break, he keeps making attempts to see me or stay in touch. I tell him I'm moving in today and that I can't meet him until later. I expected him to offer to help, but instead he says he'll call me when I'm done. *I miss you,* he says.

I set my phone down and for some reason, end up checking the last text I got from Tahoe. Eons ago, it seems.

I haven't seen him since I went to his apartment. But I asked Rachel how he was, and she told me his cast was removed, and that he's been spending most of his lacrosse games in the penalty box.

When I remember that, and the way we parted, I accidentally knock over a soda can.

"Fuck." I clean the soda up from the floor and throw the can away, then peer down at the dark, sticky stain on my shirt.

"Oh, look at that," Wynn says as she peers out the window.

I'm really not interested in whatever she's looking at. I'm too busy heading to the bathroom to clean up the mess I made. I try running water over the spot and then patting it dry with a towel. It's not perfect, but it's moving day so it will have to do.

I step back out into the living room when I spot a tall guy with a red baseball cap in my apartment. He's carrying a huge box and a dozen bags from Whole Foods, all of which he sets down on the counter.

"You are a dream," Wynn gushes as she signals to the Whole Foods bags. "We're starving."

I approach with a frown. "I didn't order—" My words cut off when the tall guy with the cap turns to look at me.

They trail off when intense blue eyes meet mine under the rim of the cap.

Oh god, I was so distracted by the mess of boxes scattered around me that I hadn't recognized him.

Now I can't breathe.

I swear to god the floor crumples under my feet and I'm falling from one end of the Earth to the other. Because I just did not expect to see Tahoe here. He's dressed in his work suit, except for that cap that covers that mane of delicious blond hair. It's almost as if the wind is extra crazy today and that's how he chose to tame his hair, rather than brush it.

His beard is a little longer, a little too sexy, and the beast has such a beautiful face that my eyes nearly ache from how much I missed seeing it.

His eyes sparkle at my expression of surprise, and he places a wrapped sandwich from the Whole Foods bag on a plate and hands it over. He smiles a little sardonically, still looking into my eyes as I take it and just hold it like a nitwit, all while I hold his gaze, hold my breath, hold onto this moment.

"Aren't you going to eat it?" His voice is low and intimate, almost as if Wynn and Rachel and all the movers aren't bustling around here.

Exhaling as I try to calm my heartbeat, I unwrap the sandwich, open my mouth, and take a bite.

The seconds seem to stretch on forever and at the same time, they seem to be swallowed up by the present when Wynn peers past my shoulder. "What is that? Turkey club? God, I want one."

"Go right ahead." Tahoe grabs one and tosses it in the air to Wynn, who catches it readily.

Tahoe's voice is lower than usual, his drawl noticeable as he looks back at me and takes a step only to lightly touch his finger to my nose as if saying, *We're good, right?*

I look up at him. He stares at my face from so close that we could almost be one. He reaches out to rumple my hair, smiles at me the way he usually does, as if I amuse him, and grabs my sandwich and takes a bite of it for himself.

I nearly melt with relief. After many nightmares, tossing and turning, wondering if whatever friendship we had was over, my T-Rex is here, and he's back.

We all gather around the kitchen counter to eat, and I'm surreptitiously looking at Tahoe's profile as we all take a little break and chow down.

Suddenly my home does feel like *home.*

Busy, and lively, and though it's still 50 percent littered with boxes and wrapped furniture, I'm not scared about being in this place all alone anymore.

He's the last to leave.

We're sitting on the living room's natural wood floor, leaning against the wall that faces my window with the best view, my couches still covered in plastic, and our legs aligned, side by side, when I toe his foot.

"Cast gone, huh?"

Pulling back the sleeve of his white button shirt (he'd discarded his jacket a while ago), he shows me his thick, tanned wrist and turns it over. "Good as new."

We smile at the same time, but when our lashes lift, our eyes aren't smiling at all.

And suddenly I have to speak what's been on my mind all day.

"Would you have liked me to throw your food like you threw my pie?" I stare out the window as I say this. I'm not sure I have the courage to look at him right now.

I glance sideways at him when he remains silent. "Why?" I ask.

A rueful grin appears on his lips, almost apologetic, but something dark lurks in his gaze. "Why do you think? Huh?" He studies me as if dissecting each and every one of my features. "Because I wasn't hungry for pie."

The rueful smile remains on his lips before he drops his head and laughs mockingly, stroking his dimple restlessly.

My stomach hurts, that queasy feeling back again in full force.

He sighs and shifts his shoulder against the wall until his torso is leaning in my direction. His dimple is nowhere in sight now. His stare as direct as a laser. And then, his voice is only a whisper that somehow fills up this whole room, this whole apartment, my whole heart.

"I want to kiss you."

He lifts his fingers to rub my lips with three fingertips.

"I want to kiss you. I look at you, with those curves of yours and that wild hair and those dark eyes and that reluctant little smile, and I want to crush you against me, fill my hands with your hair and drown in your smell. And I want to kiss you."

His eyes darken.

"I want to take off your lipstick so all you have is my mouth on you. *Fuck* Davis. *Fuck* everything but kissing you."

He exhales roughly, his nostrils flaring as he lowers his fingers.

He lowers his fingers…and my lips tingle and burn and they want to part open and my tongue wants to lick him and I want him so much, I want every bit of what he described and more.

My throat can barely get out any words.

I stare at my feet and watch my toe somehow rub against the length of his shoe. "But then what? You strip my lips of everything but your mouth on mine, and then you're gone and I have nothing. At least right now we have friendship. And it means more to me than you will ever know, Tahoe. It means so much to me. *You* mean so much to me."

He shifts his shoe until all of my toes are resting on it now. "You mean as much to me too."

"So then." I scoff at our conversation and wave a hand dismissively. "I'll give you a peck on New Year's. If you happen to be around." I smirk.

He doesn't smirk.

"I think I'll take it right now." He leans over and pecks me.

Just a peck.

On the lips.

His lips pressing on mine for just a nanosecond while my lips instinctively press back. And his lips are warm and strong and HIS. And my world tilts and everything becomes nothing, and nothing but a peck becomes everything.

Everything.

A fiery warmth oozes from the contact of our bodies. He eases back, his gaze piercing the mere few inches between us. His lips curve lightly, and though the smile touches his eyes, I can tell that his hunger was only stoked.

Just like mine…

"You available this Friday? I need a plus one."

I clear my throat and nod. I'm still so dazed and disbelieving he just did that, but I'm happy to be back on casual terms, happy to pretend his lips weren't hot and a little possessive on mine. "Done. What do I wear?"

I don't tell him that Friday is my birthday because I haven't yet made plans, and a plan with him is better than any, really.

He glances at the mess of boxes thoughtfully then digs his hand into the closest one. "This."

He grins and extracts the first thing that comes out: an apron.

"Haha." I shove it back inside.

He laughs darkly, and I laugh too, and he says, "It's a day event, wear whatever you'd like."

"Okay. Pajamas," I joke.

"I'm game." He grins devilishly.

We share a long, charged look, then I set my cheek on his shoulder and it feels so right to just sit here in my apartment with him. "Thanks for hooking me up with your friend."

"Anything for you, Regina."

His usual teasing tone is absent from his voice. He sounds somber, certain, honest. We sit there, admiring my new place, until his phone starts buzzing between us. After a while, he curses in exasperation and pulls it out, checks the screen, and I see the number 18 on his text-alert icon.

"Wow. Spurning some invitations somewhere?" I narrow my eyes in bemusement. "They really want you there."

He tucks it back into his pocket. "Yeah. Not interested."

I'm distracted Thursday night as I have dinner with Trent at Carnivale. He asked if I was available on the evening of my birthday. I'm exhausted after moving and unpacking, but he's been trying so hard that I couldn't deny him the night before.

He's trying his best to make me laugh, but I almost feel like I'm forcing it. I don't understand my mood. I remind myself about the letter at the bottom of the lake that Tahoe and I burned so long ago, knowing that Paul is fish food now. He can't hurt me now. But I can't shake off the restlessness I feel. Why I can't connect with Trent the way I do with…well, HIM.

At the end of dinner, Trent gives me a big box and tells me I can open it in my apartment. I'm hesitant to invite him over, but I also don't want to be rude when he's clearly trying so hard to make my day special. I tell him he can come up for ten minutes while I open my gift. We sit in my living room and he watches me open the box that reads MAC.

"It's all the makeup you could want for the year," he says. "So you can always look like a queen."

I love MAC.

I love makeup.

It's what I do.

But something about getting more stuff to put on my mask makes my stomach sink. It's been a battle to try to open up to Trent completely, and staring at a makeup kit, I wonder if he even cares to know what's beneath.

In the distance I spot the apron Tahoe teased I should wear tomorrow, sticking haphazardly out of the box. I feel warmth surge through me, a smile appear on my face.

It seems to give Trent the wrong impression.

"God, you look gorgeous right now. I can tell you like my gift. Get back together with me, Gina," he begs. He moves to kiss me but I quickly turn my mouth out of reach.

Even though a part of me wants to press my mouth to his because I wish that he were capable of erasing Tahoe's peck from my lips. I want to feel in his kiss just a fraction of the electric thrill I felt from Tahoe's lips, so firmly, so warmly, on mine.

But I can't do it. Nothing feels right anymore.

"Just give me time. I'm just confused. New apartment…" I signal around. "I don't know, just give me a little time."

I look at him, trying to find pieces of him to love, really trying to find something that even resembles what I feel when I'm with my playboy Viking.

When Trent finally leaves, every muscle in my body aches from hauling and unpacking boxes. I take a hot shower and after soaping up and shampooing my hair, I stand under the water with my eyes closed. I roll my shoulders under the spray, run my hands over my scalp and dig in my fingers, trying to relax the pounding in my head. Rivulets of water slide down my face. A drop of water clings to my top lip. The feel of Tahoe's lips pressed against mine returns unbidden. Soft but firm and warm and…oh god.

Right now in my quiet new apartment, in a shower that still feels a little unfamiliar, I can't believe I had the willpower to keep my mouth closed and not part my lips and taste him in a way I have dreamed of tasting him for what feels like my whole life. I picture how his lips would move against mine and instinctively I know that he would take charge, that he would be the one kissing even if I started the kiss.

The water is pounding on the top of my head and my lips are tingling and I let myself kiss him in my mind. I remember us sitting close enough for me to turn and run my hands through his hair and press into him in the way only women who really, really want sex do—nipples tight against his hard chest, hips lined up against his. I kiss him in a way I've only dreamed about, and then I'm enveloped in his arms, which feel familiar but are holding me so possessively now, and I'm transported back to Tahoe in the outdoor shower during spring break. Unapologetically gorgeous and male, so full of himself and so muscular and golden, and so very naked.

And he's just as naked right here in my shower, every inch of his naked form is pressed up against every inch of mine. My hands follow the rivulets sliding down my body, and I move them and move them, picturing Tahoe's fingers inside me. The thoughts drive me wild. Soon I'm grabbing him closer and he's got me pinned against him. I picture him moving in me, and he's kissing me everywhere I want to be kissed, and when he kisses me again—just a peck on my lips, like the one he gave me today, the real one, dry and firm and so very unexpected and so delicately powerful—a thousand shudders rock through me, one after the other.

I'm panting seconds later. I lean my temple against the shower wall. I'm standing on unsteady knees, bracing myself. I should feel better, more relaxed, sated, but though the ache between my thighs has calmed down some, the ache in my chest only feels heavier.

PLUS ONE

It's early Friday morning when Tahoe picks me up for his plus-one event, and when I step outside, he's waiting in the vintage car I saw on the book cover at his place, a silver Mercedes-Benz that looks fit for a museum. As he walks around and opens the door for me, I remember my previous night's fantasy and feel myself flush head to toe.

"Good morning," he murmurs. And there's that smile. That dimple. That devilish look in his eyes.

"Hey." I smile and try to keep my calm, but it's so hard when I feel his piercing gaze on me.

He keeps staring at me as he takes his seat behind the wheel. "Are you flushed today?"

He leans over and tips my chin up, and I push his hand away and laugh. "Of course not! Why would I be?" I ask, and hate that I feel myself flushing more as I busily strap on my seat belt.

He smiles to himself as he starts the car and pulls out into the road. We stop to have coffee first. We sit in comfortable silence while Tahoe reads the newspaper and I watch the city awaken, minute by minute as the sun rises. And by the time the

Blommer Chocolate Company opens and Tahoe is leading me toward the doors of the factory, not the store, I stop in my tracks.

"Tahoe, there's a reason I haven't used the voucher you gave me. People don't go in here for tours. I've never even heard of it, people don't do this," I say.

"They don't," he agrees with a grin, and then he keeps heading toward the factory door. "But you do."

Anticipation courses through my veins. I feel like I won the last golden ticket to Willy Wonka's factory as Tahoe leads me straight into the noisy, monstrously large building. A man who clearly has an important position in the factory, based on his clothes, greets us and walks us through the building. There are no chocolate waterfalls or Oompa Loompas. This is modern-world business on a grand scale. Huge melting tanks bigger than I am, liquid chocolate, and cocoa and sugar are all around.

The best part comes when we finally hit the store and can get our hands on the chocolates. There is dark chocolate, milk chocolate, and white chocolate; chocolate-covered cashews, pretzels, bananas, strawberries, and cherries.

"Wait for the best part." He smirks as he motions toward something behind the register, covered from view.

The man gives T-Rex a secretive smile and pulls off the cover.

I'm staring at an enormous chocolate Versailles castle. I'm beyond speechless.

He chuckles, leads me around the register, and points at it. "They even have the windows right." I can feel his gaze on my profile, taking in my reaction.

It's hard to keep myself in check.

I turn to him—happy, confused, disbelieving, humbled, *happy*. "You want me to eat my own house? You are shameless." My voice is breathless despite my words.

For a whole minute, he looks at me with this adorable smile and one lone dimple. Almost as if he's waiting for me to say more.

The stare wears me down. I drop the act, step into his arms, and hug him. I just hug him and feel him hug me back so easily, and fit me right into his frame, his arms enveloping me like a world of warmth.

I'm not a hugger, so I'm surprised by how much I'd like to hug Tahoe for a long time.

"Happy birthday, Regina," he says with a textured, drawling voice in my ear.

"Thank you, T-Rex. I didn't know you knew."

I pull away with effort and stare back at the castle, blinking away the sting in my eyes.

Ten minutes later we're outside on a bench by my apartment, enjoying the warm summer wind as we exchange an assortment of bags loaded with chocolates. I nudge him with a bag. "Try this one."

He nudges me back with his finger before he takes it and pops a chocolate-covered cashew in his mouth. "Nice."

I look away, out at the street, in a desperate attempt to resist his captivating grin.

As he walks me back home, I'm still carrying a month's supply of chocolate treats and already feeling remorse about having devoured all that chocolate.

Things feel easy again, almost as easy as before. If only my body weren't so hyperaware of his proximity.

I'm thinking about it, about him having my picture, pecking me on the lips, when his gentle nudge brings me back from my daydreams.

"Still with me?" He quirks a brow, puzzled as he looks down at me.

I nod quickly. "I was thinking that only a best guy friend would give a girl this much chocolate. Otherwise he'd have to sleep with the chocolate padding her curves."

"You're kidding." He stops walking and incredulously narrows his eyes, which gleam incredibly blue. His eyes leave mine in frustration then they come back, more piercing than ever. "Your curves are succulent. A guy could play with those for hours."

A sky full of butterflies bursts inside my stomach, and I feel myself heat up.

"Shut up," I whisper, nudging him with a scowl, unable to look into his eyes. "Everyone and everything is succulent for a T-Rex."

His eyes become hooded. "Not this one," he says.

And it's the way he says it that keeps making these butterflies flap wildly inside me.

I look at him, see the heat in his eyes, and I am so scared to get hurt again.

To get hurt a thousand times more than I ever have.

And I think that *he* knows it too. There's never been a guy in my life more protective of me than he is—to the point of protecting me from himself.

But that only makes me feel even more warmly toward him.

He follows me into my brand-new apartment. He sets my chocolate Versailles on my coffee table, and spots my MAC makeup box on the couch. I seemed to have left it there the night before.

"Trent gave me a makeup kit for my birthday," I explain.

One second he's smiling and the next he's raising his fine arched eyebrows. His eyes shutter, but then he grins briefly, with no trace of his former frustration, and he chucks my chin. "Looks like we need another evening at the Pier to color some little fishes."

What is it about this guy wanting me without makeup?

He walks toward the door.

"Now that would be a travesty," I say with a shame-on-you voice. "Almost as much of a travesty as eating my Versailles." Though I admit, signaling to it, "I might eat the little bushes."

"Eat the bushes? Alright." He laughs mischievously.

The butterflies catch fire.

I groan and shove him back toward the door.

As I do, he steals one of my many bags of chocolates. "Hey!" I call, as he starts for the door. "You're stealing my chocolates."

He turns around and starts backing away slowly, facing me. "Come get them then."

He raises the bag in the air a little bit and dangles it temptingly.

I rush at him and leap in the air, trying to grab the bag, but he wraps his arm around my waist and pulls me close—fairly crushes me to his chest—and pecks my lips again.

I start, jerking back from the shock of the touch of his lips, the renewed burst of butterflies in my stomach, which seemed to flutter up to my head.

He waits, watching me, his arm still around me.

His eyes are leveled on mine. His nose is nearly touching mine. We're breathing hard. He's not smiling; his eyes are very dark and serious. Watching me with caution and intense interest, he tilts his head, eyeing my mouth from another angle. "Is your boyfriend taking you out tonight?" he drawls out.

He waits there, as if preparing—debating, thinking—to kiss me for real. "Trent and I had dinner last night," I say breathlessly, nervously pushing at his chest. "And I...have work early tomorrow. You really need to stop doing that, Tahoe." I turn around and wipe the back of my hand over my lips shyly.

He notices, and to taunt me, he licks his lips with his tongue, his eyes shimmering in challenge.

"We'll see," he says mischievously as he walks away with the bag of chocolates, waving a peace sign.

He smirks adorably from the door, and I shoot him a dark glare, wondering if the chocolate is really what he's stealing from me.

LITTLE MAN

arly August, it's official. Rachel and Saint are having a baby boy. She's nearing her thirty-fifth week of pregnancy, and although they've wanted to know the sex for a while, the baby's position made it hard for the doctors to tell for sure. Well. The baby cannot hide his jewels any longer.

On my way to the Saints' place, all I can think about is whether or not I'll tell Rachel how confused I am about Tahoe and me. I want to tell her, but the urge to push him to the back of my mind—survival mode—is acute.

I walk into their place and follow voices to the second story of the penthouse and down the hall to the baby's room. I pause at the threshold and take in the lovely décor. There's a huge white crib and a dreamy white rocking chair, and artisan paintings on the walls of palm trees and jungle animals.

I stay still for a moment, silent for I don't know how long, because inside the room I see Rachel, Saint, and...*him*. I arrive the same instant that Tahoe hands Saint his first lacrosse stick.

It's short and wooden, and it looks old and worn.

"For when the little guy turns fifteen," Tahoe slyly tells Saint as he maneuvers the stick in a swift lacrosse move. "He's going to have to fight to keep the ball from me," he adds with a menacing twinkle in his eye, his grin at full wattage.

The sight of Tahoe giving the lacrosse stick to Saint clutches at my heart so hard I almost have to put my hand on my chest to make sure it's still beating.

"Gina!" Rachel calls.

All heads turn to the door.

Tahoe's blue eyes flare when he sees me and I can practically see him straighten. His shoulders span wider. His muscles tighten. His fingers curl into his palms at his sides. His lips curve up in a smile. He looks almost like a tiger, one just woken up from slumber, licking his lips because he's just been presented with a woman.

A woman he once called "succulent."

I force myself to breathe and I smile and instantly go hug Rachel. "If I'd known the baby would have a stick already, I'd have brought the ball," I joke to her, but instead I give her a tiny silver spoon, which was also my first.

"For luck," I say, postponing the moment when I have to turn around toward the silent men.

But I finally work myself up to it. I cross the room to congratulate Saint, and when Tahoe looks at me, it seems instinctive for both of us, it seems natural, that we somehow hug each other hello too. I flush when his arms envelop me and he says "hello" in my ear.

"Hey," I say.

I feel his lips graze the back of my ear after he speaks—accident or not?—and he steps back, watching me with those perceptive eyes of his as we ease apart. He looks like a dark prince of playboys today, dressed in gray sweatpants and a soft navy T-shirt, a duffel bag with lacrosse gear at his feet.

He's going to a game, I realize, with a kick of excitement in my stomach. And true enough, ten minutes after we've all chatted animatedly about the baby, he excuses himself to leave.

"I think I should go to your game," I cautiously say, then quickly amend when Saint and Rachel raise their eyebrows, "just so you win."

When there's only silence, I head to the door, raising an eyebrow to see if Tahoe challenges me.

He doesn't. He smirks, his eyes roiling with mischief. "By all means, if I had my way, I'd have my lucky charm with me always."

We say goodbye to the Saints, who exchange a glance that's a mix of concern, puzzlement, and amusement.

As we take the elevator downstairs, I glance at his profile. "It was very sweet of you to give little baby Saint your first lacrosse stick."

"Yeah, well. Saint's my best friend. I'm loving that little kid as if he were my own."

"You don't plan to have any?" I raise my gaze to his.

But he's watching the elevator numbers drop, and drop, and drop, and doesn't say anything more until we head to his Ghost, climb aboard, and drive over to the lacrosse field.

"I'm pumped up you came." His voice is deep and fiercely honest as he slides a mischievous look my way as his car screeches to a halt in his reserved parking spot.

"Me too."

I sense him starting to get into vicious zero-zero mode as we climb out and enter the field building. "Hey." His voice stops me a few seconds after we start down the halls, him with his duffel slung over his shoulder, heading toward the locker room, me starting in the opposite direction to the stands.

I turn to face him in the middle of the hall. He taps his dimple. I inhale for control. Then I head back and kiss his dimple. "Don't kill anybody tonight."

"Just team Black," he says, grinning as he disappears down the hall.

He *demolishes* the other team.

All I keep hearing as he works his stick, checks team Black, clicks and pops the ball, and works the game is:

"Face off!"

"Score Red!"

"Face off!"

"Score Red!"

"Face off!"

"Score Red!"

"Face off!"

"Score Red!"

We're the last ones in the locker room as he finishes changing, but rather than leave, he drops down on the bench and pulls me down with him.

"Hey. Next month…come over with me to my parents' anniversary dinner? I'm tired of the speech they give me every time I go home, same damn tune over and over."

"They want you to stop your womanizing ways, yadda yadda?"

"More like yadda yadda."

"They *don't* want you to stop your womanizing ways? Huh."

"Just come."

I flush. Not because I'm embarrassed, but because I know a man like Tahoe could definitely make me come.

The word sits in the air between us, low and soft. His eyes are dark and stormy, as they get when he's thinking about something I can only guess at, and I wonder if the word has the same effect on him that it does on me.

I really didn't need the image of him coming, but now it's in my brain. I picture his features contorting in ecstasy, harsh with effort, the way I imagine a man like him comes, and he must look so sexy, so very sexy. How he pumps, raw and ready, and I hear him laugh now and I'm all red as I wonder if he knows that my mind wandered *there*.

He tells me the exact date we leave. "I'll pick you up at nine. We'll fly down there." His eyes reveal none of his thoughts, but that does nothing to calm the flush on my face.

"What's the weather like?" I ask, trying to sound casual.

"You've never been to Texas?"

"Never."

He laughs. "It's a trip to hell in the summer."

ROOTS

It's the second Thursday of September when I climb aboard Tahoe's Hummer and we drive to the airport. Recently things have felt a little tenser between us. The air feels charged, as if our bodies are made of electricity and the space between us is a crackling outlet just waiting to be plugged in. I'm glad, though, that neither of us feels pressured to talk, and instead we listen to "Elastic Heart" by Sia and a few other songs that play on the radio.

Tense or not, we keep stealing glances at each other, and whenever we do, a smile tugs at our lips. Which makes me happy—happy that he seems glad to have invited me to join him.

He pulls us into an airport dedicated to private aircraft, where a pilot greets us and loads our luggage into the plane's outer compartment.

I follow him into the huge private airplane and Tahoe asks me to take a seat, then heads to the cockpit to take the handle, with the pilot settled in the copilot's seat.

I fasten my seat belt and admire the luxurious interior for a few minutes before Tahoe leads the airplane to the takeoff belt. Before I know it, we're speeding down the runway and taking off.

I read *Heaven, Texas* during the flight, and when my eyes start to ache from reading, I tuck my book away and alternate between admiring the blue, cloud-specked sky and tracking the plane's progress across the multiple screens along the aircraft walls.

The speakers flare. "You okay back there, Regina?"

Grinning, I peer down the plane aisle toward the cockpit to find him glancing past his shoulder at me. He's wearing a headset and has a twinkle in his eye that makes my stomach warm. He winks and says, "We'll be landing shortly, buckle up."

I check my seat belt and watch the mix of dry and irrigated Texas land patches come closer and closer. My nerves and excitement keep building. I wonder when I've ever looked forward to something as much as I do to spending time with him.

After he lands the plane effortlessly, we head down the tarmac toward a large SUV waiting outside.

Soon we're heading out of the airport and into the city and toward a sprawling two-story house set amidst oaks and cedars and a driveway dotted with stylishly cut rosemary bushes.

I'm excited to be here. As we head up the driveway, I notice that Tahoe's more interested in my reaction than anything else.

"You grew up here?"

"In the city, yes, the home, no. I bought it for my parents when I was able to upgrade them—a token of gratitude for putting up with me." He smirks then leads me toward the front door.

I soon realize that everything is definitely bigger in Texas. The guys, their hands, feet, and definitely their houses. *"Mi casa es su casa,"* he says with a smirk, drawing it out in Spanish. His hand is light and coaxing on my back as he leads me forward and it makes me feel a sense of protection.

His mother is the epitome of what a mother should look like. Warm, slightly chubby, with rosy cheeks and neatly cropped hair and a lovely old-fashioned dress. His father is tall and blond, as blue-eyed as Tahoe. Their faces light up at the sight of him walking through the front door. But his mother's smile instantly turns into a frown.

"A beard? Oh no. I like my son clean shaven, thank you very much," his mom says, kissing him noisily.

"It's not your beard to shave, Momma," he smirks, smacking her with a kiss.

"Oh, I can't stand the feel of facial hair!" She laughs and rubs his cheek, and Tahoe looks at me and gives me a smile that sends my pulse racing.

I can, I think, then I frown and push the thought aside.

"Tahoe! Did you ask Saint about my internship? I'm graduating next year." A girl of about twenty with blonde hair and a cute sundress walks in from the living room. She glances meaningfully at her watch, as if saying her time is running out.

"I told you, you can intern with me," he says, rumpling her hair.

She groans. "I want something challenging. Not my big brother cutting me slack."

"Fine then, I'll ask Carmichael. He's the biggest asshole in business this world knows. Content?"

She hesitates, then purses her lips. "Perfectly. Don't forget, Tahoe. I'm going to ride you on this," she warns.

"Trust me, I'll handle it."

He signals at me then. "I brought a friend."

His mother's eyes turn round as saucers. "Oh." She blinks. "Ohhhh, a girlfriend."

"No," I abruptly interject. "I mean, yes, a *girl* friend, but not *girlfriend*."

"My brother doesn't have girls who are friends, so you're as rare as if you were the latter," the sister says wryly. "Livvy," she introduces herself.

"Gina."

"Never brought anyone home," I hear his father say, looking at his son with shining, hopeful eyes before he comes and hugs me.

We all sit down for dinner together.

My happiness is momentarily dulled when I compare his family to mine.

I'm relieved when T-Rex drops beside me and hands me a drink, almost as if he sensed I needed it. "Thanks," I say with a grin.

When his mom and sister bring out the next course, Tahoe kicks my ankle, drawing my gaze to his. "You okay?" he asks. He's staring at me knowingly, his blue eyes sharp as tacks.

"Yes. I mean…" I shrug, and I laugh ruefully. "I envy your relationship with your parents. I can tell you're close even if you may not see each other often."

He frowns thoughtfully, and I can see him start to get frustrated on my behalf. His lips curl in a regretful smile. "How long has it been since you saw your parents?"

"It'll be two years this Christmas. I love them, and I know they love me. But it's hard to be close with so much distance. So many years of scattered phone calls. Distance creates distance and then you stop wanting to get close."

Our eyes hold in silence. He hands me his drink when he sees I've finished mine, and I appreciate him not giving me his opinion at all. I appreciate him listening—the fact that he asked.

I sit next to him quietly as everyone chats, and I take a sip, and he takes my fingers in his and squeezes reassuringly. "You've got us."

"Damn right," I say, imitating his drawl.

He laughs, and I laugh too, both of us staying right where we are, with his hand on mine.

Then we're both silent, the classical music his mother chose to play in the background tonight so soothing that it seems natural not to talk. Plus he's a guy, he seems content being silent now, squeezing my fingers between his large, callused ones.

His family notices, and because I don't want them to think there's anything going on, I pry my hand free and continue enjoying our dinner together.

His mom confesses that all of her friends told her he'd grow up to be a *heartbreaker.*

Tahoe assures her he never stays long enough to get that far.

I kick his ankles, telling him he should be ashamed of himself.

He kicks mine back and says he's not ashamed at all.

His parents watch us with these odd, happy grins that have a hint of sadness in them and pain. Not raw pain, the kind of pain that's subdued, hopeful—almost healing.

I love that their idea of celebrating their anniversary was having a quiet dinner with their children.

I'm also glad we will be staying for the weekend here.

There is so much comfort in this house. Every nook is bathed by warm lamp light and books you hadn't known you wanted to read until you spotted them. There is warmth in every corner; in the decorative throws on the couch arms; the living, breathing plants by the windows.

His parents head to bed shortly after dinner, and as I follow Tahoe upstairs, my breath catches in my throat as I look around the upstairs living room.

The room has sleek floors, white and gray marble, and huge windowed walls. I can practically see all of the Hill Country from here; white, yellow, and blue lights twinkle at us from below.

A quiet fireplace stands to my right, and to my left, a huge wall is plastered with black-and-white pictures of oil fields.

I scan the room and my eyes stop on the man who stands directly in front of me.

He looks warm. Rumpled. Strong. Hard muscles, soft skin and scruff. He has a wineglass in his hand, accounting for his wet pink lips and narrowed blue eyes.

We don't say anything. He just nods his head to the right, gesturing for me to follow him.

He leads me down a long corridor, where I can see his room through a cracked door at the end. We stop just before his door at a room on the left.

Past the door, a big white bed with light blue accents stares back at me. Silk and cotton sheets beckon me to sleep for decades on them.

"You can sleep here then," he rumbles. "Towels are right there, you've seen the living room, kitchen is downstairs—"

"Where will you be?" I hear myself ask. I regret it the moment it comes out of my mouth. I feel myself blush, and then force myself not to take it back. I force myself to stay silent until he answers.

"I'm right next to your room." He smiles, gesturing behind me to his room, peeking at me through the cracked door. Tempting me to go in and see where the T-Rex spends his nights.

I just nod.

He looks me up and down, his eyes burning a path from the top of my head to the tips of my toes. He clears his throat. "Well, uh, I'll be in my office if you need me."

He exits the room quickly. Too quickly. I couldn't ask him where his office was.

Come on, Regina, you don't need to know that.

I shake my head, take off my shoes, and lie down on the bed.

Fifteen minutes later I'm still in the guestroom bed.

Except I can't sleep.

I get up. I don't know where exactly I'm going, but I don't really care.

I wander out of the room, my bare feet and red nails peeking at me under the material of my silky nightgown. I navigate my way through the house and his office is empty. I then head back and stand at the door next to mine and tap lightly. It's partly open, so I peer inside.

Every sharp angle and smooth curve of his face is beautifully outlined in the dark. His blue eyes practically glow.

His feet are bare. He's only in jeans and a soft white T-shirt. Hair rumpled.

The way he sits at the edge of the bed with those massive shoulders hunched tell me he's tired.

I peer around his room. An old picture sits on the nightstand. He takes it and puts it facedown, then stares at the back of the frame, his jaw working.

"Who is she?"

He startles at the sound of my voice then softly says, "My wife."

"She's your Lisa? The woman you loved?"

"She was the nicest human being I've ever known."

"Now you like the dicks like me?" I try to joke.

He just looks at me, and his eyes flood with tenderness, but most of all, I especially like that I manage to make his dimple peek with a light smile.

I laugh. "I'm sorry. I can't help it." I sit down next to him. "What happened?"

"She died seven years ago."

I sense he wants to be alone. He's a wall, impenetrable as steel. I move to get up. He leans and whispers something in my ear. *"Stay."* He sounds intense. His facial expression matches the intensity of his voice.

I can barely stand the chiseled angles in his face. He is a man, human, and in so many ways he's just like me. You were dealt a bad hand and you stopped playing the game. What if we got dealt a new game…would he play for it?

I'm struck with the realization that he loved her, and unlike my situation with Paul, because she was taken early, she will always be the object of his love.

His raw, primal, male love.

A pain blossoms in my chest and I'm afraid that it's jealousy that I'm feeling. I don't know why, because I sure don't expect anything from him of that sort. "You see her in every woman, don't you?"

He laughs, then scrapes a hand over his beard. "That's right."

I hold his hand. It feels natural to, like a friend move in a moment like this. But there's fire streaking up my arm as his hand encloses mine completely and he holds me firmly in his grip. "Tell me about her."

"She used to say the oddest things. She'd notice things nobody else did. Always see the good in people." He looks in the distance, his eyes gaining a rebellious glint. "I never was good enough for her." He eyes me. "Just like I'm not good enough for you."

His eyes start dancing like a bad boy's, and I love the playful sensuality in his lips—like he doesn't take anything too seriously. Except maybe this moment with me right now. Because there, right under the playful sensuality, is a heat I've never seen shine quite so brightly. A heat that looks like the churning, burning, boiling need inside me now.

He drags a hand over his face. "She was my girlfriend when she was diagnosed. Leukemia. A rare form, PCL. The prognosis was two years, and even now, treatment is still experimental. I married her because I didn't want her to feel alone. She got sick while still a teenager. I was barely eighteen too. We were just kids."

"God, I'm sorry. So what did you do?"

"Everything. Chemo, radiation, stem cell transplant. They kept her in a glass box. To prevent infection. It was like being in a nightmare, and there was no waking up. She never came out of that box. I felt complete helplessness just watching her, not touching her, not kissing her, watching her fight all alone. She never complained, she was always smiling…you get dealt this shit hand, the least you can do is say FUCK YOU."

"She wasn't alone, you were there. And maybe she chose to fight, stayed positive for your sake."

"Oh I know that's what she did. So it was all a lie. Every day she would say she felt good when I could see her withering away." He laughs. "She died in that glass box, my little virgin wife."

"I'm so sorry."

"I left the city shortly after. It hurts to care that much for one person. She was so damn sweet, she didn't deserve it. And when they're no longer by your side, you're fucked. It takes so much to build yourself back up. I promised myself I'd never, ever go through that again."

"I can see how that would make it hard to connect with a woman that way."

"Impossible."

We sit in silence for a moment. I really don't want to impose on any time of reflection that he might need, so I move to leave. But Tahoe has lightning-fast lacrosse player hands, and he quickly snatches my wrist and squeezes. "Hey. Stay."

I look into his eyes with a growing heaviness in my chest.

There are fears in your life that neither you nor any man on this Earth can spare you from. Fears so deeply entrenched, there is no corner in your soul to hide, no way of escaping them. They grab you, own you, squeeze the life out of you, until you wake up sweating in the middle of the night, in tears, and you're frantic to touch the ground beneath you because you still feel like you're falling…and falling…a never-ending drop. Until a painfully hard surface breaks your fall.

That hard surface, for me, is Tahoe Roth.

But for the first time in my life, the need to comfort a man is far greater than any need I have for self-preservation. So I stay and entwine my fingers through his, setting my forehead against his as we close our eyes.

He whispers in my ear, dark with guilt, as if he's confessing his worst offense ever, "I picture you in my bed." He cups my face in one big palm and looks into my eyes.

"I'm here," I whisper.

He laughs darkly and kisses my cheek. "That's not what I meant."

SPOONING

'm being spooned when I wake up. I do a mental inventory and realize I'm in a soft bed next to something hard and that I'm in a pair of huge, thick arms and the one draped around my waist weighs about a ton.

I exhale and keep doing inventory.

Okay, so I'm still dressed.

And he's bare-chested and with his jeans unbuttoned.

Which is kind of a big deal because I can feel… everything.

The kind of body that deserves to be in an underwear ad, and the kind of male…anatomy worthy of, well, porn.

I need to get out of here, but I'm afraid to move.

If I move, he could wake up. And I'll have to stare him in the eye, and everything will be so awkward because…well, what now?

Exhaling, I take his wrist within my fingers, and it's so thick I can only curl my fingers around halfway. I'm not breathing as I try to lift his arm off my body. He grunts and shifts his arm downward again, to grab my hip and spoon me even more.

And he's...hard.

Fuck me. But I guess...he wants to do just that.

I'm in bed with him, and I'm trapped. There's no escape. I should probably stay here, turn around, and get one lick down those perfect abs. Get one taste of the very cock that—in all honesty—will probably bruise me. He is fucking big and he is fucking hot. How would it be to have him giving it to me hard?

I'm getting wet.

Why did I even spend the night?

I start when I feel him shift me around. With those incredible blue eyes staring straight at me.

I hold my breath, and he raises his hand and curls his palm around my cheek.

I close my eyes, dreading that he will touch me anywhere else and that I won't have the strength to make him stop.

Instead, the bed squeaks as he shifts his weight halfway on top of me, and he says in my ear, "I don't see her in you." I squeeze my eyes tighter shut as he goes on, his voice dark and almost threatening. "It's been too many women this past year and in all of them I see *you*."

He holds my face and the silence stretches, and I will myself to open my eyes to see blue, just blue, crackling and so alive—and so angry.

"You're mad that I took her memory away? Keep her. Keep her memory alive if that's what makes you happy."

"It doesn't."

He brushes his thumb over my lipstick.

I let him. "If there's anyone in this world who will understand you not being willing to go through that again, it's me."

"Do you really? Why are you driving me crazy then? Why do I need more women, more often? Why can't I get you out of my skin?"

"You feel you're being unfaithful if you slept with me because it wouldn't be her."

A mad muscle plays angrily in the back of his jaw.

"Oh wow." I blink. "You just never know someone, do you? A ladies' man like you, faithful to one girl."

We hear noise downstairs in the kitchen.

"I better go. I don't want them to assume that we..." I push at his chest and then hurry to go change. "I'll meet you in the kitchen," I say in a rush, and then stand at the door. "Tahoe." I attempt a smile but it trembles on my face. "You were always honest that you couldn't give me what I wanted but still...thank you for telling me."

"Tahoe's out with Dad," Livvy says from the breakfast table when I finally go downstairs, after heading to my bedroom to shower and change.

I join her for a meal of eggs and hash browns.

"I'm surprised he brought you here, you know?" she chattily says. "We're all surprised. Lisa died on the day of my parents' anniversary. It made the whole thing a little bitter for him, to celebrate a day when you mourn too."

"I didn't know she died today," I say, setting my fork down.

I'm suddenly not hungry anymore.

Livvy's expression saddens, then she claps in forced cheer. "Well. My mother's thrilled you're here. She wants him to have good, better memories. It was so hard to watch him. So frustrating. He doesn't like being helpless and has never allowed himself an inch of vulnerability ever since." She eyes me somberly. "He likes you. And I mean, *likes you* likes you."

She smirks, and it's so adorable, because she smirks almost like *he* does.

"He looked at Lisa tenderly, as if she were something he needed to protect. He looks at you like a man does a woman he really cares about."

I try to dismiss her words, but I'm scared because my mind actually clings to them with the kind of fervor only the truly hopeless do.

Can Tahoe's wounds really heal for him to love someone again? Can he ever even let himself feel something for me?

I'm quietly wondering when his dad comes into the house and tells me Tahoe's waiting outside to take me for a ride.

Excited by the prospect, I wash my plate quickly as Livvy ushers me out, then I head outside and into a huge barn. I take in the sight of half a dozen horses in the stalls, and I am especially intrigued when I spot a mechanical bull right in the center of the horse stables, amidst a set of mats surrounded by hay.

I take in the bull and the tall man swiping it clean with a blue cloth. Seeing him, there's a frisson of warmth running through my body.

"You have a bull in your backyard?"

"'Course. Nothing like riding a pissed-off bull." He pets the seat meaningfully while a grin flirts across his lips. He quirks his left brow. "Try it, Regina?"

"You try it," I dare.

He laughs. "I've tried it a million times."

He mounts the bull, grabs the pommel, and the bull starts thrashing. He rides it for a minute, all his muscles flexing, and then he clicks it off, dismounts, and grabs me by the waist to prop me up. "Now you."

"Oh god." I'm so nervous I could vomit.

"Come on." He pats my butt and holds me by the waist, then curls my fingers on the pommel. "Just hang on for as long as you can."

"Tahoe," I groan. "Only you."

"That's right. Live a little." He steps back with a smirk, his blue eyes dancing merrily as he turns it on. The bull begins slowly.

"Oh wow. Okay. I can do this." I hold on with both hands and then it starts thrashing wildly and there's no possible way that I can hang on. I fly, fall on the mat, and laugh from the exhilaration. I'm still laughing on the mat when he throws himself next to me and we both stare at the rafters.

"Quite a rush, hmm?" He traces his fingers over my throat as he looks down at me, and my laughter fades.

I'm breathing fast from the bull but I'm fully aware that my heart is pounding due to something else. Something close, and dangerous, and not mine to…well, ah, ride.

Flustered by his nearness, I push up to my hands and then to my feet and watch Tahoe quietly head over to the stables to saddle up two horses.

I watch the play of his muscles under his shirt with an ache. He's such a physical man. A very physical man who's never been able to love anyone he's cared about physically.

"Get over here," he says, oblivious to my thoughts.

"I don't know how to even get on that."

"I'll help you." He grabs me by the waist and ushers me forward, then cups my butt.

"Tahoe! Not by the butt!"

I squirm restlessly to keep him from lifting me. His magnetism is becoming more and more impossible to resist and his hands on me feel too good, too male, too his.

"There's not a butt so luscious anywhere but here," he teases me, and palms it then squeezes gently, and he turns me around and draws my front to the flat plane of muscles that is *him*.

We were laughing. But the smile fades from his face the instant our eyes lock and we both seem to register our position. My breasts heave against his chest, my butt is in his hands, and then he scents my neck a little as he buries his face inside my hair.

I tilt my head and grip a handful of his T-shirt.

It's as if he can't help himself. I can't either. When he lifts his head, his eyes are lightning, thunder, and blue, blue rain. He looks at me as if I'm the most forbidden, most succulent thing he will ever take a bite of.

I look at him, slowly, cautiously, nervously tipping my head upward.

When he sees that, he slides his arm slowly around my waist to draw me tighter to him.

"Come here," he says, his voice dark as he leans his head.

His breath is so close I can feel it on my face. His eyes look so dark, they're almost navy blue when he gazes into mine. He cradles my cheek in his hand.

He holds my face utterly still as he leans in.

And he gets closer,

And his nose brushes lightly over mine,
And his breath blends with my breath,
And his lips whisper over mine.

All this time I've been staring at him, motionless. Then his eyes start to close, and his lashes are gorgeous, and he smells like pine and hay...

And his lips close firmly over mine.

Softly but so possessively, I gasp as my whole body arches up to the kiss. His tongue flicks softly—opening me.

A thousand emotions and sensations ripple through me.

I'm still scared.

I still know this won't amount to anything.

I now know he may possibly never, ever come to love me.

But all the longing, all the nights, all the days, all the nudges, all the baits, all the teases, all the arguments, the games, the holidays, the chocolates, everything simmers to the surface until I feel like I'm going to explode into a million tiny, horny little pieces.

I grab his hair—hard.

A violent groan leaves his chest as he parts my mouth wider and wider. He tightens his arms around me and lifts me up against his chest almost aggressively. He squeezes me tightly but lovingly, and nibbles my lower lip, saying, "God, this mouth belongs to me, this mouth was made for me."

His hot little bite is a soft prick on my lower lip, firm enough to feel, but soft enough to feel like being bitten *all over.*

He groans again and his tongue smooths over the sting of the bite and I groan for him, moan for him, grab his hair tighter, hold him close, my heart beating a thousand beats in one single heartbeat.

When he finally eases back, he stares into my face as if searching for something he needs to see, something he's craving for, would die for, that's how intense his eyes are, how rabidly they look at me.

"I'm still on Earth?" I whisper.

His lips curl briefly, his lids heavy, eyes dilated and still fiercely searching.

"Yeah?" he asks in a voice coarsened with desire, rubbing the knuckle of his index finger over my bruised mouth.

"Yeah." I laugh.

He gives an impatient nod to the horse, and when he grabs my waist to lift me, he stops and inhales a deep breath. He smiles against my temple, and I smile to myself. I haven't seen his dimple in a while, and this time I can actually feel it against my skin.

Sometimes we use the people close to us as crutches, to keep from facing reality, or to keep from doing the hard work. We think they can do it for us or shield us from the truth. Sometimes we use our pain as a crutch too, to keep from putting ourselves out there again. I can no longer deny that between me and Trent, there always stood a six-foot-plus blond Tyrannosaurus rex, and I hadn't realized until now that nothing could have kept me from falling in love with him.

We ride across a dirt path up to the crest of a hill, where we can see the rest of the Hill Country before us. As we ride, he talks about growing up here, about the first time he fell off a horse, and I keep telling him it's so peaceful compared to Chicago. "You can almost hear your own thoughts here," I say.

"Yeah?" He raises an eyebrow, as if he intends to find out exactly what those thoughts are.

He smirks devilishly, but I smirk back just as devilishly, my eyes silently promising him he'll never know.

We head up a trail between oaks and cedars, and Trent texts me as we park the horses in a field of wildflowers and sit down to take in the view.

I need to see you.

I'm not in the city

When do you get back?

I tell him to meet me at my place Friday evening, a week from today. That I want to talk. And then I tuck my phone away, dreading the conversation already.

"Davis?" Tahoe asks as we fall back on the grass, boosted up on our elbows. He's staring out at the horizon, his jaw working.

"Yes."

That's all I say, and apparently that's all he needs to hear.

BABY

That afternoon, while at his parents' house, I get a call from Wynn saying Rachel went into labor. I leave Livvy with the flowers we were pruning and run into the house. Tahoe's charging out of his father's office and he stops when we almost collide at the foyer.

"You ready?" he asks.

I nod breathlessly, smiling ear to ear.

"Let's go."

Eight hours later, Rachel gives birth to an eight-pound, healthy baby boy.

Kyle Malcolm Saint.

He's got eyes that we all predict will stay blue, and a fuzz of light hair we assume comes from his mother.

After talking about loss and death, Tahoe and I witness this miracle of life and we are the only ones aside from the parents with red eyes.

Tahoe takes my hand in his, and then moves me closer in an instinctual gesture of comfort. His thigh barely touches mine, but I feel closer to him than when I'm physically closer to another guy. He looks down at me, and his infectious grin sets my own smile free.

"Rachel is going to be such a great mom," I vow on my best friend's behalf.

His voice is rough with pride. "Are you kidding me? Saint is going to kill it as a dad."

And I wonder if I will ever have a baby of my own to love and a husband I adore the way my best friend loves hers.

And I know. I know what I've always known. That this aching, thrilling thing I have for Tahoe won't ever go away. That I have never in my life wanted a man the way I want Tahoe "T-Rex" Roth.

That I want the kind of love that Rachel and Saint have, and if I ever have a baby, I want to be so wildly in love with the dad that my only wish is for my child to resemble him as much as he possibly can.

I've always told myself that Trent and I are good. That he's sweet and I'm happy with him. But in the middle of the hospital, watching my best friend getting kissed by her husband as they hold their firstborn child, I say—fuck good.

I want fabulous.

I want every moment to feel like it does when I'm with the man I'm sitting next to right now. Even the sad moments, the hopeless moments, the silent moments or the funny ones, or the deep ones, or the surprising ones—simply *every* moment, I want that spark that is always there, the sizzle, the light, the joy, that comes with being near HIM.

Maybe he will never want me in return. Maybe I'm a fool. But I also know that somehow, I've also been in a crystal box of my own creation for a while. And nothing has ever lured me out of my box but HIM.

I'm in love with Tahoe, and Trent will never be him.

I get to my feet and go text Trent, pushing up our meeting and asking him to come over to my place tonight.

"I have to get home," I tell Rachel.

I kiss her on the cheek, tell her to kiss the baby for me when they bring him back from the nursery, then I say good-bye to Saint, Emmett, Wynn, Rachel's mom, and Tahoe.

I say, softly so that only he hears, "I have to go, thank you for Texas." And when he smiles, I kiss his dimple and leave.

WHEN GOOD IS NOT GOOD ENOUGH

B ack in my apartment, I fall into my couch and lay my head on the back as I wait for Trent to arrive. I'm nervous, both excited about my realization and pained about it too.

He arrives with a hopeful look on his face.

"Hey," he says.

"Hey."

I lead him into my living room.

"So," he says, clasping his hands together and raising his brows as he takes the couch opposite mine.

I bite my lips for a moment, dreading what I have to say. In all of my life, I've never been the one to leave someone. I may be snarky or bitchy or grumpy or a thousand things, but I've never been the one to say I'm moving on. After being hurt so badly myself, it gives me no pleasure to hurt anyone else. But this includes myself too.

I don't know what's happening with Tahoe. Actually nothing is happening with Tahoe, but I have feelings for him that I can no longer deny.

I have been trying to find pieces in Trent to love. And there are so many sweet things about him. But what I deeply fear is that I'm not just looking for pieces of him to like. I'm looking for Tahoe in him.

I search for the words, finding it harder than I thought. I want to tell him that Tahoe likes me with or without makeup. That he nudges me back when I nudge him. In fact, he nudges me first. I want to tell him that I always dream that I'm sleeping naked, facedown, and there's a man above me, and he's licking my spine. That I wake up with a start and when I turn around, blue eyes are staring back at me.

None of these things will matter to Trent.

I hug my knees to my chest and smile sadly at him. "I wanted to change me by giving myself a chance with you. But that wasn't the recipe. I should have focused on accepting me. I don't need to change who I am for you to love me. I shouldn't," I say.

"Not everything, Gina, but making an effort for your partner—"

"I've fallen in love with someone," I interrupt. "It's hopeless and I don't think he'll ever be able to respond, but I can't keep on lying to myself about it, and you don't deserve me lying to you."

"Who is he?" he asks, leaning back. He almost looks calm about it, disbelieving, as if I couldn't possibly have found someone better than him.

I smile. "Someone who likes my ponytail."

There's not much more to say, I guess. In the end, he hugs me and kisses my cheek, and I do the same, and at least our smiles feel genuine when we say goodbye.

HALLOWEEN

I'm not ready to tell my friends that I broke up with Trent. Rachel is so busy with Kyle. Wynn may start pressuring me to go after Tahoe. I know her. She always believes that there's hope in everything. But I just don't know that there is. One kiss doesn't change anything. Tahoe kissed me and it was epic and red-hot sparks fired up as if everything inside me went haywire. That doesn't mean he wants more—that doesn't mean he can give me more. I now know why he's not interested in that sort of commitment, but that also doesn't change the fact that every time I look at him I think, *you are so loved by me, you lovely, wounded beast.*

He's been calling these past weeks since Trent and I broke up. It's almost as if he can sense I'm available. He can't stay away—neither can I. We talk constantly, he takes me out for coffee, or I stop by his office, and on many of those occasions, he looks at me with his blue eyes that pierce the space between us and say both a thousand things and nothing at all.

I don't know what's going on, but I don't want to push for more too aggressively. I sense he needs time to adjust to whatever ways our relationship is changing, and if that's what he needs, I am willing to wait it out.

On his birthday, I really wanted to knock on his door with nothing on beneath my trench coat, and just stand there, and let him see me, let him want to take me.

Instead, I hear he spends it out of town. No partying for Tahoe Roth this year. Which his social media seems to find odd.

No bash this year @Tahoe Roth? People keep tweeting.

I tweet him: **Happy Birthday @tahoeroth**

He tweets back: **Won't sleep until I figure out what you got me this year ;)**

I reread the tweet a thousand times, feeling different things each time. Amusement, excitement, outrage, arousal. I threw myself at him last year and what…he expects me to do that again this year?

Does he *want* me to do it again this year?

I decide he's just teasing me—as usual—and try to calm down my hormones.

To stay busy and keep saving up for my future apartment, I send a mass email to my friends the following week, telling them I'm free for any work they may have, including odd jobs.

My phone rings almost instantly.

Tahoe Roth.

Quelling the kick I get in my heart, I answer.

"Don't do that, Regina," he chides. "Odd jobs. Do you know how many things popped into my mind to ask you for?"

"No, I don't want to know. Not everyone's mind is as filthy as yours."

He sighs. "How much do you need?"

"What? I'm not taking your charity."

"Fine. Do my face then."

Suddenly, all sorts of X-rated ideas pop into my head too. "Excuse me?"

"I have this black-and-white masquerade tonight. Do my face. I don't wear masks, they bug the shit out of me. So you might as well paint it on me."

"Oh, ah, okay. Well I have to be done by ten, I have plans with my coworkers."

Silence.

"Eight?" I suggest.

"My place," he says.

At eight, I'm wearing my long white Halloween angel gown with a cute golden halo when I'm taking his elevator. I like Halloween. It's the only time of the year you get to be anyone but yourself.

I walk into his place and head down the hall into his bedroom, then I pause and catch my breath at the door. Tahoe is wearing a black turtleneck and black slacks. He's running a comb through his damp hair when he turns to the door and greets me with a bleak frown.

Ah. He's clearly still displeased about my "odd job" mass email.

"You know you can call me whenever you need anything, right?" he asks, his lowered eyebrows menacing.

"Yeah." I bring my makeup kit in and set it down on his bathroom counter. He has the biggest bathroom I've ever seen, with a long black granite slab consisting of two sinks spaced out by yards of smooth surface.

"Not mass email the whole city," he specifies as he fills the bathroom doorway behind me.

"It wasn't the whole city and I want the jobs." I grin then wave him in and ask him to sit on one of the two leather stools under the granite counter. "So what, did you think something kinky?" I nudge him as I prod him to sit.

"Very kinky." Our eyes meet in the mirror.

"You've got sperm in your head, I swear." I'm laughing, then our eyes hold in the mirror again and the floor starts to feel like quicksand under my feet. All in black, he is the epitome of a dark knight tonight, and if I were the kind of girl to swoon, I would swoon right now. He smells like pine, and soap, and man.

"So what's this masquerade...?" I ask as I open the bag with my face paints.

"First tell me what your plans are."

"Why?"

"Because I want you to come with me tonight."

"Ooooh...no, no, *no*." I shake my head as I start opening all of my kits in search of my black pencils, and Tahoe is staring at me intently.

"Odd jobs, huh?" he asks then, thickly.

"I'll never know what else I'm good at until I try, I guess."

His lips curl. He reaches out and strokes one finger down my jaw, his voice oddly tender. "You're good at hiding."

"Me?"

His finger traces the same path down my jaw again, the touch tingling over me. "All that makeup hiding that beautiful face." He raises his hands and cups my cheeks and turns me so that our eyes are meeting, not with the mirror between us anymore. He's looking so deep inside me, I realize no makeup can shield me from this man. Not anymore.

"You're even better at it," I accuse, softly. "You hide in plain sight. Life is all a big amusement park for Tahoe Roth, isn't it?"

"That's right." He smirks and lets go of me, the connection gone. "Regina, come with me tonight."

His voice is coaxing and oh, so very sexy. God. There isn't even a word for the things this guy's voice does to my stomach.

"Yeah? Why?" I ask, annoyed on behalf of my body as I lean over him and pick a dark liner.

"I need you." His whisper bathes warmly over my face.

"You always need me," I bluff.

He grabs my waist and squeezes as I set the pencil against his forehead. "That's right. Make yourself unavailable to your coworkers and available to me."

I ignore him and scan his features and plan my art. "I'm thinking of a black mask. Also, I forgot to mention that if you want my fabulous makeup artist services, it's sixty an hour."

He pats my waist, but his hand is so big that half of it ends up patting the top of my butt. "Tell you what. I'll add a zero to that, just because."

"Rotund no, T-Rex. But thank you."

Before I begin drawing, I spot a black mask past the open door, haphazardly tossed on his bed. "You have a perfectly good mask there. No need for makeup, Tahoe."

"I don't wear masks. I told you. Now come do me."

Come do me.

Oh god! I cannot think straight anymore.

I scowl and shake my head, but bend down again and set the tip of my pencil to his forehead. "I don't buy it."

"Do you buy that I wanted a reason for you to be here?" His voice turns husky and deep.

I lower my face and find myself inhaling for balance. "You don't need a reason. We're friends."

"Are we?" His voice is so soft, it's the merest break in the silence between us.

"I don't know what we are anymore," I say honestly.

He remains silent and I raise my eyes. His blue gaze hits me like a Taser, so electric I hear my pencil clatter to the marble floor.

I curse.

He slowly bends over and picks it up for me.

His eyes start sparkling over my expression of frustration, and he passes me the pencil, raising his brows. He smiles a little sardonically, looking into my eyes.

I hold the pencil tightly. I hold his gaze, hold my breath, hold on to this moment. The seconds tick by to the throbbing beat of my heart when he whispers, "Go on, Regina."

Tahoe's voice is lower than usual, his drawl noticeable.

He smiles a little and then when he reaches out to rumple my hair, keeps smiling with his eyes the way he usually does, as if I amuse him. Exhaling, I straighten my halo, gather myself, and start to paint him.

He watches me as I lean in with a dark pencil.

I draw the outline of a mask across the top of his face. I ease back to survey my handiwork. I've been studying his face for minutes when I become aware of that intense gaze of his, crystal clear, fixed on me.

My breath keeps leaving me.

It's not just how gorgeous Tahoe's eyes are—it's how they stare so unflinchingly at me.

I lean close enough to apply the paint and he smells so good I feel lightheaded. His breathing changes a little bit as I apply the black paint slowly to his face, around his eyes, over his skin. I change sides, and he inhales deeply as I lean over again, applying more paint. His hand comes up to grip my waist, and he shuts his eyes and just holds me as I add his mask, the moment exquisitely intimate.

"Why do you even need a mask when you wear a mask all the time?" I whisper.

"'Cause you can't go showing people the worst parts of you. They don't deserve it, and neither do you deserve to be judged for it." He looks at me very deeply for the following moment. "You would know, Regina." He tugs my costume dress. "Who are you?"

"An angel. Don't you see my wings?" I turn around, grinning. "They're invisible. What about you?"

He shrugs. My smile fades a little when he looks at me.

I picture him as the Phantom of the Opera. But his scars are not on his skin.

Silently, he grabs my waist again and pulls me closer so that I can continue drawing his mask. And I think of the Phantom, who thought the girl he loved, Christine, would end up with some other guy named Raoul, because the Phantom wasn't worthy of her.

I ache for this beautiful, wounded man that I've fallen so hopelessly for.

For twenty more minutes, I work in silence. But sometimes when my fingertips touch his face to hold him still, I sense him tense, his brows set in a straight line, jaw squaring, lips pinched as if he's controlling some unnamable force within him.

When I'm done, he rises to his feet, obviously restless. I watch him walk to his bedroom and put on his black cape, his fingers tying it expertly. I don't know why I helped him dress up, because all I want is to undress him.

As I try to quell the desire he causes in me, I hide in his bathroom, storing my makeup. When I come out with my bag, Tahoe is sitting in a chair, watching me, sitting forward with his elbows on his knees.

I step into the room. "I broke up with Trent," I blurt out without thinking.

There's a long pause, as if the Earth stopped moving.

He narrows his eyes. "Do you want me to say I'm sorry you broke up with him? I'm not."

"No." I shake my head. "I didn't come here to talk about my failure in relationships."

A sad smirk appears. "Hell, Regina, I'm the last one qualified to judge anyone's relationships."

I duck my head, unable to look him in the eye.

I think he mistakes that for sadness, for when he speaks again, he sounds frustrated as he rises to his feet, walks up to me, and takes my shoulder in one hand, lifting my chin with the other. "Come on. That motherfucker isn't worth it. You deserve so much better, Regina." The admiration in his eyes nearly undoes me.

I want his lips. I want his hands all over me. I want his heart. His wounded beautiful heart he's put on a shelf where nobody can reach it.

Being with him lately only hurts, only makes me realize nothing of what I've ever felt before was real, nothing was like this, nothing compares. It was a little flicker compared to a wildfire. A tiny prick of pain compared to a whole throbbing, all-consuming ache.

"You look even more beautiful when you're upset," he says softly, seizing my chin again, eyes perceptive and deep. The warmth of his gaze echoes in his voice. I'm enthralled by what I see there, swirling in his eyes. There's a primal ferocity in his look, a hunger like I've never seen in a man's eyes before. "Though I'm not too happy for you to be upset over a guy like Davis. A guy who…hell, any guy doesn't deserve you being upset over him. Do you hear me?" he says in warning, his left eyebrow rising a fraction.

I groan. "You act as if I'm this perfect little thing. I'm not. Okay, now I'm leaving, grumpy," I say.

"No, you're not." He grabs my shoulders, guides me back into the bathroom, and forces me to face the mirror and look at my own reflection. After a confused moment, I look up at his.

Sternly, he says, his voice brushing warm just above my earlobe, "Now her."

"I'm not going to your silly masquerade party…"

"Come on, Regina. I'm imagining a beautiful silver mask here for this beautiful lady." He touches my cheekbone, once again looking at me through the mirror.

He's so tall. The most striking black mask with silver and gold swirls covers the top of his face. The rest is scruff, and blue eyes, and chiseled and male.

"What am I supposed to mask myself as?"

He grins a mischievous smirk. "Exactly what you are now. An angel." He leans to whisper in my ear as he tugs playfully on my halo. "Soon to be fallen." The corners of his lips curve into a demon's grin. "Come on, let's go."

I groan in complaint but feel a reluctant smile on my lips. "I'll go, but I'm not painting my face."

He's surprised by that, I can tell.

I guess I'm just as surprised.

"I'm tired of painting my face, Tahoe." Suddenly I just want him to see me, the real me, all of me, bare.

And I want him to like what he sees...

I don't know where the thought comes from. It surprises me so much that I keep it to myself.

I text my coworkers to let them know I can't make it. I leave my stuff at his apartment. We take the elevator downstairs—me dressed in white, him in black. Me with curly black hair, him with beautiful blond hair. Opposites, really. Him tall and muscled, me shorter and curvy.

So why does it always feel so right?

The party is in an apartment in Tahoe's building, five floors below. The moment the apartment door opens and we step into the shimmering crowd and the pulsing music, a girl rushes him. She pries Tahoe's cape off his neck and twirls it around herself, but he just laughs and retrieves it and swings it around his shoulder.

I try to ignore the sensation of having swallowed a brick. He's a ladies' man, and ladies' men attract ladies, effortlessly, that's what he does.

He makes such a wicked demon, and a beautiful phantom, but as we walk side by side through the costumed crowd, all I see is Tahoe Roth. The man I think of constantly. The man who lights me up.

Jack-o'-lanterns stuck on fake pikes flare with electric candles all across the room. People dance, drink, and make out.

We head to the dance floor and as girls start recognizing him by the eyes, the beard, the height, they start yelling happily, shouting, "Trick or treat?" and trying to get a kiss.

I walk away—sick of seeing the guy I want kissing everyone but me—when I hear him say, "Not tonight," and when I turn around, I realize he's pried free of them and is heading my way. The look in his eyes makes me breathless.

Is it chilly in here? My nipples stiffen under my top. I've never seen Tahoe stalk so slowly, but reach me so fast.

He curls his hand around the back of my neck and guides me to the dance floor. "Dance with me," he whispers in my ear.

He grasps the neck of my heavy gown and tugs me forward until our bodies are flush and warm against each other. His body heat envelops me, head to toe. I slip my hands up his shoulders and into his hair. And we move...his eyes caressing me...making love to me in ways no man I've ever been with ever did with his whole body...

Dancing always makes me feel sexy. Dancing with Tahoe, however, has a whole other level of sexy attached to it. His fluid moves and the animal magnetism he emanates make me not only feel sexy, but *sexual.*

I dance and let go but at the same time, I try to repress the feelings of longing and desire awakening in my body.

His cape billows around us. He holds my back and looks at me, only me, as we sway. I know that I'm not classically pretty. I'm considered more sultry, but Tahoe's stare right now makes me feel as if I'm both—as if I deserve to be deliciously fucked and wonderfully protected. And as if he wants to be the man to do both.

For the first time I don't feel guilty about being held by him in front of the world. I don't feel guilty that my fingers want to crawl deeper into his hair, and I press my cheek into his chest and he presses his jaw into my hair, in the center of my halo, and inhales me.

"You want to know something?" he says with a sly smile, tipping my chin to his. "All the work put into dressing up, right now I just want to be me. And I just want you to be you." He tugs on my halo and loosens it from my hair, smiling in mischief as he drops his cape along with my halo and sweeps me around the dance floor, leaving them behind.

I punch him and tell him, "You're so silly," but when he grabs my face and rubs my lipstick a little bit, as if he wants to get rid of the little makeup I'm wearing tonight, I ache.

He's my best friend. The only person I love to be with, want to be with, always. He's the only man I've ever wanted like *this*.

I stop his hands and lower them.

I step back so I can look into his eyes, and his smile wavers on his face—he's still standing there with that black mask, but his eyes are all him, all blue, and all on me. I feel a prick of wetness in my eyes as every single feeling that I have for him flames and burns inside me.

"I love you." I try to hold his gaze with all the honesty and strength that I can muster. "Touch me now. Hold me now. Love me. Let yourself love me. I'm scared too."

My voice breaks, and suddenly, as his stormier-than-ever blue eyes look at me, I feel more bare and naked than I have ever felt in my life.

And the next thing I know, I gasp in a rush.

"I can't believe I just blurted that...Tahoe, I'm sorry, I... I have to go."

And I turn around and shoulder my way to the front door, wishing that I indeed had wings that could fly me out of there.

My beautiful apartment creaks and croaks all night. Or maybe it's just my conscience, or my mind, replaying every detail of the evening. Tahoe, Tahoe, Tahoe, *Tahoe*...

I don't sleep one wink.

I miss him already. I feel like I lost him already. His incredibly honest friendship. His addictive teasing of me. His sporadic appearances in my life, which always lit me up and made me aware of how glum the second before he appeared actually was.

My makeup kit, my cell phone, everything of mine is still at Tahoe's place. I was lucky I had given the extra key to my new apartment to one of my neighbors. I know I'll have to get my stuff back soon, but luckily I've got a credit card tucked away and some cash on hand too. I feel weird without my cell phone—but I can't find the courage to stop by and pick it up yet.

In the morning, I go see baby Kyle at the Saints' place to try to clear my head. I've got so much on my mind and such a heavy sensation in the center of my chest that holding him makes me feel better. Holding a baby always does. I also simply craved seeing Rachel. She's my best friend, and no marriage or babies will ever change that.

I tell her that I've broken up with Trent for good. I know both Wynn and Rachel have probably suspected that I've had strong feelings for Tahoe for a long time, though I'd never actually told them that I do.

I think they both knew that I was not ready to admit it, even to myself.

"And I told Tahoe I loved him yesterday," I say quietly as I set the sleeping little baby back into his crib.

Rachel's eyes widen in surprise.

"I didn't say it so that he would say it back or anything, but I felt like a hypocrite, being friends and yet not being able to just tell him how I feel. Now…I don't know if I regret it."

Rachel heads across the baby's room—beautifully decorated with a jungle painted on his wall and a plush giraffe as tall as I am—and she grabs the Kleenex on top of his changing table.

"No, silly, don't. I'm not going to cry." I wave it off, but only because I *refuse* to have the option of using them. "I didn't go to work," I add. "I asked Martha for a few days. I want to think things through. After what I said, I don't know what's going to happen, but I don't want to lose his friendship."

"Saint went to see him this morning."

"Oh. Saint went to see Tahoe?"

Rachel nods. "He called him at two a.m. saying he needed to talk." When I say nothing, she shrugs. "I'm not sure that they'll talk about anything, really. When guys are bummed, sometimes they want to sit and drink in silence and just have a buddy nearby."

"I guess," I say.

"You know what? I think you need to just be with yourself while you sort out things in your head, Gina. You've been so busy with work, and Trent was another distraction from maybe figuring out what it is you really want—and what you want to do about it. Please, if you don't take anything else from me ever again, please just accept going to our house in the Hamptons, Gina. I'll arrange transportation—just go clear your head."

And so I take her advice, and that afternoon, I accept her offer to fly me up to the Hamptons for a weekend.

CHECKED

The following morning I decide to sit down on the window bench and read *Gone Girl* with a cup of hot coffee by my side. I had French toast for breakfast and am enjoying this time on my own to regroup and think about how to maybe, slowly, try to rebuild my friendship with Tahoe.

I've wondered endlessly whether or not I did the right thing in telling him I love him. I feel like the world opened up and swallowed me, but I also feel relief that I finally came clean, even if what I said was not what he wanted to hear.

I'm still thinking of the look on his handsome face when the words left me, the shock and almost concern (for me, I'm sure it was for me). I can't concentrate on the book on my lap. I've been staring at it for a while when I hear the sound of tires and a rumbling car motor.

I peer out the window and watch a tall man emerge from a silver Audi rental.

He's wearing black jeans and a black long-sleeved crewneck. It's hard to breathe when the man walking to the front door is the one I wanted to get away from this weekend.

A familiar triple knock startles me.

I force myself to put the book down, walk to the door, inhale deeply, and open it.

He fills the space outside like he is a god and like he is at the center of everything. Our eyes lock, and I suddenly realize I'm makeup-less, in my pajamas, my heart flipping helplessly at the sight of him.

I can't think when he looks at me, with wounded blue eyes and a thoughtful frown.

I press my lips tight with nothing to say, then turn around and let him in.

I don't know what's happening, what I was getting into when I told him I loved him. Two broken parts can't make a whole and I know it.

We were friends. And now how can we be friends after what I said?

He's silent and so am I, two broken people, a little angry at whatever hurt them, having nothing to vent and no one to punch, not really.

The wood floor creaks as he stalks so close at my heels that I can almost hear my personal bubble pop. My lungs strain for air as he stops me and slips his fingers up my cheek and cups the side of my face.

"Don't," I warn.

He kisses my cheek.

"Don't."

He kisses my other cheek.

"Tahoe, don't."

He goes for my mouth and I turn my face away. His kiss lands on my cheek, and against my skin, he inhales.

His arms come around me, stronger than if they were steel.

The feeling of being engulfed by something uncontrollable seizes me.

"Are you upset with me?" he asks fiercely in my ear, turning my face.

I'm trying to talk without allowing my voice to reveal any of the chaos I'm feeling. "Why would I be——"

"For being such a messed-up fuck." He looks at me. His perfect face is only an inch from mine. He sets a peck on my lips and my breath leaves me in a hurry.

"You're not. I'm not upset. I just want to be alone a little bit, okay? We're okay. You and I are okay, we're friends and we'll always be friends."

He holds my face in both hands as if to make sure I won't avoid him this time. "So easy, you give up on me, huh? You tell me you love me and run away—why? Did I not have a right to say something back?"

I press my lips in stony silence.

"Well, you're going to have to hear it, lady."

I exhale.

"First I have to say I missed you," he says, his voice dropping. "You're like an insistent little trickle of water, soaking into every inch of my life. I can't look anywhere without noticing your absence, Regina."

Just hearing his voice makes me oddly emotional and makes my throat ache. "I missed you too, Tahoe."

He drags a hand over his bearded jaw, drops it and fists it at his side. "You just up and disappeared. Don't do that to me again, Regina."

"I didn't disappear, I've been right here. I didn't think anyone would mind."

"I'm not anyone, and I was worried about you."

He looks restless, all of his energy crackling around him, around *us* as he silently wills me to understand with his gaze.

"Okay," I say.

"So," he spreads his arms out, "girl," he laughs, "you've checked me so hard I can't even think straight anymore. You've been checking me left and right this whole year and I fucking can't even think straight anymore, Regina.

"I love you." He looks at me. "I love every part of you. I could be a thousand miles away from you, stay away from you my whole life, put an ocean between us, take a million other women in my arms, and you're still the one I want, the only woman on my mind."

He scrapes his beard. He seems nervous, rubbing the back of his neck restlessly.

"See, I was in love once. I never thought I was good enough for her. We were kids, puppy love." His voice lowers. "But even in puppy love, love shouldn't be like that. It shouldn't need you to change." His eyes shimmer like blue lightning. "I've learned that with you. Love should make you feel good about yourself and about the person you are when you're with the one you love. Love should make you feel accepted as you are."

His stare bores into me. "You know my every side, you've seen me in every way, and you let me see *you* the way you let no man see you. And somehow we still crave to be with each other. Not because I'm broken and I make you feel good about yourself…because I'm *not* broken with you. You get me and I get you. I accept you, I *cherish* you. I fucking revere you. Just as you are. I want no other woman in my life and I want you to have no man but me. So I love you." He exhales rapidly. "And I fucking love the way you look right now. I love that smile of yours most of all."

I'm both smiling and crying and getting the little makeup I'm wearing all messed up. "Did you have to say this right now?"

His arms engulf me in the most delicious way. "Yes. Now."

He rubs my lips with his thumb. He lifts me and twirls me like he did when he said I was his lucky charm, then he stops and slowly lets my body drag down the length of his as he sets me on my feet.

Our eyes latch, so intently and with such hunger that our laughter drifts off.

His smile fades as my own smile fades.

A pool of yearning swirls in my stomach as I notice the shifting blues in his eyes until I can hardly see anything at all, only his pupils, dark as night and eating me alive.

He squeezes the arm around my waist. He captures my face in his other hand, looking at my mouth. His palm is warm.

I lift my head.

Before I know it, I'm kissing him.

We both make a sound; he makes a deep, hungry sound, and I release a startled whimper, but we won't tear our lips away. He takes my hand in one of his and puts it on the back of his neck, drawing me closer. And he nibbles my lips, and he kisses my lips, and everything I knew about kissing is shattered as sparks shoot throughout me, fire races in my veins, my toes curl, my heart pumps, my whole body is one giant aching ball of need.

He gathers me close and I can't stop kissing him.

He scrapes his thumb over my lips as if to make sure there's no lipstick between us, only his lips and my lips. He looks at me, his chest stretching his shirt with each breath.

I could not possibly be more receptive as he starts to move his hand down my curves, savoring me.

My hips roll achingly toward his body.

He nibbles my earlobe, unleashing shivers down my spine. "Tell me you want me. Or I'll make you tell me. Tell me now, Regina."

"I want you, T-Rex."

"And I love you." He grabs my face in both hands and kisses me, adds teeth to the kiss. He nibbles my lip and then he sensuously bites it and tugs it gently before releasing, and it feels sore and loved and I want him to do it again. He holds my face framed in his callused palms, his eyes boring into me. "I revere you. I'm addicted to you. Tell me you know that. Huh?"

"I know that," I say, with effort.

He hugs me to him and inhales my hair, then tips up my face, smoothing his tongue over my lips to open them.

I open my lips farther, lost in the feel of being in his arms and being kissed like this and feeling his hair between my fingers and how much he wants me.

I can't get over the taste of him. The heat of him, and how it seeps through our clothes and to my skin. His hands trail over my backside, spreading to engulf all of me.

We take a moment to breathe and watch each other with an intensity that makes his breath become deeper, mine faster, and we're both so completely serious. As serious as we've ever been.

He spreads a hand over my face, looking at my mouth, his palm engulfing nearly half my face, and I lift my head to kiss him again.

I aim for his jaw, but Tahoe turns his head just the necessary inches to catch my lips with the center of his mouth.

He growls softly when he's got my mouth under his and I don't move away, instead letting him mold his lips to mine.

He holds my face, his hand open, and uses his thumb to pull my chin down so that my lips part and he can dip his tongue into my mouth...right where I want him, where his taste brands itself in me, and bubbles of pleasure race down my nervous system. His hot, soothing taste fills every tiny nook and corner inside me.

Sensations crackle through my bloodstream. I am liquid and warm. "Tahoe," I whisper.

"God, say my name like that, just like that," he murmurs as he trails his lips up my jaw.

He nibbles my earlobe, unleashing shivers down my spine. He groans and squeezes me tighter to him, as if he's waited for this for too long.

He grabs my waist and shifts me so that he has access to my entire backside and I'm flat against him, kissing him as hard and fast as he's kissing me.

"Tahoe, Tahoe..." I moan.

"I know," he groans huskily into my mouth, "I know."

His tongue smooths over mine as I tip my head back and open my lips farther. I want him to taste me all over, to take everything.

The heat of his chest against mine is burning me to ash. His hand trails over my abdomen, my heart aches when I see the raw lust on his face as he watches his fingers steal under my pajama top.

Fingertips stroke all over my belly. He leans closer. His mouth brushes over mine and he gives me one light peck on the lips, like the ones he used to give me.

I tremble.

Another kiss—this one he punctuates with a small, delicious bite on my bottom lip. I clench all over with need. He nibbles me so tenderly, seizing my lip, gently biting, gently tugging, gently releasing, heatedly licking.

I slip my fingers under his shirt, wanting to touch him.

He seems to want my touch too because he shrugs off his shirt and tosses it aside. His hair ends up all mussed and I love it; I run my fingers over it and kiss his mouth again. Lick my tongue across the soft scrape of his beard and up to his glorious, minty, hot mouth.

Breathless at the sight of his magnificent body in its semi-nude state, I toss my top and send it flying across the room. I'm wearing no bra, and the next instant we're pressing up against each other, pressing our lips together.

He scoops me up and carries me upstairs, stalking the house with quick steps.

He turns into a room, leaves the light off, the door kicked shut. Sunlight streams through the window. And I am grateful because I want to see.

And I think he does too because as he sets me on the bed, he is doing nothing—nothing—but laying a thousand pounds of heat on me with his eyes.

Before I can beg him and ask for it now now, *now*, he's crawling over me, his lips settling possessively back on mine, tongue sliding inside. I claw him closer, flesh to flesh, the thickness of his erection pressing against his jeans and settling perfectly between my thighs.

He's so big and so hard, and I'm so ready I'm quaking. He tugs my shorts down my legs and leaves me only in my panties. Green striped ones. He takes them in as he takes in all of me, naked and so very bare for him.

And he could not look more pleased as his eyes roam my every curve, my every inch.

He makes love to me with just his gaze. After a long, sinuous path, his eyes stop and smolder on my face. "So gorgeous, nothing has ever been this gorgeous," he huskily declares.

He slides his warm palms over my rib cage and covers my breasts—my aching, heavy breasts—in his gentle palms.

No one has ever held my breasts with more reverence.

His thumbs caress the peaks at the same time, and Tahoe watches my expression as he does. I gasp in surprise; waves of white-hot lightning roll through me. His eyes darken as he takes in my reaction, flashing as if the white-hot lightning lives and breathes inside *him*, and he does it again, curling the hardened little tips. Caressing me with the utmost care.

"Tahoe," I purr, and I arch and grab the back of his head, fill my hands with fistfuls of his hair, and I press my lips to his. "God, you feel amazing. You *are* amazing," I groan against his mouth.

This kiss is a bit wilder now, more out of control. We're both getting breathless. I can feel him getting restless, getting hungry. His stare is hungry, the feel of his hands wandering my body is hungry, the way he's gently biting my lips, earlobe, and throat is hungry.

He unfastens his jeans, tosses them aside. His muscles ripple with his movements as he crawls back over me, and deep inside me, in the parts of me I've tucked away for too long, I feel a ripple too. A ripple of longing and desire and love, I almost don't know what to do with this mix of feelings, but I lie on my back and look at Tahoe and I know that this man needs to be physically loved, and often. He has jumped from bed to bed never really knowing what it is he needed. I've held back, afraid that I'd never find what I need. Now this man is here and he is all I need. And I want him to find everything that he has ever wanted in *me*.

I sit up in bed and kiss his lips, and he kisses mine, smiling down at me with my favorite smile, one that is very male, a little cocky, a little arrogant, and a lot tender. "Do you want me?" He cups my face with both hands, his look wild and demanding. "Do you?"

I nod without hesitation. I feel him tug my ponytail free. My hair tumbles to my shoulders. He looks at the wild curls with appreciation and then runs his fingers through them as he fists a handful of hair, leans down and entwines his tongue with mine. "Then you'll have me."

He slips his free hand into my panties, his fingers sliding over my damp folds. "Are you ready for me? Say you're ready for me, 'cause I cannot possibly be more ready for you," he growls. His drawl is evident. I've never seen him so turned on.

The push of his middle finger inside makes me gasp, and a storm of ecstasy takes hold of my every breath. My concentration, my whole attention, leaps from my hands sliding on his skin, to his finger moving inside me, back to my fingers on his chest, then to my mouth trailing down his neck, and to his mouth nibbling at my ear, back to what his fingers are doing, my body rocking and combusting.

I'm lost and he's all there is. *All* there is.

His chest jerks with his breaths that fall over my face. "You have no idea how much I want you. You have no idea how many times I've thought of this. Done this in my head with you," he drawls.

His hand holds me down by my hips as he continues expertly, lovingly fingering me, the sensation of fullness making me moan as he lowers his head to one of my breasts, up in the air in offering. He sucks, and then, against my skin, thrusting a second time, slower and deeper, "Regina...you're so perfect, Regina."

I could not possibly be wetter.

I pull his head down and latch on with my lips. I feel his smooth, warm skin beneath my fingertips. His mouth more voracious over mine. Tahoe pulling me closer. Tahoe's weight on me. My mouth on his jaw, his neck, my fingers on his hard, muscled chest.

His lips sucking my earlobe. Him whispering that he craves me wet, that he craves me "*this* wet," and his fingers easing inside me, then outside me, stroking my folds. Entering me again. I'm gasping against his throat as he inserts two fingers, then three.

One thing I'm quickly learning about Tahoe Roth is that he is a little bit of a biter.

He bites everything before tasting it.

Bite...tug...release...lick...full-on kiss. All on the same spot. In so many spots.

It's madness-inducing.

I bite his lip and pull for a second, doing the same.

A grin touches his lips as his eyes catch fire. "Naughty girl," he kisses me, "you sweet naughty girl."

He pulls out a foil packet and tears it open with his teeth. He looks down at me for an intense few seconds as he slips it on.

I can't catch my breath or stop my racing heart as he grabs his erection in one hand and holds my body pinned in bed with the other wrapped around my hip.

We pause for a moment. It's that one moment where I realize—this is it. This is it, this is it. And we both want it too much. Have been waiting too long.

He enters slowly, taking his time—his exquisite time—for me to adjust to him.

I think he is savoring the feeling of me, of my body hugging him, just as I am savoring the feeling of him, driving inch by inch inside me.

I am no longer empty. I'm no longer lonely. I'm so full I could burst. I'm so happy I want to cry. I'm so aroused I'm buzzing head to toe and afraid that if he moves just one inch deeper, I'm going to come.

He eases back as if he senses how close I am to exploding. And then he slowly drives back inside, entwining my fingers with his. My breaths jerk fast as he fills me, hard and steady. He whispers as he looks at me, "I love doing this with you, nearly as much as I love you."

He drives forward completely. I thrash and move my hips, desperate for more. He throws his head back and utters, as if he can't believe this is real, *"Fuck me,"* in the hottest way I've ever heard any man curse before. It's that thick drawl.

He pins me in place and drives into me again as if he wants to bury himself in me and possess me whole.

The noises he makes drive me crazy, his kisses obsess me. The warmth of his breath on my cheek arouses me even more as he holds my head to kiss me. His kiss is nearly painful, it is so raw, and he slows it down until it's unbearably worshipful and tender.

I soak it all up. The feel of him. The increase in his speed. Faster and faster. I'm holding his jaw and pulling him to me, closer and closer.

The sound of me, crying out.

His heavy breaths, as fast as mine.

And the moment I lift my eyes to find him staring straight into mine with that dimple peeking out and I know that he's loving this moment as much as I am…

My nails sink into his back, my face in his throat, and suddenly I'm not smiling anymore.

I'm taken to a shattering climax, one where nothing else exists but this feeling of belonging.

Convulsing, I'm twisting and shaking, and crying a little it's so intense, the way I come in his arms. I hear the sound of his breath jerking in his chest and I feel him tighten his body as he comes. He ducks and sucks my nipples, then my lips, his fingers traveling up the grooves of my ribs as he croons that I'm so hot…so very hot…

We're a tangle of delicious limbs when we come back to reality. He brushes my hair behind my shoulder, exposing my neck so he can gently kiss my throat.

The sound of silence settles in the room.

I lie naked and sated, his arms holding me.

He shifts me in a way that he's still inside me, and we lie quietly together.

He cups my cheek and forces me to look at him.

One year ago, all I wanted was to be his—a thousand moments later, I still do.

Millions of smiles in the world, and his is the one I love most. The one he's wearing now is particularly cocky. "What?" I ask.

"Nothing."

I groan and nudge him. He nudges me back and pulls me tighter into his arms, laughing as he bites my earlobe.

NEXT MORNING

I wake up in a big bed with white cotton sheets when I hear the sound of the shower being turned off. Minutes later, it smells like coffee. Vanilla?? Coffee. Definitely some vanilla.

I moan and roll over to find the sun streaming in through the windows.

White cotton sheets cover my naked legs.

I feel lazy and smooth.

And it smells more strongly of coffee.

I stretch my arms over my head and smile, looking around me.

Tahoe.

Tahoe…

With that thought, with the thought of that *name* and the man attached to it, I jerk up out of the bed, slip into my nicest pajamas, and practically sprint out of the room.

My stomach is a bundle of nerves and my sleepiness is slowly lifting with every step I take on the white limestone floor.

Tahoe hears me coming into the kitchen and I swear I can practically hear him smirk from where I'm standing, five feet away.

"Morning, sunshine."

He's wearing his PJs too.

He packed a bag when he came over? The thought warms me when I realize he meant to stay.

Dark blue pants with white stripes. Shirtless. I gulp.

Tahoe takes me in from where he stands, admiring me in a melon-pink silk sleep dress. I blush and smile.

I look over his shoulder to find the coffee machine dripping sweet chocolaty-brown deliciousness.

He follows my gaze and smirks. "If you want it, you're going to have to come and get it."

I narrow my eyes and slowly make my way toward him.

I am met with a wall of hard muscle.

He smells like mint and coffee and soap and Egyptian cotton sheets and like…me.

He smells like a lazy Sunday morning.

I breathe him in and look up into his sparkling blue eyes. I get up on my tiptoes and whisper in his ear, "Step aside, baby."

I feel his muscles tighten and his breath catch in his throat at the endearment. "Not yet," he croons, slipping his arm around my waist and trapping me there.

I run my hands up and down his chest. "Please?" I answer.

I don't know who I'm teasing anymore.

Him or me.

His nearness maddens me. The memory of last night maddens me.

He exhales roughly and before I know it, his hands grasp the backs of my legs, lifting me up, and I'm sitting on top of the marble kitchen island.

He pushes my legs open and stands between them. He smirks down at me and lowers his head to mine. "Give me a kiss," he whispers, teasing me with his breath on the side of my neck.

"What?" I gasp, trying not to focus on his lips sliding along my flesh.

"Kiss me, Regina." He continues rubbing his lips along the curve of my jaw. He plants a kiss on my pulse point below my ear.

"Give me a good morning kiss, *baby*," he continues, looking heatedly at me.

"Ha…" I try to laugh through his teasing but I'm having difficulty thinking of a good comeback. "I'm not used to being charged for coffee I can make on my own."

"Really?" he asks, his hands pushing my little silk dress up my thighs.

His hands are warm, and a little rough, and so achingly familiar. Warm on my skin as he holds on to my thighs, dangerously close to my ass.

I find myself wishing he would go higher.

God, Regina, get a grip!

I laugh at myself and Tahoe smiles against my neck. "What? You can't handle a little kiss?" he taunts me.

"I can, I just don't think you can," I whisper.

He lifts his head from my neck and cups my face in his big hands.

Big blue eyes stare down at me.

Pink lips taunt me.

His blond, scruffy beard rasps and tickles my skin as he plants a kiss on my cheek.

I breathe a little harder.

"Just one kiss?" I breathe.

"Just one," he says, still cupping my face with one hand while the other rests on my thigh. His thumb rubs circles on the inside of my knee.

He looks down at me with sparkling, burning eyes.

He looks hungry. Sleepy. Strong. Ready.

I tilt my head up. My lips are inches away from his. The sun is warm on my bare back. I lean back a little more and pull him in closer to me. I wrap my legs around his waist. His hand tightens on my thigh.

He nuzzles me with his beard. Running it along my jaw, rubbing it against the tip of my nose.

He kisses my chin. My forehead. My cheek.

I wrap my arms around his neck.

I let my lips touch his. I don't move. We're both breathing hard and I can feel him through his PJs.

I force myself not to moan.

I open my mouth against him and give him a light kiss.

His mouth tastes like toothpaste and him.

Now, I do moan.

He smiles against my lips. "Is that all you got?" he taunts. "I was expecting more from you... Let me get a real taste of you, Regina," he murmurs against my lips.

I practically melt in his arms. I nod my answer.

He smiles lightly, leans in, and pries my lips open with his. He takes them leisurely and gives me a soft, wet kiss. I can feel his tenderness in the soft skin of his lips and in the tips of his fingers as he cups my face and slowly kisses me until I forget how to breathe.

I hold him closer and he moans against my mouth. He slips the tip of his tongue against mine and wets my lips. He keeps kissing me and I swear I never want him to stop.

Soft, wet, warm lips moving against mine in the most tender, sweet, lovely kiss I have ever been given.

He kisses me in a way I have never been kissed the morning after.

He kisses me like I am the first drop of rain after years of drought.

He kisses me like I am the first and only bite of chocolate he is ever going to get.

He savors me. Tastes me. Sucks on me. Pries me open with his tongue and gently, slowly moves his lips against mine.

He slips my nightgown up my hips and I realize he'll soon discover I'm not wearing any underwear. I scoot closer to him and the scent of his shampoo and his cologne hit me.

I almost start crying right there because this feels so perfect and so forbidden and so lovely I could die.

I rock my hips against his erection.

He lifts his head. "Regina?" he mumbles. He looks at me. His lips parted, his blue eyes glowing, surveying, exploring, probing me. Almost asking me to say the words.

He looks expectant. Warm. Waiting for me to do something.

I just nod. "I want you," I whisper mischievously in his ear. I take his arm and wrap it around my body.

That was all he needed.

"Regina…" This time it doesn't sound like a question. It sounds like a prayer.

It sounds like a growl.

He takes me in his arms and drags me to the edge of the counter, between his parted legs.

He frames my head with his hands and looks at me with those blue eyes.

We look at each other for what feels like years until he reaches out his hand and rubs my chin with his thumb.

I feel a knot in my throat, but I force myself to ignore it.

Why the hell do I want to cry right now? God, Regina, breathe.

Breathe...

I keep telling myself that as I feel him shift above me so the hardest part of him fits right between my legs. I moan.

He drops his head and kisses my collarbone. His lips are incredibly warm and wet, as they trace a leisurely path from my collarbone to my jaw.

He teases his fingers into my sex.

He kisses along my neck, soft, lingering kisses. He traces my lips with the tip of his thumb.

He kisses my chin. My forehead. He rubs his knuckles across my cheek. "You're so soft…"

He gives me a look that could instantly melt metal before he heads to the bedroom.

I'm dazed, watching as Tahoe lazily walks back to me while tearing open a condom packet.

He swiftly unties the drawstring of his pajama pants, releasing himself. Then he slips on the condom, stands before me, drags me back up against him, crushes my mouth beneath his, and he enters me…and it's perfect. His voice is rough and smooth at the same time. Dark and light. Thunder and lightning.

I cup his face and force him to look at me as he takes me.

His eyes look incredible. His bearded jaw sexy. His lips wet from sucking on my skin.

I run my fingers through his hair and bring him down to my breast, pulling down the material of my nightie.

The kiss is wet. Raw. Warm.

He lifts his head and pushes his tongue inside my mouth and I practically melt in his arms.

He kisses me for a long time. Sucking my moans into his mouth and getting to know every part of mine as he continues pumping.

He sucks my lower lip into his mouth gently, and bites it with his teeth, and then he takes my mouth and gives me a lazy, long kiss.

I feel incredibly loved.

I feel cherished. I feel adored.

There are no other words for it.

He takes my arms and pins them above my head, clasping both of my hands with one of his.

He runs his other hand down my side, my waist, my hips, until he reaches my knee and grasps it to wrap my leg around his waist, bringing him in deeper.

He kisses down the inside of my arms, which are still held above my head.

He rubs his thumb against my nipples.

He kisses my lips.

He sucks on my neck.

"You're a fucking dream. You're a fucking dream and I can't believe I'm not dreaming you right now," he whispers.

He slips his hand behind me and cups my bottom and my eyes burn when he uses his hand to pull me, grind me against his cock as he enters again. I roll my hips and take every inch that I can, kissing his face, then kissing a path to his lips.

"You look so fucking gorgeous, I could eat you up," he growls.

When we come, we come even harder than before, clutching and twisting against each other, our mouths biting and tasting and kissing each other.

When he finally pulls away, I don't know my name.

I look up at him and we are both quiet.

My heart is beating so hard in my chest. My whole body is vibrating.

He's breathing hard. His muscles are warm against my body. His hand remains on my lower back, holding me still.

He looks down at me and lays his forehead against mine.

These are the kinds of moments that make you realize that you never really need to hear the words I love you. Right now the words are all over me, all over us, in his touch, his gaze, the way he breathes me in, the way I breathe him too.

We stay that way for a couple of long, exquisite minutes, satisfied, happy. At peace.

When he pulls away I swear he takes a piece of me with him, but he comes back with a boyish smile on his face and gives me my cup of coffee.

"Good morning, Regina," he finally says.

"Good morning, Tahoe," I say back.

He winks and leans over to kiss me on my forehead.

"What do you want for breakfast?" he asks, turning his back to me and taking out some pans.

"Hmm…are we fully stocked? Of course we are. How about…pancakes?"

"Mm...I like how you're thinking," he answers. "Pancakes it is."

After checking the ingredients in the fridge and debating whether we should add blueberries or dark chocolate chips, we decide on both.

We have coffee next to each other on a small breakfast table, the sun coming up through the big windows of the Saints' house.

We talk about our schedules, trying to figure out if we need to head back today or Sunday.

We settle on Sunday night so we can be at work on Monday...and we can enjoy each other until then.

And when I start flipping pancakes with Tahoe's hand on my butt and his lips nibbling my ear, I smile the whole time.

It's still, even now, *especially* now, so damn easy with him...

TEXTS

When we arrive back in Chicago, I update the girls and they both nearly bust my eardrums when they yell over the phone.

They want details.

Wynn screams, "I knew it! Finally we can talk about it!" and Rachel laughs and says she and Wynn had been having conversations that alternated between fretting about us and actually praying that we could make it work. Rachel says that soon after I left for the Hamptons, Saint returned home and urgently asked her where Tahoe could find me. In that instant, she says she *knew*—because Tahoe came with him—that it was clear that T-Rex wanted me no matter what.

"Something about the look in his eyes was so fierce, like he'd tear a building open to find you," Rachel says.

I get a message early one morning that week from my parents.

Mom: So your father and I have been talking and we thought it would be a good idea to travel into town and fi-

nally meet this man you've been dating so we're making it home for Christmas to meet Trent!

Tahoe shifts in his bed and bites my shoulder. "Who is it at this hour?"

"My parents. They're probably in a very different time zone right now," I whisper.

His fingers are callused, his eyes warm, as he strokes my hair and peers into my phone screen. He reads the text and raises his brows.

He leans back, fully relaxed and fully hot, as I text back my mother. I show him the text.

Me: Actually, Mother, I'm dating Tahoe now. :)

He laughs approvingly and reaches out to caress my bare arm. He raises his hand and tugs at a loose strand of my hair, his eyes loving. His hand slides up to stroke his thumb along the back of my neck. I exhale and close my eyes until my phone buzzes, and I read the text. I show Tahoe her reply.

Mom: What Tahoe? The Texan Tahoe ROTH?

He gives another rumbling laugh. And then there's that twinkle in his baby blues. God, he rocks that dimple, that face. I'm probably one of thousands who have fallen for it, one of hundreds for sure.

Over a year ago I'd already been trapped, and he's only ensnared me more and more, especially with those hot looks he gives me, like he wants me and only me.

Laughing at my mother's panic, I kiss him. Set my lips right on his, then I smile. My father has always been a sucker for the who's who in the business world; my mother a sucker for the who's who in social circles around the globe. Why am I even surprised that they know who he is?

I text my answer and feel him grin as he nibbles my shoulder and sees what I write.

Me: The very one. He says he looks forward to meeting you this Christmas.

Mom: Regina men like that don't settle!!!! Give me 5 minutes I'm calling!!!!

"She's calling. Wow," I say, looking at him in amazement. "Your reputation precedes you. Do you know how many times she's actually called me?"

"Happy I'm good for something," he smirks as he nibbles and bites my earlobe. I sigh and turn my head, kiss him softly. He drags his beard down my throat, my belly, down there— and he turns his face to my left inner thigh and nibbles his way to the center between both thighs. His lips stroke me, barely grazing my clit. Then his thumb circles me and dips inside my folds.

He lifts his head as he raises his thumb and shoves it into his mouth, licking me off him. His eyes shut, and he growls softly and lowers his head again to taste me at the source, the feel of his beard against my thighs tickling and arousing me.

He bites on my clit, and twirls his tongue in just the perfect way. And then his tongue dips inside me, then out, his whole mouth kissing and tasting me. His hands slide down my thighs to keep me open, to widen my legs apart...

And it takes my mom a little longer than five minutes to call, which is just perfect. By the time my phone rings, we've made hot, delicious love, and we're both sated and relaxed in bed when I lazily answer. I tell her that I'm dating Tahoe and that he is exclusively dating me.

He laughs on his side of the bed, shaking his head over his reputation, then leans over and bites my shoulder again before taking the phone from me.

"Mrs. Wylde, I assure you, my intentions with your daughter are honorable. I've fallen in love with her, and nothing will give me more pleasure than meeting you both during the holiday."

Well. He really knows how to charm just about anybody.

XMAS & NEW YEAR'S

We spend Thanksgiving with his parents, laughing and eating turkey, where I get to hear anecdotes of Tahoe as a mischievous little boy. Never content with anything. Even older ladies used to fawn over him and his dimple and his blue eyes.

For Christmas, we decide to stay in Chicago. My parents come and finally get to meet Tahoe over a delicious steak dinner at Chicago Cut.

I can tell that my parents were spending time at the beach. A warm glow shines on their skin as they head toward our table. "Come here and let me look at you," my mother says, drawing me to her.

She lifts my arms and takes in my jeans and sequined sweater.

I'm embarrassed by the fact that it's obvious my parents haven't seen me in almost a year.

"So nice to see you, darling." My mother finally hugs me, then sets me aside before excitedly asking, "And who's the man?"

I glance at my dad, who's grinning at me proudly. As if only now that I've found the approval of a man, I'm worthy.

"Tahoe," I say, pointing at the Viking next to me as if they hadn't already spotted him from the moment they walked through the restaurant door, when Tahoe and I stood up to welcome them.

Tahoe shakes their hands and greets them warmly.

I glance at Tahoe, a part of me wanting him to like them. Which is irrelevant, I guess, because sometimes your loved ones don't love each other. But his smile is genuine, and my parents are obviously so impressed they're nearly tripping on their words.

Mom is dressed fashionably as usual, her dark hair like mine pulled back into a neat bun, tons of faux pearl necklaces draped around her neck. "I have to say, the news came as a shock to us, a shock," she admits, as Tahoe pulls her chair out.

I'm so tense, I'm relieved when Tahoe takes his seat and summons the waiter and motions in my direction for someone to get me a drink.

Rachel is the opposite of me. She's so close to her mother that she's always wanted that kind of connection for my mother and me, but you can't force these things. And yet I'm surprised by how much we enjoy the evening together. Tahoe simply has a way of putting everyone at ease, and I think that seeing me so happy actually makes my parents more receptive to me somehow.

I can really tell that my mother is charmed by Tahoe. Not being one to mince words, she tells him that he's just the man she's warned me about all my life. That he has the smile of a bad boy and the face of a *heartbreaker*.

It amuses me that she sounds a little bit like his mother did. I nudge his ankle under the table and chide him. "Such an incorrigible ladies' man, shame on you."

His foot toes back my ankle and he smirks. "Yeah, but *you're* my lady now."

My mom can't seem to resist kissing Tahoe on the cheek before they leave. She pats his beard and thanks him for being so good for me.

"Did you hear what she said?" I frown as we climb into his Ghost. "Good for me? Not *to* me?"

He leans across the car console and kisses my temple, his dimple forming a little nook against my cheek because I suppose he really liked that stroke to his ego. "Yeah, I heard."

I roll my eyes but I smile to myself. Because I know, I'm good for him too.

For Christmas, I give him *me*…wrapped in nothing.

He gives me a key to his apartment.

I'm not ready to move in, but when I tell him that, he pats my butt and says, "Well hurry, 'cause I am."

So on December 27th, I take a few things over. And I haven't slept in my apartment since.

On New Year's, there's a party hosted by the high rollers Tahoe, Callan and Saint hang out with.

We dress up, go out, and mingle. But Rachel and Saint stay home with Kyle, Emmett and Wynn are spending New Year's traveling, and Tahoe and I are far more interested in sexy times than mingling, so we don't stay at the party for long.

The party was held close by so we're able to reach his apartment in fifteen minutes. I kick off my shoes and drop my clutch on the sofa, then gaze out the living room window while Tahoe takes a bottle of champagne from his collection and sets it in an ice bucket to chill. He then drops down on the couch.

"Come here." He crooks his finger in the shadows, his eyes glowing.

I gulp. "You should get a pet; it's like your favorite phrase: 'come here,'" I say.

But I start walking forward, helpless as a sleepwalker.

He rises to full height as I reach him. "I only like *you* to come here. Come right," he pulls me into his arms and kisses my lips, adding a little tongue, "*here*." He brings his hands to my face and starts removing my lipstick.

I groan and halfheartedly try to squirm free. "*Don't* remove *my makeup*."

"Don't put it on then." He smirks and holds me more firmly.

I frown at him. His gentle fingertips soon ease the frown away.

I find myself standing utterly still, studying his face as he has his way and erases my makeup until my face is bare. His eyes shine with tenderness, sky blue and so raw that I feel raw too. I feel wanted and accepted and untouched by life, hopeful and in love, and I never thought I'd feel like this again.

I won't cry.

I won't cry I won't cry Iwon'tcry.

Lifting his jacket, I duck underneath and pull it over the back of my head and hide myself as I press my bare face against his shirt buttons. My cheek pushes flat against his pecs. His chuckle rumbles against my cheek as he spreads his hand on my back. My fingers tug his shirt free of his waistband and slide underneath to tease a path up to his pectoral muscles. And his nipples.

I finger his nipple. He makes a sound in his throat that rumbles really deep. I open a few buttons and push his shirt aside to expose his other nipple. And I suck it.

His chuckle over my mischievousness fades to a groan. He shrugs off his jacket, then he finishes unbuttoning and shoulders off his shirt, frowning laughingly down at me. "Are you hiding from me? Don't hide from me."

Groaning, I put my hands over my cheeks. Through the spaces between my fingers, I meet his gaze.

His eyes are dancing in amusement.

His laugh fills the room. He's enjoying seeing me like this and he shamelessly forces my arms to my sides. His voice darkens with lust. "Come on, let me look at you. You look edible right now."

I leave my arms at my sides.

He holds my gaze as he tugs my sweater dress over my head, then lowers my strapless bra, and one of my nipples appears. He takes it in with hot male appreciation. He frees my other nipple and leaves them there, exposed.

He bends his head. He nibbles first. Bites the tip of one a little bit. The gentle tug of his teeth causing the tip of my nipple to swell and my sex to ache with an absolute craving to be filled. He turns his attention to my other nipple, biting it gently. He tugs, releases, licks it, then full-on kisses it. When he covers it with his mouth and sucks, I buck in pleasure. I arch and clutch at his back, raking my nails over his muscles.

"*Tahoe*," I groan, mindless with arousal.

He's clearly aroused too. He makes sure to grind his erection against my belly, letting me know it. I'm not sure if I imagined it—did it pulse harder when I said his name?

He drags his teeth over my nipple and bends down to lick it again, rasping, "So succulent," and then sucking gently as his hands caress me, "Touch me, Regina. Take my cock in your little hands."

He guides my hand over his slacks and sets it over his length, and he's stretched to the limit, hard and massive. My mouth dries up and I lick my lips as I stroke him, and he groans.

And suddenly we both lose control.

He jerks on my bra, rending it open. He pulls down my panties while I unbuckle and unzip him. I drop his pants and he lifts me, carries me to his room, and sets me on his bed. He waits at the foot of the bed, getting an eyeful of me, and in the meantime letting me get a complete and totally amazing eyeful of him.

My mouth waters as I stare at six feet plus of tanned, naked Tahoe before me.

Naked and so, so *hot*.

I forget everything when he leans over me and murmurs in my ear with an amused smile, "Come here."

I hold on to him and whisper back, "I am here."

"Yes you are. But get closer," he says.

I try to get closer as he sets his knees on the bed, leans over me, and spreads my legs open so I have room for him.

I push him to his back and straddle him.

He sits up and runs his hands along my curves and cups the side swells of my breasts. "Closer," he says. He plays with my breasts, with my pussy, as if they're all made for him.

I hug him tighter, kissing him the way he makes me want to kiss him, with all of me, mouth and teeth and tongue and heart, whole body rubbing and feeling his.

He groans appreciatively, squeezes my ass. "Closer." His voice is dark now. Textured.

A part of me wants to keep making him ask, keep my guy on his toes for me, yet I'm affected by his nearness to the extent I can feel only one thing, the urge to please him.

So I kiss him harder, filling my hands with the scrape of his beard, and when he opens his mouth with a smile, I lift my body and lower myself down on him.

"Oh god," I groan.

His smile fades against my lips and he kisses me softly but then more urgently.

"I love you," he says, now pressing his lips to my cheek and kissing me there.

I move over him slowly and run my fingertips over his chest. Against his lips, I whisper, "Don't hurt me, Roth, ever."

And when he simply and confidently says, "Never," he grabs me by the hips and kisses me again, moving beneath me, filling me up, filling me in.

He rolls me to my back and spreads me out on the bed, and then he's all over me, inside me, as close as he can get.

And he moves, and I move.

He whispers thickly in my ear, and I realize that I believe every word this man has ever told me and each one that he says right now in my ear.

"You feel so right..."

"I'm so wild about you..."

His hands and kisses echo what he tells me.

He takes me with precision and also with strength, our bodies flexing to get closer, his body overpowering mine enough for me to get fucked as hard as I've ever been fucked but not get broken.

I sense when he's coming, because his body tightens deliciously, his sounds become more erratic and deep and primal.

My orgasm hits. My body blazes like the core of the Earth, then I'm shuddering in an explosion so great it's almost frightening. Tahoe holds my face still and gives me the hottest kiss I've ever experienced as I come, devouring me gently as he quickens his pace and meets me there. The low growl that rips up his chest as he comes is the hottest thing I've ever heard.

We share a series of lazy, appreciative kisses as we both recover.

He pokes my nose with the tip of his finger, his dimple popping out. "You look so gorgeous like this," he says, so much ferocity in his eyes. He takes me in with his gaze and brushes a tendril of damp hair from my forehead, then rubs my lips with his thumb.

"You're amazing," I say.

We sigh simultaneously and then just stare at the ceiling, dazed and at peace.

As I start to doze off, waiting for the New Year, he nudges my feet under the covers. I kick him in response. He nudges me harder to get my attention. "Hey. I love you," he says, and then he grins at me with that adorable dimple.

In the distance I hear the fireworks blast across the city as the new year begins.

We share a smile and kiss and he says, "Happy New Year, Regina."

"Happy New Year, Tahoe. Oh wait!" I scramble out of bed and bring the grapes we bought specifically for this occasion, along with two full glasses of champagne from the bottle we'd been chilling.

We pluck grapes and add twelve, one for each month, into our champagne glasses.

"To what do we drink?" I ask.

"Your navy-blue panties."

"Come on."

He lifts his glass. "To my lady. May she have success in all her endeavors, health and friendships, and may I not take my own last breath until she takes hers. May she always know I love her."

It's not just the words, but the way he says them and the way he looks at me, that make my eyes water. "Whatever I say now will pale in comparison," I say.

"It won't pale."

"Yes, it will pale," I say.

He looks at me questioningly, his lips curling at the corners while his eyes darken somberly. "Just tell me you love me."

"I love you." I fling my arms around him, then recover and lift my champagne glass in a toast. "To my guy. May he win every game he chooses to play, have many reasons to laugh, more successes than he can remember, and as long as he loves me, always have me."

His eyes darken with emotion. We *clink* glasses, he drinks, and I drink, and as I set my glass aside, and he sets aside his, Tahoe grabs the back of my head in one wide hand and we kiss long and slow as he rolls me to my back and loves me again, too drunk on each other to want anything else.

DEAR READERS,

If you'd like to read what's next in the MANWHORE world, please be sure to keep an eye out for Callan Carmichael's story, coming in 2017!

I can't wait to share his and Livvy's story with you!

And watch out for a brand new series coming this year. It's a surprise that has me completely obsessed, and I hope it will completely obsess you too.

XOXO,

Katy

OTHER TITLES BY KATY EVANS

Manwhore series:

MANWHORE
MANWHORE +1
MS. MANWHORE

Real series:

REAL
MINE
REMY
ROGUE
RIPPED
LEGEND

ACKNOWLEDGMENTS

I am so lucky to be surrounded by such an amazing team of people who motivate and inspire me to keep writing and sharing my stories. This book would not be possible without the support of my family, who sometimes has to deal without me for days when I find myself immersed in the cave. Thank you to my beloved husband for his unwavering belief, support, and love. My son, for his ever-amazing song suggestions; my daughter, who is always my first reader and #1 fan; and my daughter's boyfriend, whose expertise in lacrosse helped me so much. I also have to thank my dad for my love of writing, and my mother for being everything a mother should be.

This story would be nowhere even near readable if it weren't for the fabulous group of people who help me make it shine. So an extra huge thank you to my agent, Amy Tannenbaum, and everyone at the Jane Rotrosen Agency, who've always supported and given my stories a home; to my super editors Kelli Collins and CeCe Carroll, my copy editor Lisa Wolff, my proofreader Anita Saunders, my beta reader Kati D, and the tons of author beta readers whose encouragement and insight helps so much. Monica and Kim, especially, I couldn't have done this without you!

To precious Dana, thank you for Chicago.

Thank you to my fabulous audio publisher for bringing *Ladies' Man* in audio to my "listeners" and to my foreign publishers for translating my stories so that they can be read across the world.

To Julie at JT Formatting and my cover designer, James at Bookfly Covers, you did an amazing job!

HUGE, heartfelt thanks (and CHOCOLATE!) to all of the bloggers out there: you are incredible in your efforts to promote the books you love and so passionate about making sure that readers know about them. Thank you for taking the time to share and review mine.

And very especially, I am so grateful to my readers. Without your eyes on these pages, my book wouldn't come alive in your hearts and minds.

Thank you for your support, your messages, and your interest in my work and characters.

Hugs, and big Tahoe Roth love,

Katy

ABOUT

New York Times, *USA Today*, and *Wall Street Journal* bestselling author Katy Evans appeared for the first time on four different bestselling lists with her 2013 debut book, *Real*. Since then, all of her titles have been *New York Times* bestsellers. Her books have been translated into nearly a dozen languages across the world, with over a million copies of her books sold worldwide. She lives in Texas with her husband, two kids, and their beloved dogs. To find out more about her or her books, visit the sites below, she'd love to hear from you.

Website: www.katyevans.net
Facebook: https://www.facebook.com/AuthorKatyEvans
Twitter: @authorkatyevans

Sign up for Katy's newsletter:
http://www.katyevans.net/newsletter/

68975194R00179

Made in the USA
Columbia, SC
13 April 2017